THE MYSTERY
OF RIO

Alberto Mussa

THE MYSTERY OF RIO

*Translated from the Portuguese
by Alex Ladd*

Europa
editions

Europa Editions
214 West 29th Street
New York, N.Y. 10001
www.europaeditions.com
info@europaeditions.com

Copyright © by Alberto Mussa.
Published by special arrangement with The Ella Sher Literary working
in conjunction with Villas-Boas & Moss Literary Agency & Consultancy, LLC
First Publication 2013 by Europa Editions

Translation by Alex Ladd
Original title: *O senhor do lado esquerdo*
Translation copyright © 2013 by Europa Editions

Acknowledgements
I am grateful to Reginaldo Alcantara for his many contributions
and valuable insights. And to Selma Marks for her generous assistance.
Finally, many thanks to John Sherman for his skillful revisions.
Any errors or omissions are, of course, my own.
Alex Ladd

Library of Congress Cataloging in Publication Data is available
ISBN 978-1-60945-136-3

Mussa, Alberto
The Mystery of Rio

Book design by Emanuele Ragnisco
www.mekkanografici.com

Cover photo © Nikada/iStock

Prepress by Grafica Punto Print – Rome

Printed in the USA

THE MYSTERY OF RIO

The House of Swaps, formerly the residence
of the Marquise of Santos, São Cristovão, Rio de Janeiro

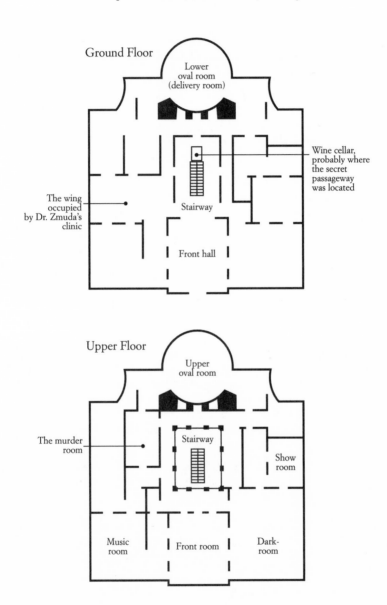

Ground Floor

Lower
oval room
(delivery room)

Wine cellar,
probably where
the secret
passageway
was located

The wing
occupied
by Dr. Zmuda's
clinic

Stairway

Front hall

Upper Floor

Upper
oval room

The murder
room

Stairway

Show
room

Music
room

Front room

Dark-
room

*This is the story of one
who kills, then dances.
Beware! A true hunter
first lures, then pounces.*

I t is not the geography, it is not the architecture, it is not the heroes, or battles, much less so the chronicles of customs, or the fantasies conjured up by poets. No, what defines a city is the history of its crimes.

I am not, of course, referring to run-of-the-mill crimes. Ordinary, predictable, and petty criminals exist everywhere in the world. I am speaking of foundational crimes, necessary crimes, those that would be inconceivable, that could never have existed, anywhere but in the cities to which they belong.

I arrived at this conclusion by way of the Unesco Standing Committee on the Theory and Art of the Police Novel, headquartered in London and financed by Scotland Yard.

I was on the Fourth Panel, whose task it was to study the criminal annals of the great world capitals and list examples of "perfect crimes" that occurred in real life but whose nature was on a par with their literary counterparts.

Although I was troubled by the inapt description, I accepted the Committee's rules and pulled up a large number of cases for Rio de Janeiro, the city I was assigned to investigate. I was about to conclude my report when I noticed that one crime stood out from the rest.

It, too, was a perfect crime. However, its "perfection" lay not in the infeasibility of uncovering evidence, but rather in the logical impossibility of accepting the solution. I was not content simply to include material such as this in a bureaucratic report.

My meetings in London did not go well. Not only is the city

not in the tropics, I was not prepared for how exotic its natives were: they were incapable of grasping notions of chance or disorder; they were ponderous, restrained, punctual; they did not react well to spontaneous emotions. I left the Committee's headquarters without a job, but I did not hand in my notes.

This novel is based on those notes, following, of course, the template of a detective story. But it can also be read as an adventure story, a "treasure hunt" of sorts, filled with duels, ambition, and revenge. It is thus closer to Dumas than to Melville or Conrad—a similarity that betrays the city's French leanings.

Others will read it as a tour through Rio de Janeiro, in both time and space, because one cannot understand or interpret a crime outside of where it was committed.

And since crimes define cities, it is also the myth of Rio de Janeiro. The foundation myth, although not chronologically so. I now realize that the concept of city is independent of the concept of time.

Many will say that I have veered, once again, into the realm of fantasy. I reject this assertion. This is a real story, and an autobiography, although it may seem like fiction. For in order for literature to be interesting at all, it must differ from life.

So then they asked Tiresias.
"If you divide pleasure into ten,"
the Seer said, "of that number,
surely, nine belong to women."

They asked the Prophet too.
Mohammed spoke not of ten:
"Of a hundred parts," he said,
"ninety-nine belong to women."

The crime, whose victim was the Secretary to the Presidency of the Republic during the Hermes da Fonseca administration, was committed in the old imperial neighborhood of São Cristovão, on the old Imperador Street (now Pedro Segundo Avenue), where the legendary mansion known as the House of Swaps once stood.

The House of Swaps, once the residence of the Marquise of Santos, and later the property of the Baron of Maúa, had been awarded in a court of law, after all appeals had been exhausted, to the Polish doctor Miroslav Zmuda. The doctor, a controversial defender of abortion and female sterilization, took possession of the mansion in 1906.

This fabulous little palace at one point was also headquarters to the Ministry of Health, as well as the Fourth Centenary Museum. Today it houses the Museum of the First Empire. On the day our story begins—Friday, June 13, 1913—it seemed to house the Polish doctor's imposing clinic.

I say *seemed* to house. I overstate the point: Doctor Zmuda's clinic, along with a very rarely used delivery room, did in fact function in that house during morning hours, in the left wing of the ground floor. However, behind its façade, there also existed a magnificent brothel, whose mysteries were concealed on the second floor.

Doctor Zmuda's brothel was the most exceptional establishment of its kind in the city. For it was not merely an establishment where men rented the services of prostitutes; women could rent the services of men there, too. As a matter of fact, every imaginable arrangement, combination, and permutation was allowed there.

And it was not always a matter of prostitution: the House was also frequented by lovers, there of their own free and spontaneous accord (in fact, the price charged to give them cover was among the highest). And there were those who went there seeking random liaisons with strangers, which would give them access to the orgy nights—collective lovemaking sessions for couples only. And that is how the mansion became known, to this last group, as the House of Swaps.

If not for the fact that Dr. Zmuda's clinic was frequented by people of prominence, run with the utmost discretion, protected by the authorities, and above all loved by its clientele, it would not have withstood the tremendous shock of the death of the president's Secretary to the Presidency of the Republic.

Witnesses were unwavering and pointed to only one suspect: the prostitute known as Fortunata.

Fortunata had been in the room with the secretary. She was one of the "nurses," as they were called in the House—full-time prostitutes who had their own private clients. Her activities on that day were routine—she saw two gentlemen before the victim and, when she received the secretary at 4 P.M., she quickly began tending to him in one of the rooms. Moments later, she came down for glasses and a bottle of red wine.

No one thought it odd when Fortunata, at around the time of the Ave Maria, rushed into the oval parlor on the top floor, where the nurses normally went to relax. She said she was very late, and rather rudely refused a glass of cashew liqueur, before exiting through the front door.

It was only two hours later, after it occurred to them that the secretary's nap seemed unusually long, that they knocked on the door. Fortunately, the nurse who discovered the crime did not scream.

The victim's wrists and ankles were tightly bound to the iron bedposts in such a manner that, according to the forensic expert, he could not possibly have untied himself. The neck still exhibited the murderer's deep thumb marks. The coroner's report (marked "Confidential") confirmed that the *causa mortis* was strangulation, even though the force applied exceeded that normally exerted by a woman.

Apparently, no objects of value were missing—the gold ring with its flashy ruby was still there, as were the pocket watch and its long chain, made of the same metal, the tie clip with its inlaid ivory cameo, plus eleven *mil-reis* in cash—which early on ruled out the possibility of a robbery.

One circumstance was cause for embarrassment: the president's secretary lay gagged and blindfolded with a thick strip of black cloth and a whip with a silver handle was found on the floor near the bed, which explained the deep lacerations on his legs and pubic region.

According to an old legend, underneath the House of Swaps, which had been especially remodeled to become the residence of the Marquise of Santos, there were several tunnels connecting it to the palace at Quinta da Boa Vista, as well as to other nearby houses, so that Emperor Pedro I could come and go without arousing suspicion.

This is one of the ironies of the city: in a building endowed with secret passages, criminals could exit through the front doors, as Fortunata had done. This would never have happened in London, Baghdad, or Buenos Aires, to name only a few examples.

While authorities tried to quash the scandal, an enormous contingent of police officers scoured the streets of São Cristovão and the neighboring bars to arrest a woman named Fortunata, of whom they had only a cursory description, taking care not to link her to a murder.

The police were hoping that the fugitive had not made it far, and that she had sought refuge in the home of a lover or a friend. Just the same, civil guards and public safety officers rushed to the ferry terminal and the railway stations to try to prevent the killer from slipping away.

Fortunata rented a room in a second-floor apartment on Conceição Hill. Her landlady, who ran a sewing school on the first floor, was horrified when the police came to search her tenant's quarters, and stated that she had not seen her that day, having assumed she was still on night duty at the Polish doctor's clinic. Her statement seemed consistent with the facts, since the probable killer's personal effects were still in her room.

The searches of the street and of the suspect's room were unfruitful. To police officials, who initially believed the fugitive would be arrested in a matter of hours, the failure of these efforts was becoming a source of consternation, and increased pressure was placed on the officers. That is, until a fortuitous turn of events a little past midnight in Gamboa changed the course of the investigation.

A police officer reported that, while going down one of the slopes of Favela Hill along the edge of the English Cemetery, he saw a moving shape, perhaps that of a man, a grave robber, trying to jump over a wall from inside the cemetery via a rope tied to a *camboatá* tree, whose branches extended over the wall onto the street.

He did not blow his whistle to summon his fellow officers because he was not entirely certain about the existence of ghosts. He had the distinct impression, however, that the man, or whatever it was, after noting his presence, retreated. It was enough for him to show his mettle. Grabbing hold of the same rope that the shape had intended to descend with, he climbed the wall and jumped into the cemetery.

In those gloomy surroundings, spiked with trees whose

canopy of leaves cast shadows everywhere, the fearless policeman searched for the footprints of the desecrator. And, to his
despair, he saw an apparition pass below where the chapel
stood. Filled with panic and already regretting his decision, he
managed to utter that he had a warrant, and he threatened to
come closer. It was then that the being betrayed its true nature
by fleeing once again, this time behind a headstone.

Every predator's courage grows in inverse proportion to the
fear exhibited by the prey. With the policeman it was no different. He thus leaped in pursuit of someone who could only
be a grave robber.

There was no struggle, so to speak. Straight away, the officer arrested an old man dressed very plainly, with a large cloth
sack worn bandolier-style across his chest.

"I came to do a job. It's for a private client. Don't ask me
his name."

At the Mauá Square police station, the seat of the First
District (with jurisdiction over the port as well as northern
downtown, from the old wharf of the Mineiros all the way to
the Mangrove canal, near Formosa Beach), they found the following objects among the old man's possessions: shells, stones,
tiny implements, wood chips, stubs of magic *pemba* chalk, tal-
low candles, macerated leaves, tiny vials with mysterious
brews, cartridges of gunpowder, as well as other small things.
They also found a bottle of cachaça and fragments of animal
bone.

But what most surprised authorities were the gold pieces.
Specifically, a pair of earrings in the shape of seahorses. The
sergeant on duty, who earlier had received a description of
Fortunata—brown-skinned, tall, approximately five feet six
inches, wearing a turquoise taffeta dress and gold earrings
shaped like seahorses—concluded that this could not be mere
coincidence, and that those earrings had not long ago been on
the ears of the woman they were pursuing.

"That's payment for my services."

He was known to police, the old man was. He went only by Rufino, and he was reputed to be a great sorcerer. An old-time character in the city, he lived high in Santa Teresa, in a remote area where there were half a dozen shanties by the entrance to the forest, but he was frequently seen at Rosario Church, at the Pedra do Sal, at Lapa Square, and Misericodia Hill, where even the wealthy, in search of prayers, potions, and amulets, could find him. He rarely saw clients in the hills, except for serious cases, procedures that needed to be performed on the patient's actual body.

Word had it that he was over 100 and the owner of a vast buried treasure, although few gave credence to such legends. In fact, he was feared and respected, and his power derived from the odd trait that he had never told—and was, in fact, incapable of telling—a lie.

The sergeant, however, was the skeptical type. He wanted to know when and where Rufino had obtained jewelry belonging to a fugitive sought by a direct order of the chief of police.

"A man gave me this gold."

It was not his answers that surprised the sergeant, but rather the solemn and reverential reaction of his subordinates.

"Believe him, chief. The old man doesn't lie."

Rufino revealed that the earrings had belonged to the man who had hired him for the job, given to him in appreciation for his trips to the cemetery, and that this man would be visiting his home, high up in Santa Teresa, within two weeks' time, in order to complete the spell.

After wavering, the sergeant had him arrested until he had further word from his superiors, whom he had notified. The jewels were retained as material evidence in a possible crime tied to Fortunata—although he had no idea what she was actually wanted for.

The sorcerer objected, saying he was being robbed. Before

he was led to his cell—escorted with great respect by the officers, who even went so far as to apologize—Rufino looked one
of them in the face.

"If you ever need my help, sir, don't bother."

The old man was brash.

Interestingly, the day after the murder, the obituaries
reported that the death of the Secretary to the Presidency of
the Republic was due to a case of sudden cardiac arrest.

No mention was made of murder or of the incident at the
English Cemetery. No mention was made, either, of the
searches in Conceição Hill, and the name of Fortunata was
never brought up. Only one newspaper was more astute than
the others and published a brief article that made reference to
a "strange death," "ignored circumstances" and "the silence of
the authorities." However, no further suspicions were raised.

Since this is a police narrative, it is important that the
reader know exactly the way things transpired. Let us then go
back to the night in question, so as to know the exact chronol-
ogy of facts and to understand how such a scandalous tragedy
could have been concealed from the public.

It is true that Dr. Zmuda's influence, because of his ties to
people in power, was decisive in covering up the crime. The
first measure he took, as soon as he confirmed the absence of
breathing and a pulse, was to order that nothing be touched.
He also instructed that no more clients be let in that night and
that all the nurses remain in the oval parlor until further notice.

Fortunately, it was a Friday, a slow day. The Polish doctor
said goodbye to the remaining clients, who did not suspect a
thing, and a little after 8 P.M. he telephoned the chief of police.

Since 1907, the chief of police of Rio de Janeiro was directly
subordinate to the minister of justice, who appointed him.
Below the chief of police there were three auxiliary chiefs, followed by, in decreasing hierarchical order according to rank

and seniority, the district-wide captains and lieutenants—not to mention, of course, the officers.

In this instance, the chief of police might have had the backing of the minister, because certain actions needed to be taken immediately. Due to the case's political overtone, he did not allow an inquiry to be launched in São Cristovão, where the crime had occurred, and he assumed personal control over the investigation, arriving at the House of Swaps before 9:15 P.M.

From there, on the telephone, after hearing a brief report of the incident and writing down a description of the suspect, he ordered the searches, which began around 9:30 P.M.

Time was against the chief of police. He could not delay notifying the family for too long. But he did not want the relatives to see the body in that state, before the bruises could be hidden, especially around the neck.

On the other hand, an examination of the crime scene, even a cursory one, was essential. After all, there could be sinister motives behind the assassination, and extremely serious political implications. It was while in the throes of these thoughts that he asked the doctor, "Tell me something, Zmuda: which men from the department come here?"

The Polish doctor never gave out such information. He hesitated for a moment. In this situation, he could not withhold the information without putting his own position at risk. Not including those that went to the House infrequently, he replied, the following were regular clients: the police captains of Lapa, Botafogo, Gávea, Tijuca, Santa Teresa, Mem de Sá, Madureira, Meier, and Bandeira Square; one lieutenant from Vila Isabel, who had ties to the *jogo do bicho* lottery, and a fingerprint expert.

Some coincidences really help the novelist—the chief of police happened to know this expert. What's more, he held his ambitious nature and keen intelligence in high regard, so much so that he had made him head of the criminal identification services.

Thus, while the search for Fortunata was in full swing, the chief hurriedly called this important individual, who will yet shine on these pages. And it was to this individual that the chief of police assigned the investigation of the case, to be carried out with the highest level of confidentiality.

While the expert exercised his duties at the scene of the crime, the chief of police had no trouble convincing Dr. Zmuda to provide a false statement for the death certificate as to the *causa mortis*. After all, it would not be the first time that the Polish doctor had committed a criminal offense. And because he trusted—with the guarantee of the doctor himself and his head administrator—that the nurses would not dare reveal anything to the contrary, he was able to construct a final version of events: the secretary, after leaving a classified meeting with high-ranking government officials, suddenly fell ill as he passed through São Cristovão in a cab, and he asked the driver to take him to Dr. Zmuda's residence—the closest medical clinic that it would occur to anyone to go to at that location. The Polish doctor attempted emergency procedures, but the patient finally succumbed.

This was the story they told the widow, the children, other relatives, and the press. When, at around 4 A.M., the body arrived for the viewing at the Catete Palace, it was already prepared and dressed in a beautiful high-collared robe. No one could detect any evidence of the crime.

The residence of the marquise—the lover of Pedro I—is not the only building in this city rumored to have secret passageways. In fact, the most notorious cases involve two of the oldest religious orders in Rio de Janeiro: that of São Bento, located on the hill of the same name, and that of the Jesuits, who erected a college on Castelo Hill.

The Benedictines were accused many times of promoting smuggling through a secret tunnel, which even had a wharf inside. Late at night, every so often, a rock would be moved to allow small skiffs or even boats filled with merchandise to pass through and furnish supplies to ships anchored near Paquetá.

The Jesuits, on the other hand—as has been long known—had opened similar passageways: one that began at the high altar of the college's old church and then branched out into various tunnels (one of those mouths was discovered in 1905, during construction on Central Avenue) and another that connected the priests' library to Calabouço Point. It was through this latter one (so they say) that they managed to carry off their fabulous treasure, shortly before they were expelled from the city after putting up a resistance, in 1760.

There were others too. For example, in 1831 a narrow hideout was discovered beneath the planks of one of the customs piers, which would have served as a hideaway for capoeiras and rebel fighters to then escape to the Atlantic.

The flight of these captives and convicts onto waiting galleys was promoted by an extensive network of so-called "enticers of slaves"—in actuality a criminal organization made up mainly of free Africans, in cahoots with a brotherhood of blacks and members of the military who served in the terrible prison of the navy's armory, where detainees were submitted to forced labor in the quarries of Cobras Island.

What is incredible about this story is that, once in the basement of the customs building, the fugitives would proceed through an underwater tunnel—the first in the world of its kind—to the arsenal, where they would then be smuggled onto the galleys.

It is also said that a high-profile Carioca murder is tied to the secret passageways, one involving Jean du Clerc, a captain in the French Navy. The renowned pirate was defeated and imprisoned during his failed invasion of Rio de Janeiro in

1710. Detained in the lap of luxury at the home of a local nobleman, du Clerc was killed by a band of masked men who curiously gained entrance into the house without being noticed by the sentinels.

A few months after the crime, in 1711, another important pirate, Captain René du Guay, taking advantage of a dense fog, was able to attack at Gamboa Beach with more than five thousand men. This time around, the invasion of the city succeeded, thus avenging du Clerc's defeat. Although he managed to extort a fabulous ransom, René du Guay did not find what he had been looking for—Lourenço Cão's lost map, which had been in du Clerc's possession when he set sail from La Rochelle.

This map not only untangled mysteries concerning a hypothetical discovery of Guanabara Bay by Phoenicians, it also showed the way to the precious Irajá mines and the location of a city of women, as well as many other important sites, including the mouth of the underground lagoon that contained the brackish water of immortality, which one could reach through a vast stone tunnel (most likely a natural concavity in the rock), the entrances to which were so hidden that they were unknown to the Indians themselves.

A secret tunnel also figures in the history of Rio de Janeiro's most illustrious crime: the murder of the ruffian Pedro the Spaniard in the dungeons of Aljube, where he was found dead on the morning of the day he was meant to be hanged.

Pedro was a Galician, not a Spaniard. The nickname was given to him by the common folk of Rio in order to get under his skin. His sad story began at a very young age in his native Galicia, where he killed friends and relatives. He fled to Portugal, and there he violently killed a rich and beautiful lover who had showered him with gifts. Then he fled to Rio de Janeiro.

Pedro the Spaniard was never a capoeira: he killed through

treachery, almost always from behind. He would kill benefactors, eliminate fellow gang members, and commit unnecessary acts of cruelty against helpless victims. It was not a matter of greed, or lust, and much less so ideology. I will leave it at that. Those who have the intestinal fortitude and wish to know the details can read José do Patrocínio's novel.

He enters Rio's criminal annals not as a murderer but as a victim. On the morning of the day he was to be hanged, Pedro the Spaniard was found dead in his cell. There was talk of witchcraft and poisoning; there was also talk of secret passageways. However, there was no official inquiry into his death, and in fact they may not even have realized that he was already dead.

For, against all of the laws of nature—or perhaps deliberately—they led the prisoner in that state to the gallows at Prainha. A large crowd witnessed the execution of the abominable bandit, who shook and swung just the same, hanging from the rope as he died a second time.

Days before leaving office, in November of 1910, President Nilo Peçanha inaugurated the Central Police Palace on Relação Street (corner of Inválidos). It was designed by Heitor de Melo, perhaps the principal exponent of the French style, which had been so in vogue for major city buildings ever since João VI.

The historical importance of the building transcends art, for it was at that same palace that the new forensic departments were located, whose mission it was to give technical support to the precincts, employing the most advanced forensic and criminological methods then available. It was also where the College of Police Sciences and the fascinating Crime Museum were established.

The museum's collection is truly amazing. The objects on exhibit, all of them, were taken from real crime scenes or seized as evidence to be used against suspects. There were weapons and projectiles for ballistic analysis, instruments used in celebrated murders, objects with fingerprints (still a novelty at the time), shoeprint molds, pieces of fabrics (for comparative analysis), even letters used to illustrate the latest techniques in graphology.

The museum also had a gruesome collection of human organs, removed during the autopsies of crime victims and then preserved in formic acid for forensic studies.

Also notable were the significant number of exhibits related to illicit activities, such as samba, Candomblé, and gambling: roulette wheels with cheat pedals, loaded dice, tarot cards with arcane characters, and the vast arsenal of religious objects of the *mães-* and *pais-de-santos*—among which I would highlight the most varied types of drums, including the oldest *puíta* manufactured in Rio de Janeiro, which is different from its African counterpart because the stem is on the inside.

Lastly, there was a section for documents: transcripts, reports, crime statistics, photos of murder victims, and anthropometric identification cards (the type championed by Alphonse Bertillon), which would soon became obsolete as forensic science began favoring more modern techniques, which prevailed in Argentina, the United States, and England.

The entire collection was under the care of Sebastião Baeta, who, in spite of being born out of wedlock into humble beginnings, had traveled to London, New York, and Buenos Aires, where he had studied techniques employed by forensic experts in those countries, specifically the use of fingerprints.

He was recognized as one of the most talented forensic investigators, and was a pioneer in the photographing and dusting of fingerprints.

It should come as no surprise, therefore, that the police high command chose their best forensic expert, and the chief of that division, to secretly collect and analyze the evidence in the murder committed at the House of Swaps. The reader must have already perceived that it was Baeta whom the chief of police rushed to call on the night of the crime.

Baeta had a great calling for the forensic sciences. Although he was not a doctor, he had acquired a solid understanding of anatomy and physiology and was rarely wrong when identifying the *causa mortis* and other circumstances surrounding a homicide.

Therefore, the coroner (hand-picked by the minister of justice himself), after a cursory examination, signed off on the expert's conclusions, forwarded in advance to the chief of police, which stated that the secretary had died of asphyxiation caused by constriction of the respiratory cavities of the neck, and that, because of the decline in temperature and the first signs of mandibular and cervical stiffness, strangulation must have occurred shortly before the approximate time when Fortunata exited the building.

Fingerprint analysis, particularly of the wine bottle and glasses, revealed that two people were drinking in that room— the secretary and one other individual. According to the nurses, who had witnessed the comings and goings of the suspect before the murder, Fortunata had grabbed the bottle and glasses and took them with her into the bedroom. Therefore, it stood to reason that the second set of fingerprints was hers.

At a given moment, probably in the bedroom, the bottle was grabbed by the body and not the neck. The size of the hand that did so coincides with that of the person who strangled the victim. Therefore, it was the prostitute who killed the secretary, there being no reason to assume the presence of a third individual at the scene of the crime.

This conclusion, however, was not without controversy: Baeta could not help but wonder about Fortunata's hand strength, which would have to be exceptional for a woman, and capable of fracturing the laryngeal cartilage of the secretary, a man with a robust and relatively adipose neck. Not to mention that she would have had to snap the cervical curvature at the fifth vertebra. Perhaps feeling a tinge of professional jealousy, the coroner chose to overlook this objection.

Of the objects seized from Rufino, the ones that most interested authorities were the earrings in the shape of seahorses; however, the overlapping fingerprints on them made precise identification difficult.

Sebastião Baeta also paid a visit to the English Cemetery. The first thing that caught his attention was the remnants of a bonfire, put out at least twelve hours earlier, which included not only ash, but also charred leather, probably from a shoe.

There were no signs of disturbed graves, or of overturned soil, except in a remote area, on the extreme right, on a slope, where, days before Rufino's arrest, a mass grave had been dug. In that grave, the bodies of ten sailors, who perished during a quarantine of a British cargo ship, were buried. The ship had come from Ceylon and perhaps brought with it a plague of some sorts.

The episode with the cargo ship had caused a rift of sorts between the Anglican community and Brazilian authorities. The English intended to accept only those sailors who were subjects of the British crown and who adhered to the Anglican faith. The city, however, decided that they would either bury all eleven dead—which included Indians, Africans, and Malays— or they would all be sent to a common grave at another burial ground.

Forced to admit Muslims and idolaters onto such holy ground, the cemetery's administrators were outraged and tried to block the exhumation, which they considered disgraceful, delaying the work of forensics by about ten days. Finally, on June 23rd, the mass grave was opened before a lieutenant from the First District and one of the expert's assistants. No female cadaver was found, and thus they rejected the hypothesis that

Rufino had killed Fortunata, stolen her earrings, and buried the body.

Baeta added the wine bottle and a photograph of the secretary's neck (which did not show his face), highlighting the region where the prostitute had choked him, so that the comparative analysis employed could be taught to students at the Police Academy.

I had almost forgotten a key fact: the silver-handled whip, which aroused so many malicious comments, had on it fingerprints that forensics concluded belonged to the woman. However, since it had not been used as a weapon, it was not added to the museum's collection.

Perhaps Sebastião Baeta's greatest merit as a forensics expert was his previous experience as an investigator. He had joined the police force as an officer, stationed first in the fifth district, in the most dismal area of Lapa, a favorite location for the practice of capoeira and a breeding ground for bandits. He soon showed talent in solving complex cases, using a simple methodology, which could be summed up in a phrase that he himself had coined: "No one can withstand a continuous and exhaustive investigation."

For Baeta, a crime scene said a lot about the criminal, who invariably left his "signature" behind. For him, ideally, the work of the forensic police consisted in discovering and identifying these signatures, without having to resort to the fallibility or even the venality of witnesses, the traditional tool for gathering evidence.

The expert's enthusiasm for dactyloscopy, therefore, was to be expected. His most ambitious project was to create fingerprint records for the entire population of Rio de Janeiro so as to be able to immediately identify a perpetrator after a crime had been committed.

Nonetheless, in 1913 criminal identification techniques

were still very new. Without properly hiring and training personnel, police authorities had no way of obtaining data for all of the city's inhabitants, but rather only for those who passed through the precincts. And even then, not all suspects were taken to Relação Street to be processed.

It was thus that Baeta first came face to face with Rufino. On the afternoon of June 23rd, when the inspection of the English Cemetery had been concluded, the chief of police called the precinct at Maúa Square, and ordered that the sorcerer be freed after being taken down to Relação Street and undergoing the customary processing. The captain at the precinct balked at the order, but the decision had already been made.

"That man's bait. Behind bars he won't be of any use to us."

Both the chief of police and Baeta were convinced that Rufino had not killed Fortunata, for one very simple reason: The old man's run-ins with the police in the past had all been for 399s—loitering. Everyone knew him, what he did for a living, where he lived. Which was precisely their great hope: that there might be some tie between him and the prostitute, so that they could track her down. If she were dead, on the other hand, discovering the motive of the crime, or who had ordered it, would be almost impossible.

The only problem—or, at least the only problem Baeta could see—was how to keep hidden the tie between the death of the secretary and the search for Fortunata. Especially since the earrings had been found in the possession of the sorcerer.

That was why the expert was extremely dismayed at seeing Rufino arrive at the police headquarters accompanied by an officer and the captain of the First District himself.

"I need to have a word with you, sir."

It was a delicate situation. Baeta, who would have preferred to be questioning the old man, left the job up to his subordinates, and he invited the captain into a private room. The expert looked askance as the officer followed them in.

"Don't worry. In the First District we're all brothers."

The captain thought it very important that he know the crime this woman known as Fortunata was being sought for. The expert, naturally, said he was also in the dark, that he worked in a bureaucratic area of the police, and who was he to question his superiors. The captain looked at him suspiciously.

"What's the lady have to do with the old man?"

The situation was not only delicate, it was also dangerous. If Baeta did not act quickly, the Maúa Square people might get their hands on Fortunata. And of course they would force her to talk, and then the whole story would go public. The expert, thus, turned the tables and abandoned his defensive stance.

"You've had the old man for ten days. More than enough time for a confession."

This time, to the surprise of the expert, the officer interceded, producing Rufino's statement, where he alleged he had not received the earrings directly from Fortunata, but from a certain man.

"That man will be at his house, next Friday."

The expert noticed a look of skepticism on the part of the captain. But the officer insisted.

"Wait till Friday, boss. The old guy doesn't lie."

Baeta had heard the legend before. To get them even further off track, he thought a slight taunt was in order.

"The last resort for a liar is to claim he doesn't lie. Rather obvious, don't you think?"

Officer Mixila was almost offended by this. And he began to recite stories about the sorcerer. He was one of the officers most responsible for spreading the mythology surrounding Rufino, telling incredible tales: miraculous cures, disconcerting predictions, spellbound individuals acting against their own will, or others who suddenly became rich, or managed to contact dead relatives.

And he referred to personal experiences, that he had a

corpo fechado, because of the old man's work, which protected him from metal weapons and bullets, which had saved him fantastically, in confrontations with the worst criminal elements, and that everyone had witnessed this, even the captain.

"I owe him my life."

Mixila opened his shirt to show the scars. Just then, someone knocked, saying that they were done with the old man.

Baeta could not resist asking Rufino, who looked at the captain with disdain, one question: "What's the relationship between this woman and the man who gave you the earrings?"

Rufino, with an air of insolence, did not hesitate.

"Just that they came from the same belly."

So, then, that was it: it was simpler than anyone had imagined. Perhaps it was worth waiting for the brother to be picked up; perhaps he really would appear on Friday at the sorcerer's home.

Baeta, then, told the old man that he was free to leave, and he formally returned the earrings to him. To his surprise, however, this greatly upset the captain: "This man was arrested in my jurisdiction. Any evidence of a possible crime, whatever that crime may be, stays with me, in my precinct."

Without waiting for an answer, the captain turned his back on Baeta, followed by Officer Mixila.

In 1890, during construction of the Central Post Office, in the old Imperial Palace, a coffin was dug up containing the skeleton of an adult male.

Due to the fact that he had been buried in one of the Palace rooms, due to the fact that he had been buried in a coffin, due to the fact that there had never been a single murmur of a murder committed in the privacy of that building, those with very active imaginations have imputed the crime to the emperor himself—more specifically, the first emperor.

Perhaps the suspicions were founded: Pedro I was impulsive, a good swordsman, he knew the rudiments of capoeira, and had affairs with countless married women. According to the most common rumor, the skeleton belonged to an outraged husband, or to a father seeking revenge, who had had access to the palace.

The much-discussed case of the skeleton, also known as the "crime of Bragança," was the subject of satirical and sensationalist newspaper serials, such as one by Vítor Leal (a pseudonym shared by Olavo Bilac, Aluísio Azevedo, Pardal Mallet, and Coelho Neto), who gave the story its current and definitive shape.

There are, however, plausible objections to this hypothesis. According to newspapers of the time, an analysis of the coffin revealed that the body had not decomposed inside. It was a second burial, after the remains had been exhumed a first time. Since the statute of limitations had expired, there had been no investigation or forensics performed. Therefore, it was never proved conclusively that the victim was a male.

This hypothesis, that the bones buried in the palace were those of a woman, ties the case to the tenebrous mystery of the witch buried alive behind a wall.

To make a list of the witches of Rio de Janeiro, both male and female, from the earliest of times would be an impossible task in a novel such as this. Lima Barreto, who had been an occultist, wrote many of his short stories based on cases he had studied: for example, the case of the French alchemist who arrived on du Clerc's fleet in 1710 and claimed he could transmute human bones into gold, which resulted in a slew of desecrated graves throughout Rio de Janeiro and was told as fiction in the classic *The New California*.

It was Barreto who uncovered the case of a local male witch whose life's work was to create an elementary library—that is, literally, a library composed of a single book—wherein it would be possible to read all the stories theoretically conceivable to the human imagination. These are the real facts that formed the basis for his short story *The Man Who Knew Javanese*.

I could cite other examples: *The Cemetery, The Number of the Sepulcher, The Sorcerer and the Police Captain*. Lima Barreto's work was tremendously informed by witchcraft, but he forgot about the walled-in witch.

In fact, the legend of the witch has truly been forgotten in time. She disappeared suddenly, in 1699, leaving no trace after cursing the Jesuits, who had enslaved her, and the entire kingdom of Portugal, and prophesizing the Lisbon earthquake.

For the purposes of this book, the importance of the witch—or, to use a more dignified word, sorceress—is not merely due to the happenstance that she and old Rufino belonged to the same lineage of African *gangas* and *mulójis*, and thus were heirs to the same arts and knowledge, but rather because the walled-in sorceress was the first in the city's history to add the ancient heritage of the Indian *pajés* to that rich tradition, and to the persistent tradition of European witchcraft.

As a slave in Lisbon, she memorized the content of the books of Saint Cyprian, particularly the teachings of the infamous witch Evora, of whom this saint had been a disciple when he lived among the Chaldeans.

In Rio de Janeiro, as a slave of the Society, having served in the mills for years (thus explaining her extensive contact with indigenous people), she came to master all of the uses and applications of tobacco, the native techniques of dream interpretation, and the method of temporarily uncoupling the soul in order to have direct contact with dead spirits.

It was also on Carioca soil that she learned about the gypsy doctrine and made friends with the New Christian and the kabbalist Semeão de Arganil, having helped that wise man to make a short-lived golem—the only recorded one in the city's history.

Like Rufino, she was almost a century old; and also like him, she did not tell lies, was incapable of telling lies—proof being that she had never been wrong about a plague or a prophecy. Those who know magic now know in what branches of knowledge this sorceress dwelled.

And it was precisely for devoting herself to these less noble divisions of witchcraft that the walled-in witch sealed her fate: on Ash Wednesday of 1699—the first summer day after the dreary storms that lasted through carnival—the sorceress shook up the city, making a great scandal at the door of the City Hall, demanding punishment for some priests who had supposedly physically abused her during the previous three nights.

Her story was not given the consideration it deserved, however, perhaps because the matter was not deemed to involve the plague, or perhaps because they judged her to be too disfigured, even for a bunch of old priests. She was arrested the first time when she foresaw grave omens against the Jesuits at the Largo da Sé.

Punished, she returned to the streets shortly thereafter, spouting curses in which she described, in an animated and impressive manner, the seismic events that would blight the capital of the kingdom in little more than half a century.

She was detained this time right at the Terreiro da Polé, next to the pillory, while addressing a large crowd. She was brought before a judge and sentenced to a public lashing—disappearing shortly afterwards without witnesses.

The disappearance was notable for one sole reason: she was bound tightly to a thick pole at the pillory, and had just received fifty lashes. Word spread that she had died during the ordeal due to the negligence of the authorities, for a surgeon or doctor should have accompanied the enforcement of the sentence to avoid such accidents. The executioners themselves would have disposed of the body, thus absolving themselves of any responsibility.

To counter this version, the priests themselves spread the rumor that she had vanished into thin air, as real witches did, and that she had plunged straight into Hell.

Certain truths, however, leak—albeit partially. And the story that has remained since then is that the witch had been buried alive inside a wall at the college at Castelo Hill.

Coincidentally, that same year construction began on the Mint—the architectural nucleus of the future Palace. In the administration of Gomes Freire, later the Count of Bobadela, the building underwent significant renovations, including the addition of a second floor, meant to be the governors' mansion and later that of the viceroys. Soon after, they began tearing up walls to make way for stairways.

Here is my theory: the foul-mouthed witch was removed from the pillory still alive, but not by her executioners. Esteemed citizens, gentlemen who had witnessed the ordeal, realized that she would not resist long. And they seized the opportunity to enclose her behind the walls—not of the college, but of the building under construction, right next door, at the Terreiro da Polé.

The first ones to discover the corpse—four decades later, when the Mint was undergoing its renovation to become the Palace—decided, without fanfare, to clean the skeleton and put it in a decent coffin, and they reburied it in the same structure.

These were foremen, stonecutters, street pavers, carpenters, housepainters, and masons of all sorts, much utilized on that job. And among the ancient traditions of their professions is the one that says it is necessary when constructing large buildings to entomb a live person in the walls, preferably a woman, to assure the structure will not collapse. They would not run the risk of removing such a protection.

We have seen how the first contact between Sebastião Baeta and old Rufino transpired, and how, during that brief interview, Baeta could not resist one question about the relationship between the prostitute Fortunata and the individual, still conjectural, who had given the old man the earrings in the shape of a seahorse.

The expert's anxiety should come as no surprise to the reader: the investigations up until that day had not linked Fortunata to anyone outside her circle at the House of Swaps—except, of course, the woman who ran the sewing school, from whom she had rented a room.

According to all witnesses, she had no friends or relatives in the city. The landlady was particularly emphatic on this point: that for her (before the police search), her tenant's great virtue was precisely that. Be it on a Sunday or a public holiday, she hardly ever left the house. She would not go on day trips, or meet up with girlfriends, or go out on dates. She seemed exclusively devoted to her work, and despite being pretty and well dressed she was not in the habit of blowing her money on Ouvidor Street.

She came to Dr. Zmuda's clinic referred by one of the nurses who had been at the House longest, an extremely trustworthy girl. Madame Brigitte—who was from Espirito Santos, but pretended to be French, and who supervised the girls—was a very cautious person and confessed to Baeta that, at the time, she had found the referral odd, because normally the initiative to hire new girls was her own. Baeta wanted to know the name of the girl who had made the referral.

"You probably remember her—Cassia. She married a client, a judge, and then they ran off to Europe together."

Baeta remembered the girl because he had been with her shortly before his final trip to the United States to study forensics. He persisted: had Cassia given references? Had she said something about Fortunata's previous life? Madame Brigitte was visibly uneasy.

"She was so persistent. She had so many positive things to

say about her, she gave me so many assurances, that I ended up taking pity on her."

Fortunata's initial interview was in the wing to the left of the lobby, occupied by Dr. Zmuda's clinic.

Madame Brigitte insisted that they follow the clinic's official protocol. She asked about her qualifications as a nurse, purposefully keeping her on her toes. In the end, not only was she obliged to recognize the beauty of the applicant, she took a liking to her too—her mischievous look, her smile which made it clear that she saw through the charade perfectly well.

They made arrangements to obtain papers from the Holy House of Mercy, as they had done on numerous other occasions. It was the only document containing any information on the prostitute, and it was minimal: "Fortunata Conceição, a native of Rio de Janeiro." That was it.

"You must understand, the letter is a fake."

The first client was an importer of agricultural supplies, a man of routine sexual appetites. Though not violent, he was rather vigorous and very well endowed. Madame Brigitte really wanted to impress Fortunata, so she would assimilate well to the vicissitudes of her new profession. What she had not counted on, when she entered the bedroom after the client had left, was the stain of blood on the sheets.

"It was my first time."

Madame Brigitte was dismayed by this, and even moved. She never did discover the real motives that led that beautiful twenty-something woman to seek out such a life so freely.

Fortunata, however, did not make a big deal about it. She was there of her own accord. And she had a talent for this.

She was permissive, enjoyed her line of work, and did things with the demeanor of one who does good deeds. She disproved the biased and untrue theory—still held by many intellectuals—that prostitutes never feel pleasure in their line of work. Fortunata had intense and beautiful orgasms.

She was, however, very reserved: she did not share episodes from her personal life; she never spoke of her family or mentioned the reasons that had brought her to the House. Soon she became better known and respected, and it was not long before she was invited to the parties. Fortunata would work with other women, couples—nothing was out of bounds for her.

The expert was taken aback by Madame Brigitte's final words to him: "She liked to get some, that tramp."

Baeta also heard from the nurses. They did not find the violent whipping strange at all; it was actually to be expected with the secretary. The only pertinent fact, which did not really say much, was their shared perception that Fortunata had been very agitated in recent days and had acted aggressively on more than one occasion—even unintentionally biting a client's lips.

The expert also spoke with Miroslav Zmuda himself, but he did not make much headway on that front. On the contrary, he almost had a run-in with the doctor because he insisted on a list of Fortunata's principal clients.

"Should I include your name, too?"

The expert laughed, easing the tension. He had met the prostitute under unusual circumstances. It was in the famous "darkroom," one of Madame Brigitte's inventions. Once a month, always on a Monday, the Madame would gather all of the nurses on the right wing of the upper floor and block out all of the light. The clients would then be permitted to enter. The most fascinating perversions would ensue.

He was unaware that Fortunata was the name of the woman who had attracted him that night. Seated casually beside her on a cushioned rosewood settee, he sensed her presence by her perfume and the warmth of her skin, and moved in on the mystery woman.

He pulled back in disgust, though, when he noticed there was someone else there, a third person, a man seated on her other side, touching the same parts, disputing the same spaces. But she was irresistible, the texture of her skin, her flesh, and Baeta tried again, wanting her to choose him. But Fortunata did not, and the two men shared her.

Insecure, jealous, suspicious, the expert felt a sense of failure, because the mysterious partner had climaxed with the other man. When he left, he knew he would come back—as he in fact did—to find out who she was, to be with her again, because he could not accept a secondary role for himself.

He concluded that that woman—capable of taking a man like him to such extremes, so compliant and yet so perfectly in charge—did not need to kill to get what she wanted.

In the early morning hours of Friday, June 27th, the caretaker at the English Cemetery made his rounds with lime paint and a brush. He cleaned gravestones and pruned the trees, and was a kind of chief gravedigger. On his way to give a coat of lime to the wall of the memorial chapel, he was shocked when he saw a low-flying vulture preparing to land near the jambul tree to the rear of the cemetery.

Still attempting to grasp what was happening, he followed the bird. He could not believe his eyes: one of his shovels was resting on a mound of earth, near the sailors' mass grave.

The stench, the sound of beating wings, led him quickly to deduce what he would see moments later at the edge of the hole: partially exposed bodies in advanced stages of putrefaction serving as a meal for the throng of black butchers.

He immediately grabbed his shovel and began to refill the grave, which did not have the intended effect of scaring away the birds, which is when he realized that this might be a case for the police, and decided to alert the authorities.

It was a great embarrassment to the cemetery administrators, who had resisted the presence of the forensic experts so vehemently just two weeks earlier. Now there was no doubt:

the cemetery had been violated in exactly the same location that had aroused suspicion the first time.

To sift through that rotten matter again, after so little time had elapsed, was essential. With a mask that barely held back the odor, Sebastião Baeta personally oversaw the inspection this time, along with one of the lieutenants from the First District.

If, days earlier, the goal of the examination had been to discover the body of Fortunata—possibly murdered and thrown into this ditch by the murderer—now the main question was whether any cadavers had been stolen by whoever had done this.

Baeta thought to consult the cemetery's records, to compare them with the number of dead buried in the grave. The answer raised even more questions: on June 9th, eleven sailors had been lowered into the pit, and exactly eleven bodies remained buried on the 27th.

Nearby, the expert also identified remnants of candles and a pile of ashes containing pieces of a white sheet. It was a detail that incriminated Rufino, because a similar residue had been found during the first investigation and in almost the same place.

Unfortunately, when the head gravedigger witnessed the attack of the vultures, he was overtaken by the impulse to fill in the grave before warning the police. This hampered the analysis of footprints, a problem exacerbated by the large number of people who visited the scene after the incident was discovered.

Still, Baeta ascertained that at least one individual had been there in bare feet, and that it was probably the same person who had opened the grave. This footprint, of course, was one more clue against the old man, who had not lost certain habits from his time in captivity and never wore shoes.

From investigations carried out in the vicinity, an old woman, a practitioner of *macumba*, reported that shortly after the Big Hour (midnight) she lowered gifts to the Lord Skull, at the gateway to Little Kalunga (the graveyard), consisting of manioc flour, firewater, snuff, and seven black candles.

The Lord Skull had commanded her to sing and trace twenty-one *quimbanda* points (witchcraft lines), seven times each. And should she see anything, she should close her eyes. And should she hear anything, she should not respond.

To visit a cemetery at that time, the Big Hour, is not for the faint of heart. But the old woman had faith in the *catiços* (the entities), especially in Lord Skull.

So, when she finished tracing her lines with the *pemba* chalk at the gate, the last point having been traced at about 2 A.M., she heard footsteps getting closer and closer. She kept on singing, though almost at a whisper, lowered her face, and clenched her eyes shut. When she could almost feel the man's breath, she heard a mocking voice:

"Good evening, ma'am!"

Her statement, of course, was never officially taken down. Baeta asked one more question: "Can you remember with certainty whether these were the footsteps of someone wearing shoes?"

The witness did not have to think very hard before answering yes. However, her statement—which could have cast doubt on the intruder's identity—did not prevent the captain of the First District, after receiving a note from the lieutenant who was accompanying Baeta, from taking the only reasonable measure in his opinion: ordering the arrest of the individual to whom the evidence pointed.

Rufino was arrested by three officers that same day before 11 A.M., while walking down Santa Teresa Hill, at the corner of Riachuelo.

At the precinct, the captain ordered some of his men to return to Santa Teresa in order to break into the suspect's home and conduct a search.

"I didn't dig up those bodies."

Rufino's denial did not convince the captain.

"Were you or were you not at the English Cemetery last night after the gates closed?"

Rufino did not answer, claiming that his profession demanded complete secrecy. The sergeant insulted him, threatened him, and even kicked at him violently, but the officers restrained the sergeant. When push came to shove, they would defend the old man. Such was their fear of his power.

"He didn't do it, boss. The old man doesn't lie."

The captain doubted Rufino, and the claim that he never lied, for the simple reason that he considered it impossible for human beings to withstand the weight of the absolute truth. But he developed a very logical line of reasoning, beginning with the following premise: if he did not lie, if he was incapable of lying, his silence was tantamount to a confession. Therefore, the old sorcerer had been at the English Cemetery the night before to commit the crime specified in Article 365.

The officers, however, protested, and a major meeting was called to prevent the issuing of an arrest warrant. The captain respected his men, his brothers in the First District. He did not want to act without consensus, and he tried to convince them that something major was afoot in the Mauá Square jurisdiction, and that they were being kept in the dark by the chief of police.

Just then, the sound of loud voices interrupted the discussion: the officers tasked with entering and searching the sorcerer's house had just returned, and they brought with them a man they had arrested trying to enter the shanty after calling the old man's name.

"That's the man who gave me the earrings."

The first record in the history of Rio de Janeiro of the desecration of a cemetery is a 1551 letter by an anonymous Jesuit priest addressing the Provincial Superior in Lisbon, a document that Serafim Leite attributed to Father Nobrega.

The story is more or less as follows: a group of Tamoio Indians, proud and well-armed, left the village of Uruçumirim to capture Maracajás who lived in Paranapuã. They landed in what is now Ribeira Beach and soon spotted the enemy.

The fighting was fierce, but the Tamoios had the advantage right up until more Maracajás from other regions arrived and began repelling the invaders. The Tamoios then fled, taking a few prisoners with them. The scene is described in very lively fashion, complete with the whistling of arrows and the thump of war clubs—proof of the "furor with which the Brazilian natives attack their adversaries."

But what most impressed Father Nobrega—if indeed he was the author of the letter, because there is evidence that he was in Pernambuco at the time—was not the violence of the combat, but rather the ignominy of the revenge.

A brief digression is in order. The Tupi, contrary to other peoples—such as the Portuguese, the Gypsies, and the Ethiopians—do not accept that death occurs simply when life is interrupted. With the exception of the great Tuxauas—avengers and cannibals, like Cunhambebe, for example—a person dies only when the skull is fractured. From that moment on, the soul begins a dark journey through death's paths, battling the *anhangas*, the cannibal spirits, so as to overcome annihilation and achieve absolute eternity in the Land of No Evil.

So, the Maracajás (Father Nobrega tells us)—knowing or sensing that the Tamoios would return to the battlefield in order to break the skulls of their fallen comrades, and thus guarantee their tally—instead of burying their own dead, buried the Tamoios that they had slaughtered as if they were Maracajás.

Thus, the skulls that the Tamoios split five years later, on that same battlefield, were those of their own relatives.

It was said later that it was this act of fratricide that weakened them, until they were finally vanquished by the Temiminós of Arariboia (who are Maracajás too), in the war that culminated in the founding of the city.

Rio de Janeiro, thus, arose from a desecrated cemetery. And the tradition continued. By 1567, even though the city's founding landmark had been transferred from Sugar Loaf Beach to Castelo Hill, the modest little mud-and-thatch church (which also housed the sacred icon of Saint Sebastian, the city's patron saint) remained in the old town. And this little church was almost ruined in a landslide during heavy December rains. In rebuilding the church, it was discovered that the tomb of Estacio de Sá, who had been buried with a huge gold cross on his chest, had been violated.

The cross, of course, had vanished. And years later, in 1583, when the mortal remains of the founder were finally transferred from the original chapel to the city's new site, they noticed the second outrage: Estacio's head had been shattered—surely revenge by a Tamoio defeated at Uruçumirim, who had opened the grave not to steal but to obtain credit for one more dead.

And the city's fate continued to unfold. In the 1660s, shortly after the Cachaça Revolt, a cult of fanatics emerged who were in the habit of digging up slaves, since they did not recognize their right to a burial. They would scatter their bones in public places as an affront. These sacrilegious attacks mainly targeted the cemetery created by the Franciscans for the burial of the order's own slaves.

I have already mentioned the case of the obscure French alchemist who traveled with du Clerc's fleet and caused similar disturbances. But the great terror begins in the nineteenth century, when a wave of necrophilia hit, whose apogee was during the Parnassian period. It was perhaps this coincidence that gave rise to the charges against the poet Bilac. His detractors never understood him, and make an analogy that seems a bit cruel: that Parnassians and necrophiliacs care only about form, ignoring content.

This era also saw the systematic trading of corpses, stolen from graves and then sold to the schools of medicine and surgery. The most interesting case was that of Paiva, a recently graduated medical student and a close friend of Álvares de Azevedo, who unknowingly dissected the remains of his own sister.

The nineteenth century also saw the first appearance of the living dead—or *cazumbis*—who have nothing to do with Semeão de Arganil's golem. True *cazumbis* are dead who are resurrected in order to be their creators' slaves.

Some experts say that they come from the *jeje* kingdoms of Dahomey. No one can ignore the power of *jeje* magic. Both mummification and the resurrection of *cazumbis* were sciences of ancient Nubia, which were assimilated by the pharaohs of Egypt and various secret societies that began to flourish in the region of Lake Nyanza, particularly the blacksmith clans of Bantu-speaking tribes.

In their tremendous march south, the Bantus spread. Although much was lost in this diaspora, certain peoples were formed based on all of this knowledge and on these secret associations. The most notable example being the *caçanjes*, from Angola.

That was the race of the walled-in witch, but neither the captain nor Baeta suspected that Rufino also belonged to these people.

Ever since he had ordered Rufino's release on the 23rd, the chief of police instructed that the men of the seventh district in Santa Teresa should keep him under observation, and should always communicate to him any strange occurrences, any actions that broke with the legendary sorcerer's well-known routines. This would not be an overt surveillance; the aim was to know who he was looking for, or who was looking for him, and whether he was frequenting different locations than his usual ones.

So, on the morning of the 27th, as soon as the officers of Mauá Square arrested the old man on the corner of Riachuelo, the police chief was notified, and knocked on Baeta's office door, which was in the same building on Relação Street. It was then that he learned of the raided graves and of the somewhat vague clues used to justify the warrant.

If he were not forceful, even despotic, with the First District, he would lose control of the case. And he resolved matters with one phone call, which caught the captain by surprise just as this new individual was being brought in.

"I'll interrogate the two of them. Personally. Right here on Relação Street."

The statement by Aniceto—the man arrested trying to enter Rufino's house—would close promising avenues and would virtually shut down the entire investigation, increasing the mystery surrounding the murder at the House of Swaps.

Aniceto was born on San Antonio Hill and had lived in Gamboa, Saúde, Pinto Hill, and Pedra do Sal. He was born to a single mother, who gave the child to his godmother to care for when he was not even ten days old, and disappeared shortly thereafter into the far-flung corners of Bangu. The boy's name was Aniceto Conceição—and his last name was not the only coincidence he shared with the prostitute Fortunata. Baeta, who sat next to the chief during the interrogation, detected in Aniceto many features of Fortunata's physiognomy.

"She's my sister, boss. Twins. She left with my mother. I stayed behind."

It was a typical story. Aniceto became an assistant typographer, in his father's company. His father took him in without ever acknowledging that he was his son. When his father died, his brothers threw him out. From then on, he lived around the docks, doing odd jobs. He never saw his mother again, and only recently had he reestablished contact with his sister.

He did not have a police record, but the officers who escorted him to Relação made sure to mention that Aniceto was well known in capoeira circles, although he had been missing from the *rodas de pernada* lately.

"I was up in Alagoas, boss. It's been about a month since I've been back."

The capoeira confirmed what Rufino had said: the seahorse-shaped earrings were payment for a service rendered, and before that they really had belonged to his sister. Obviously, such a statement, even if it did not directly cast suspicion on the witness, demanded plenty of explanation. The expert wanted to understand the relationship between the twins, since the nurses and the landlady were completely unaware of Aniceto's existence.

Aniceto told the story as follows: Between June 3rd (the day of his arrival) and 13th (the day of Fortunata's disappearance) he resided in her room, and in fact she had given him the keys, giving him access to the entire second floor. His days were spent in the room, with the door locked (the landlady could not suspect his presence), and late at night he would go out to stretch his legs and have his fun, always returning before dawn.

Fortunata had promised to help him secure some type of job through influential clients of hers. At this point in the interview, in a very suggestive tone—but a veiled threat, nonetheless—the capoeira revealed that his sister's other life was no secret to him.

"I knew where she worked, boss. I know very well what she did there."

Finally, on the 13th, at around 7 A.M., Fortunata entered the room, desperate to get money and other objects, saying she needed to disappear immediately. Without any explanation, she gave him some of her jewelry and wrote a letter to be delivered to Madame Brigitte—a desire he was still reluctant to comply with, because the hastily written missive contained a confession.

"I didn't tear the letter up. It's probably with the stuff she gave me."

Aniceto left the second-floor apartment shortly after his sister, and—since he had long harbored the desire to submit himself to one of old Rufino's spells—he immediately sought him out, giving him the earrings as payment.

The old landlady, who ran the sewing school and owned the apartment, was subpoenaed to testify. She was categorical:

"I've never seen this scoundrel before."

Aniceto could prove otherwise. First, he described the house in detail: the rocking chair, the mahogany table, the statue of Saint George, facing the door, the niche in the bedroom with Saint Anthony; and the hallway niche with Saint Francis of Assisi. He also spoke of the flowerpot with its horrible yellow ribbon and of the rusty carving knife. What is more, he showed an extensive knowledge of the landlady's habits: that she went to bed early and woke up at sunrise. He knew the names of two or three of her students, and that Sunday lunch was chicken with okra.

The sewing teacher—who was not in the habit of prying into Fortunata's life and did not have a copy of the key to her room—was speechless. Aniceto took the opportunity to return her keys to her. She exited, pale, trembling, cursing her former tenant's treachery and lack of morals.

The capoeira had recently moved into a rooming house near Harmonia Square. Officers escorted him there in order to examine the evidence. And, sure enough, there was the letter, which said the following: "I made a silly mistake. It wasn't on purpose. Please forgive me. And thank you for all you've taught me." It was signed, very visibly: "Fortunata." Below, in a postscript of sorts, the prostitute prayed for the secretary's soul, citing the deceased by name.

Later on, witnesses from the House of Swaps recognized the jewels found in Aniceto's possession as having belonged to the prostitute. Baeta was also able to attest that the signature on the letter was authentic by comparing it to the forged reports that Dr. Zmuda regularly asked the nurses to sign, as a precaution.

The expert also asked if the capoeira could give the names of any of his acquaintances who were also friendly with Fortunata.

"I never mentioned her, boss. Who mentions a sister who's a whore?"

In one of those old taverns in Santa Rita Square—or, more precisely, on the corner of old Cachorros Alley, in a dark and smoky room, where voices were never elevated above a whisper—the Brotherhood of the First District, sucking on their cigarettes and drinking cachaça after a strenuous day on the job, discussed the case of the English Cemetery.

The first lieutenant, who had been present at the forensic analysis of the allegedly violated grave, was lamenting a fatal error, which, according to him, could definitely have compromised the investigation.

"The first time around, we didn't count the bodies. We just checked to see if they were male."

This was his thesis: the police had started from a false premise—i.e., that Rufino had killed the prostitute and hidden the body in the mass grave. After forensics had done their job, since no female cadaver had been exhumed, the conclusion was that no crime had been committed. However, the lieutenant had a different theory: the old man had opened the grave and robbed a corpse to carry out some abominable spell, and for this he received the pair of gold earrings. And then, before the 23rd, he returned the body to the grave. Therefore, during the second inspection, the number of dead matched the records.

"And why didn't you ask for a count?"

It simply had not occurred to him. Perhaps the sinister environment, the fear of contracting the plague, the disgust of seeing those bodies piled up, explained the urgency with which everyone had dealt with the situation.

"And where does Fortunata fit in?"

She did not. For the lieutenant, such speculation was not acceptable. Rufino had to be arrested for multiple counts of grave robbery. And he reminded them of the public commotion over the recent cases, never solved, of stolen cadavers, in which suspicions were raised about the presence of necrophiliacs inside the police morgue.

"It's time to put that thief behind bars!"

The officers, however, believed the old man. These were honest cops, almost all of them, but possessed of an excessive honesty, bordering on mysticism. The fact that they came, most of them, from the same environment, were raised amid those same criminal characters they arrested, still weighed on them. Many consulted *alufás* and *mães-de-santos*, cropped their hair close, attended *jira dos catiços* to call on spirits, lit votive candles on Mondays. They had associated with capoeiras, gone to the *batuque* and *pernada* circles. They had, naturally, acquired the vice of gambling, and they did not just bet on the *jogo do bicho*, they also played in illegal card games with heavy pots. Intellectually, they were *malandros* too.

"It wasn't him, lieutenant. The old man doesn't lie."

Their argument was simple and very rational: in his interrogations, Rufino either gave compromising statements that put himself at risk—for example, revealing that the capoeira who had given him the earrings would be paying a visit to his home—or he would remain absolutely silent.

He kept quiet when it would have been natural, or at least less suspicious, to answer evasively. For example, questions like "Do you know Fortunata, the prostitute?" the sorcerer simply did not answer, when it would have been much easier just to answer, "No." Thus, it became clear that the old man was tacitly admitting knowing Fortunata—a woman sought by the police, and whose acquaintance could only bring complications. Not answering, "I've never heard of her," had, in a sense, been foolish.

The police, who had dealt with all sorts of street-smart criminals over the years, knew the customary procedure of those people. If Rufino had said nothing, it was because he did not—could not—tell lies.

The captain, for his part, disagreed with everybody. A truculent and idealistic type, he boasted of never having detained an innocent suspect, never having failed to substantiate a hunch. As far as he was concerned, Rufino *did* have ties to Fortunata and was being protected by the chief of police. And his main argument revolved around the gold earrings, which belonged to the woman and were found in the old man's possession.

"Think about it. Ponder the facts. In less than six hours, a woman, a fugitive from the law, gives a pair of gold earrings to a man, and a little while later those earrings end up in the hands of a sorcerer. It makes no sense, I'm sorry."

The men, accustomed to police reason, could not refute his argument through logic. The captain felt he was close to prevailing. And he plowed ahead. For him, the nature of the crime committed by Fortunata mattered little. Whether or not Rufino practiced his magic at the English Cemetery did not matter. He wanted to know what interest the police had in that old man and that woman. He insisted on that point, and that something big was afoot—that the entire Mauá Square Brotherhood was being left in the dark on purpose.

The captain reminded them that on the 13th, Rufino was surprised at the English Cemetery with the gold earrings in his possession, and that between the 26th and 27th he had also been there (forensics had found the bare footprints, very likely his). If Rufino had been paid one pair of gold earrings for his first job for Aniceto, on this latest occassion he must have received something of equal value.

Obviously, the old man must enter and exit cemeteries at every time of day, and at least twice a month (an average they had just ascertained), because everyone knows cemeteries are not protected. So, if he really were over a hundred years old, as the officers themselves claimed, by now he must have accumulated a vast fortune in gold pieces—or gems, silver, or even cash—whose value must be immeasurable.

This gave a great deal of credence to one of the legends spread about him, the only story that, unfortunately, his own men seemed to deride: that Rufino owned a magnificent treasure, buried somewhere in the city of Rio de Janeiro.

Then, suddenly, it happened. It all made sense to them. Because this is the effect, the virtue, of treasures, which for hundreds of centuries have driven human history.

What was at stake was not honor or integrity; it was not a dilemma concerning moral concepts. Nobody wanted to steal, or even thought of it. The First District police always refused any type of bribery. They would never commit a crime for money.

But they were men, too. And none of them—none of us—can resist the ancient fascination of a treasure hunt.

And the discussion continued, and the policemen remained there, drinking and smoking, completely infatuated with that mirage, with that concrete possibility, with the material existence of that legendary treasure—which they had only vaguely heard about, which they maybe even believed in, but which they never imagined they could be so close to.

There is no faith, there is no truth, that has so much power to move people. Especially in Rio de Janeiro. And so, just past midnight, Mixila himself slammed his fist on the table's grimy marble:

"Damn geezer!"

The first treasure to disappear in Rio de Janeiro was probably not buried in the earth but rather was lost at sea, near the mouth of Guanabara Bay, in a Spanish galleon weighing over three hundred tons. Reportedly, the ship was returning from an expedition to the Rio de la Plata, laden with Inca gold, and was dragged adrift by a formidable storm, bursting its hull against giant rocks, possibly Cagarras Islands.

A few of the survivors—who had escaped in rowboats or floating on planks—were picked up days later by another vessel from the same flotilla, which had temporarily gone off route, thereby escaping the fatal storm.

These are all sailor stories, backed by very little documentation. But if the shipwreck did in fact occur, and if we take the Inca gold as fact, it makes no sense to imagine that one of those survivors would have been able to battle the breakers on a piece of wood while clinging to a chest filled with dozens of kilos of precious metals, only to bury it ashore.

So, these legends of lost treasures summarize the essence of humanity. It was this legend, the treasure of the Spanish galleon, that brought the first pirates to Guanabara Bay, and, years later, in 1531, led Martim Afonso de Souza to drop anchor at the western rim of the bay, opposite the mouth of the Carioca River, and to erect a fort and organize futile expeditions in search of that gold.

This circumstance—the galleon's treasure that has never been found; the fact that treasures in general are never found—is, for these hunters, the greatest proof of its existence. The fame of perhaps the greatest treasure in Carioca history—

the one belonging to the Jesuits, which has been missing ever since they were expelled in 1759—is based on similar foundations.

There is little doubt that the treasure exists. What is not certain is whether it was hidden beneath the college at Castelo Hill. After a lengthy resistance put up by priests, the building was finally evacuated, and then slaves, students, bands of soldiers, and a throng of people from all walks of life searched the building, probing all of its entrails, never finding a thing.

That was when talk began about a secret passageway connecting the college to Calabouço Point. Society informants would have alerted the priests in Brazil in time, who would have preemptively loaded this immense fortune onto clandestine brigantines, whose whereabouts today are impossible to ascertain. Let's face it, this story borders on fantasy literature: no ship at the time would have been able to cross the entrance to the impregnable bay—which only once in its entire history had been overtaken—without being detected.

Therefore, I do not think the thesis that the treasure was smuggled out has any merit. The Jesuits' treasure stayed in Rio de Janeiro. Another indication of this is that it continued to be actively sought during all major construction projects requiring excavation in the city, particularly during the razing of Castelo Hill in the 20th century.

It should come as no surprise that a second (totally fictional) version of this legend links the Jesuits' treasure to alleged Phoenician inscriptions on Sugar Loaf Mountain, which (fraudulently, in my opinion) make mention of a Prince of Tyre. That great treasure, so the story goes, initially belonged to the Templars, and before that to King Solomon, discoverer of the mines of Ophir.

The Jesuits, by virtue of their erudition, would have been the first to identify the Carioca tomb of the Asiatic prince, discoverer of the Atlantic route to Guanabara, later hiding the treasure found next to the sarcophagus in a location that remains hidden.

One detail of the story is particularly noteworthy: even after they were arrested, deported, and tortured, which indeed the priests of the Society were, none of them ever revealed the hiding place of the treasure. This is another feature of those who bury vast riches: their code of silence.

Such was the case of a treasure of emeralds brought to Rio de Janeiro before Garcia Rodrigues Paes had opened his trail—proof that the Cariocas joined the fray for the mines around the same time that the fierce São Paulo prospectors did.

Even before the city was founded, there were already rumors of precious green stones in the hinterlands. Martim de Góis, who left in 1695 to go up the Inhomirim and reached as far as the Piabanha, had no other goal than finding these famous stones. Perhaps he made it as far as the headwaters of the Tocantins. Martim de Gois, however, never came back. He was killed, along with several of his men, by a faction of rebels led by the *mameluco* Nuno Esteves.

The *mameluco* and his men reached Rio de Janeiro, bringing back bodies of several Indians wrapped in hammocks, all with their heads crushed.

Nuno Esteves' story was hard to believe: that while passing by an Indian village on the banks of Iguaçu, three days' march from the city, they had surprised a mob of savages ready to cook those dead, whom they had just sacrificed in their fashion.

The dead must have been from the Jacutingas Nation, previously catechized, as the village had its own cross. Nuno Esteves and his followers managed to drive away the cannibals, recovering the bodies of pious Jacutingas in order to give them a proper burial.

Despite the nuisance caused by the odor, the *mameluco*

insisted on holding a wake for the Indians, claiming that he had vowed to do so. It was this strange show of devotion that alerted people that something was amiss.

The next day it was discovered that, besides the broken skulls, the bodies had been torn open from the base of the neck to the bladder, and that their guts had been totally emptied out.

He could have explained everything away: that they had been eaten by the other savages, and that their entrails had already been removed. However, someone pointed out that the victims were not properly painted, according to tradition. This was evidence of the fraud perpetrated. And sure enough, while handling the corpses, an emerald slipped out of one of their throats.

The men of the expedition were tortured, but they never revealed where the stones were hidden. The *mameluco* Nuno Esteves also never admitted to the murder of Martin de Goís and those who had been faithful to him. They all died on the gallows, in a dignified manner, shortly thereafter.

What about those treasures that cannot be found even though it is known where they are buried? Such was the case of the celebrated Manuel Henriques, the Gloved One—a nobleman bandit who tormented travelers along the the gold roads and trails, stealing heavy loads of the metal mined in Minas Gerais that had to be brought down, as the law stipulated, to the city of São Sebastião.

The story of the nobleman is interesting. In love with Queen Maria, the Mad, he once was allowed to stand in a receiving line to kiss her royal highness' hand, but only managed to touch the tip of her fingers. From that day on, as a pledge of his love, he never took off his glove.

They say Queen Maria began to lose her wits from that moment on, and that this angered the court, resulting in the persecution of the Gloved One. Even if the incident did not truly make the queen mad, it did lead her would-be lover to seek consolation in a life of crime.

Manuel Henriques was the terror of the northern part of the state of Rio de Janeiro and the southern part of Minas Gerais during the last decades of the 18th century.

He grew rich like a king. But he never did win the love of his life.

His treasure is in a cave lost in the confines of Vargem Pequena, on the edge of the Guaratiba parish, in a seemingly impenetrable place in the Grota Funda hills called Cova de Macacu. I even went there myself when I lived in Recreio, and I have foraged through those woods. They say the slaves who carried the treasure, the only witnesses who knew its hiding place, were murdered shortly after they buried it.

The most extraordinary Carioca treasure, however, is that of the king of the Ivory Coast—or, better said, the treasure belonging to Chica da Silva. The theme here is the subjective value of the treasure, not the impenetrable secrecy that surrounds it.

The king of the Ivory Coast was actually a prince of the mighty Ashanti Empire who came to Brazil to expand the slave trade, dropping anchor in Rio de Janeiro. Here, he praised the beauty of the women and, quite naturally, wanted to meet the queen of the land.

Coincidentally, Chica da Silva had just arrived from Tijuco Township to see the sea for the first time. And she was introduced to the Ashanti embassy as the sovereign ruler of Brazil, which was not exactly a lie.

It seems that the contractor João Fernandes de Oliveira, Chica's husband, slept well during the night the two of them spent aboard the prince's galley. And at the farewell banquet, hosted by the slave trader Manuel Coutinho, Chica da Silva received a huge gift in African gold, jewels, and rich pieces carved in ivory, which astonished all of the guests.

This treasure, however, never made it back to the Castelo da Palha in Tijuco. When João Fernandes ordered the chests opened, he found only sand and shells. The contractor was in an uproar. He summoned his slaves and threatened to kill the responsible party. Chica da Silva took no notice: for someone who would never see the immensity of the sea again, it did not seem like such an unfavorable exchange.

When the expert Baeta left the House of Swaps at five in the afternoon on Wednesday, June 18th, he had already concluded a series of formal interviews with the doctor, the nurses and house manager, and thus had amassed all of the available information on Fortunata, even the secret list of her major clients—obtained with great difficulty—which would undoubtedly have been of interest to the chief of police, for it included some well-known military and political figures.

That's what the expert thought. But Madame Brigitte, evidently, had not revealed everything. She had omitted one essential fact: that she had detected a contradiction—a lie, actually—told by nurse Cassia, the senior nurse, who had referred Fortunata and insisted so vehemently that she be allowed to work there.

Fortunata and Cassia had been neighbors. Their mothers were each other's godmothers, and they themselves had been childhood friends. Madame Brigitte noticed that the two did not show much affection, and never exhibited much intimacy, but she did not pay it any mind; she attributed the behavior to modesty. After all, Fortunata was very reserved with all of them.

The time arrived, however, for Cassia to get married. A former client had asked for her hand three weeks after her childhood friend had come to the House. That excited the imagination of the other girls, who were very hurt when they did not receive an invitation to attend the ceremony. Not even

Fortunata was invited, which did not escape the notice of Madame Brigitte.

Madame Brigitte, however, did go. As the guests were congratulating the couple, she was introduced to Cassia's mother. She asked her about her friend, and she discreetly mentioned Fortunata. The mother's look of confusion said it all: the story of the childhood friendship was false. And Madame Brigitte, though upset, did not make a big deal of it. She concluded that the lie was well-intentioned, and that it was not worth provoking disagreements with a nurse already so well established in the House and who had shown herself to be so good-natured.

Madame Brigitte regretted having told the expert that Fortunata's admission process had deviated from the norm. It was a rare occasion—perhaps even the only time—that such an oversight had occurred: a nurse hired without a corresponding job opening, without a demand for a new nurse. For this reason, Madame Brigitte blamed herself for the secretary's murder. Miroslav Zmuda, of course, did not know any of this, and asked no questions when he saw her, soon after the expert's departure, writing a letter whose content he had no interest in knowing.

Madam Brigitte, in fact, was more than simply a house administrator. She first met the doctor at the old clinic in Glória, shortly before the court order transferred to him the ownership of the Marquise of Santos' house. At the time, Madame Brigitte was a recent arrival from Espirito Santo, residing on Lapa Street at a boarding house for young actresses, and she had not yet adopted the French moniker.

When she took her clothes off and lay naked before the doctor, she felt she could not resist; she ended up betraying herself, unable to conceal the subtle contractions in her gluteals. Dr. Zmuda, experienced in these matters, understood the offer. And, without neglecting to examine her, he satisfied her in just the right spot.

Miroslav Zmuda visited the Lapa street address and became a client, and made of her a kept woman, taking her away from that life once he became a widower. By the time he took possession of the House, Madame Brigitte—already going by that name—was his sweet concubine.

The Marquise's House was a find, for both of them. Ever since she had first moved into the boarding house, the dream of that humble girl from Espirito Santo had been to be French and to own a brothel. Not only for the money: the future Brigitte was fascinated by the sexuality of others. She loved to know the small perversions that made up personalities. She believed that it was possible to predict the behavior of people based on their sexual character.

Miroslav Zmuda, for his part, was what we would today call an obstetrician or gynecologist: he performed abortions, sterilizations, and treated venereal diseases. Although not a sexologist in the classical sense, he had a special interest in the physiology of coitus. He was one of the first Western scientists to study the phenomenon of sexual attraction. Born in Krakow, he naturally preferred Rio de Janeiro.

And so the House of Swaps came to be, and Madame Brigitte was its prime mentor. The architecture of the building lent itself perfectly to its purpose: to the left of the imposing main entrance there was a gate for carriages, which drove down a lane lined with giant strangler figs and royal palms, all the way to the rear, where two elliptically curved iron staircases took guests directly to the second floor. There were so many trees between these staircases and the small lake that graced the garden that visitors who exited there could rest assured they would not be seen by anyone outside the House.

Madame Brigitte wanted the House to be a secret institution whose existence was known only to those whom it served. Thus, she was not merely satisfied with copying similar establishments, whose doors were essentially always open. She devised a space both open and closed, where women and men could give free rein to the most abstruse desire, immune from social disapproval.

Therefore, discretion was the basic rule. The most common type of clients—men seeking prostitutes, for example—never knew that boys were also available, unless they requested them. Group nights were also promoted in secrecy, and nurses who were not invited did not even suspect they existed.

All sexual idiosyncrasies were kept strictly confidential, and only the parties involved knew about them. Madame Brigitte also catered to risky desires; in such cases, though, it was necessary give the personnel the day off and suspend all activities, which required very high financial compensation, as was the case with the lady who wanted to be with four men at once (Madame Brigitte demanded that she be masked), or the gentleman who enjoyed mistreating young men in uniform (usually foreign sailors, recruited at the piers).

Madame Brigitte trained the girls, developing in them the ability to discover inadmissible drives and propose to clients the most exotic adventures. Therefore, the success of the House of Swaps depended on the selection of its nurses, to which Madame Brigitte gave special importance. She wanted only women of great talent with very reputable pasts. In the case of Fortunata, she had failed in her evaluation of this second trait.

Although it was already too late, after the expert's visit, Madame Brigitte decided to set the record straight regarding certain matters, even if it meant saying a few harsh words. So, she sent off the letter, addressed to a distant ranch in the vicinity of Encantado.

The letter arrived at its destination, but from there it was forwarded to another address in Europe. It lay there a few months, until the addressee returned from her summer travels. When the answer came—in late September, well after the point where the narrative is now—Madame Brigitte had a big surprise, and an even bigger disappointment.

In fact, Cassia was not Fortunata's friend. She did not even know Fortunata. She just wanted to leave the life, and sought someone versed in the magic arts of *mandiga* to win over the heart of the judge, who was a good man and an old client. The sorcerer Rufino demanded a diamond ring, and that she place a person of his own choosing—the prostitute Fortunata—at the House of Swaps.

The minimally experienced reader knows that in police novels, or mystery novels in general—at least when there is an honest relationship between the narrator and his readers—there comes a point when the reader has enough information to solve the mystery.

When the reader intuits that this point has been reached, the reader feels compelled to anticipate the end, guessing the narrative ploy that gives coherence to the plot—usually revealed only in the last pages. Therein lies the pleasure of the literary game.

That is precisely the point our story has reached. Although some facts remain hidden, all the clues have been provided, some directly and others symbolically. Nonetheless, for the expert Baeta, I believe it is still impossible to solve the crime of the House of Swaps.

This was the conclusion that Baeta himself had reached, in the confidential report he prepared and signed for the chief of police in early July.

On June 13th, 1913, at about four o'clock in the afternoon, the secretary of the presidency of the republic arrived at the House of Swaps and was greeted by the prostitute Fortunata. Minutes after they entered the room, Fortunata went downstairs to get two glasses and a bottle of red wine in Dr. Zmuda's makeshift wine cellar beneath the grand staircase, where, leg-

end has it, there is a secret passageway built by Emperor
Pedro I.

The following fact should be emphasized: the nurses at the
House at the time saw Fortunata pass, holding the bottle and
glasses. So, the fingerprints found on these objects that are not
the secretary's belong to her.

At around 6 P.M., Fortunata passed the Upper Oval Parlor,
where her colleagues were gathered. She was in a hurry, and
reacted in an uncharacteristically curt manner to a kind gesture, before leaving through the front door. She was wearing a
blue taffeta gown and had on the pair of gold earrings shaped
like seahorses.

Shortly before eight, taking note of the secretary's unusually
lengthy stay in the room, Madame Brigitte asked someone to
wake up their illustrious client, which was when he was found
dead, bound tightly to the bedposts, with deep thumb marks
on his neck. The police report confirmed the cause of death as
asphyxiation, with no signs of robbery.

According to the capoeira, Aniceto, the prostitute's brother
(a fact that did not need documentation due to their extremely
similar physiognomy), Fortunata returned to the building
where she rented a room, in a hurry, saying she had made a silly
mistake and needed to escape.

She left a letter addressed to the House manager, Madame
Brigitte, which was never delivered. The sister also left the
capoeira money and jewelry, including the famous earrings.
Witnesses identified the other pieces as also belonging to the
prostitute.

According to forensics, Fortunata would have arrived at
Conceição Hill between half past six and twenty to seven—in
other words, after dark. The owner of the building did not see
the prostitute enter or exit, although she could not remember
whether or not she had retired by then. She was unaware of the
true profession of her tenant (who had intentionally kept her

in the dark) and had never noticed a man staying with her in her room. Although she was forced to admit that Aniceto had described the house perfectly.

The capoeira's version was also corroborated by the authentication of Fortunata's handwriting and signature in the letter to Madame Brigitte, which were compared to the fake nursing reports required by the Polish doctor.

The police search of the second floor apartment occurred around 9:30 P.M. Aniceto had left at around 8 P.M. (shortly after his sister) and had immediately gone to Rufino the sorcerer's house. He used the earrings to pay for certain services. Rufino was surprised after midnight in the English Cemetery with those same earrings, as well as other objects he claimed to use in his activities. His testimony was highly credible and confirmed the capoeira's.

Baeta pointed out that the old man, although he would occasionally clam up, had always been unwavering in his statements. He even announced that Aniceto would be appearing at his home, a fact that was later confirmed.

Unless a body was found, the theory that Fortunata had been murdered and robbed seemed to have little credibility. If there was a body, it was not in the English Cemetery. Forensic investigations performed on June 23rd found no evidence of tampered graves, and in the mass grave—opened on the 9th of that month and showing signs of recently overturned earth—all of the corpses were male.

It had not been possible to establish a connection between the crime in question and the fact that on the 27th clear evidence of tampering had been found in the mass grave, although no bodies had been stolen. Fresh footprints indicated the presence of a barefoot male at the scene.

Since the footsteps heard by witness around 2 A.M. on the 27th were those of a male wearing shoes near the cemetery gate, no conclusions could be drawn. One theory was that it was another of old Rufino's clients (or that of some other sorcerer), who had just finished some magic rite. The incinerated waste found did not clarify matters any, but it was very likely that it was linked to those rituals.

The report concluded by suggesting that Fortunata's most important patrons be investigated. The expert's theory was that the crime had political motivations. Fortunata had simply been used to carry it out, and those who hired her must have helped her escape.

The theory that the death had been an accident, the result of excessive zeal in the simulation of torture to which the secretary liked to submit himself, was somewhat weakened because the assassin had employed great strength—indeed, unusual strength for a woman.

The crime at the House of Swaps was by no means the only one of its kind.

Since this book's thesis—that the history of a city is the history of its crimes—cannot be proven merely by presenting one case study, I have decided to mix into the larger narrative certain reports of crimes that, in a sense, foreshadow it. They are what I would call "predicate crimes." I will begin with one that might have been titled *The Birth of the Tragedy*.

In the 1800s, in the coastal region of Gávea Parish (known as Praia Grande do Arpoador), in wetlands crisscrossed by inlets and mangroves, between the sand bank of the lagoon and the Dois Irmãos cliffs, just below the settlement of Pau, there was a hamlet of *caiçaras*—fishermen and shellfish gatherers who inhabited fifty rustic huts, from the time when the gunpowder factory was built on the lands of Rodrigo de Freitas.

For nearly three centuries they lived rather secludedly, almost lost in time, in a strictly endogamous environment. And though they had regular contact with the townspeople, bartering fish for tools and household instruments, and though they barely spoke their ancient gibberish anymore, they had still managed to preserve their somewhat exotic customs, which often were in conflict with the laws of the Empire.

Two of those customs are of particular interest: that of providing graves only to those who died of old age and of natural causes, while ingesting the flesh, blood, and ashes of the victims of any kind of accident; and that of submitting women to the control of a particular caste of men: the shark hunters. Saying "hunters" here is not inappropriate, because these animals were caught by hand.

It was an amazing feat: the *caiçara* who truly coveted a particular woman needed to take a stick with a stiff, razor-sharp tip and swim into the ocean, naked, to wait for an attack. He could take bait (for example, a guinea pig or a baby paca), and bleed it out on the high seas.

When the shark attacked and bared its teeth, the *caiçara* would jab the sharpened stick perpendicularly into the jaw, locking the shark's teeth shut and capturing the prey.

From that moment on, this *caiçara* was entitled to the woman he wanted (if she were available). For a girl, to be chosen was considered the highest honor.

Men who did not undergo this test would only get a wife if a father, an uncle, or a brother were sufficiently generous. Women obtained in this fashion, in general, were of lower quality.

That is what happened in 1830 with one of these *caiçaras*, Conhé, who won the virgin Merã, a young, restless, and misty-eyed woman. Life can be funny: Conhé already had a first wife, given to him as a present by an uncle, but it was Merã, and not the first one, who soon became pregnant.

Conhé exhibited with pride, for nine moons, the necklace and harpoons made of shark's teeth. Merã did not have much to her name, but she had a beautiful smile.

The change happened on the day she gave birth: when her water broke, Merã writhed in pain, and the child would not come out. The first wife sat back and watched the ordeal unfold, and when she sensed the outcome, she rushed out laughing and began spreading the news to the neighbors.

Those *caiçaras* considered any incident that diverged from the natural course of events and that could cause any kind of harm to an individual, especially death, to be demeaning. In a word: they disdained misfortune.

Thus, anyone who drowned, was murdered, was attacked by predators or poisonous snakes, lost their honor. This is why, if they were fit for consumption, they were eaten—even the ashes of their bones. Therefore, neither Merã nor anyone else in that situation would be considered worthy of saving. And the vengeful first wife ran through the entire village looking for Conhé.

The shark hunter learned of the disgrace while bartering at the Três Vendas Square with the slaves of architect Grandjean de Montigny, of the French Artistic Mission, who since 1826 had lived nearby in a sumptuous manor house in the shadow of the forest.

Conhé's reaction was unexpected: he asked the slaves for help. Merã was rushed to the estate's slave quarters, followed by an out-of-control Conhé. The midwife, an old slave woman, did not hold out much hope.

"The child is sitting up, half-strangled by the cord. I'll do my best to save the mother."

That was when a bewildered Conhé pleaded:

"Please, the child first! Don't let the child die!"

Merã, though driven mad by the pain, could not help but listen. Life really is very funny: the old midwife managed to save both mother and daughter—for it was a girl, who would be given the name Vudja.

When they returned to the village—with a heavy sack of

coffee and dried meat donated by Madame de Montigny, who also pledged to be the girl's godmother—the reception was not the best. That same night, Conhé's brothers-in-law, the first wife's brothers, paid him a visit to let him know they had taken her back, with the uncle's consent.

Conhé cursed them, but his attention was on Vudja. So much so, that he did not react when, the next day, some boys stole two of his harpoons, which were decorated with the teeth of the shark he had caught barehanded.

When Merã finally recovered from her fever and puerperal inconveniences, Conhé—happy because Vudja had survived—once again sought his wife. Then came the surprise: Merã rejected him, forcefully. Repeatedly so, on the second, third, and fourth attempts. Conhé insisted almost every day, and he was always rebuffed.

And that was not all: whenever he would show interest in any other woman, old or young, the other shark hunters would step in, alleging that the desired woman was unavailable and pointing to another hunter, who supposedly had chosen her before. It was an informal way, the only one they had, of banishing him from the caste. Conhé was the first among them to know this infamy.

Merã, for her part, besides scorning Conhé and enjoying her shellfish, found secret pleasure in practicing small cruelties against Vudja, pretending that they were minor accidents. Several times she burned the girl or scratched her skin with fish bones. One time she went too far and broke her daughter's leg, leaving her lame for the rest of her life.

And Vudja grew up, and had her period. However, no shark hunter would consider her. The lame and crippled virgin was jealous of the girls who got married, all the while watching as Conhé's overtures were consistently rejected by her mother, forcing Conhé to sulk alone in the opposite corner of the hut. Such was Vudja's childhood.

It is important to say that Madame de Montigny kept her promise. Once a year, Vudja would go to her godmother's house, always returning with some trinket or other. When she was thirteen, still ignored by men, she was astonished to see, behind the barn, one of the coachmen mounting one of the cooks.

She returned to the village very upset, mainly because the woman's behavior had been very different from Merã's. That same night she suddenly moved out of the hut, irritated by her parents' ceaseless fighting.

Vudja's plan was simple: one afternoon, while Conhé slept in the hut and Merã collected shellfish in the Preto River, she went to a nearby swamp, where she captured an enormous *cururu*, also known as a cane toad, or *bufo marinus*.

When Conhé felt that thump on his chest and on his mouth, his reaction was just what Vudja had imagined: startled out of his sleep, he pummeled the beast, and opened his eyes wide—which is precisely where the toad squirted his venom.

Vudja knew that until the inflammation died down Conhé would be blind. What happened next is not hard to imagine. That night, his eyes covered with macerated rue leaves, Conhé was unable to pursue Merã. Thus, he was stunned, but also as happy as could be, when he once again felt the moistness of a woman's body.

The next day he asked Merã for water; and tried to touch her affectionately on the forearm. His wife jumped back, flinging the drinking gourd far away. They exchanged insults and Conhé reminded her of the night before. Merã stammered in disbelief. Finally she denied it, forcefully, and left no doubt that what he was saying was impossible.

That is when Vudja entered, carrying her basket full of crabs in one arm and her father's harpoons in the other. She had caught no fish with the harpoon; she looked at her mother with eyes even mistier than hers.

It perhaps comes as no surprise that our true story begins now and will revolve around the four main characters: Fortunata, Baeta, Rufino, and Aniceto. Or, to be more precise, around the three men, since Fortunata will only reappear in the end.

The first character that we should get to know better is the forensic expert Sebastião Baeta. Born out of wedlock, on his father's side he came from one of those traditional Minas Gerais families. His mother's lineage was also *mineira*, but she was the descendant of the ex-slaves who worked for that same family.

Sebastião's parents remet in Rio de Janeiro: he was an engineer; she was a washerwoman. Their passion was so spontaneous that they registered the boy as legitimate, even though by then the engineer was already married to a grade school teacher from Viçosa. Such a situation, of course, could have resulted in lengthy legal battles concerning the future forensic expert's inheritance rights.

The family, however, decided upon an amicable resolution, granting the washerwoman some child support, specifically for the education of the child, who would also be included (or so it was promised) in the engineer's will.

And Baeta, an outcast to his paternal relatives, was born at the foot of Turano Hill and raised in Catumbi in a modest home near the São Francisco de Paula Cemetery. To grow up in Catumbi means, naturally, to be in close contact with the streetwise toughs from Estácio. And Baeta acquired certain essential life knowledge from them.

His great callings were women and books. Thus, he rose through the ranks quickly at the police department, and before long he was married to a girl with fine calves—a standard of female beauty of the time, destined to dominate the mainstream aesthetic of Rio de Janeiro for the rest of the century.

Baeta was not a bad husband. But the influence of the

orthodox street smarts from his childhood did not allow him to assume the risks of monogamy. Therefore, besides his wife Guiomar—who was faithful and was coveted by all the neighbors—he also carried on about half a dozen affairs throughout the city: on Ajuda Street, on the Livramento Hill, and in the Largo da Lapa.

He liked to frequent the House of Swaps, where he was quite successful with white women. And he became the client of about half a dozen nurses, even Fortunata herself—a fact that significantly influenced the investigation, as we shall see.

If this were a psychological novel—or one that inhabits the characters' interior life, emphasizing subjectivity at the expense of action and concrete facts—we would reflect at length on one of the expert's traits: his abandonment of his roots in order to seek affirmation in superior social circles.

But it would have been a waste of time. Suffice it to say that Baeta's reimmersion into the primitive world of the streets was a key moment in his biography. It happened when the chief of police, after reading the first report, insisted that the expert continue working the case as an investigator, so as to find Fortunata's brother Aniceto, in the hopes that he would take them to her.

So far, Aniceto's daily routine had consisted of visiting Ouvidor Street, where he seemed to look for work and try to sell off Fortunata's jewelry, raising the small fortune of almost ten *contos de reis* (although the pieces were worth even more than that).

Baeta and the chief of police knew that following him during the day was not enough, and that the surveillance needed to go undercover: discreet forays at night to the piers, the hills, and the dives of Gamboa and Sáude—the capoeira's stomping grounds—would be necessary.

There was, however, one potential problem: the area was under the command of the First District, the Mauá Square

Brotherhood, which undoubtedly would put up a deafening and fierce resistance to Baeta's presence in their jurisdiction. The trick, therefore, was not to arouse their suspicions.

So, practically the entire month of July was spent implementing the following strategy: Baeta frequenting taverns, making occasional trips to the port, and paying visits to the headquarters of the Rancho das Sereias on Camerino Street, where, with his broad shoulders and manly expression, he won over the head dancer and flag-bearer, who lived on Favela Hill. Of course, such a relationship went a long way toward justifying the expert's presence in the area.

The first incident that would change the course of our story happened in one of those old eateries on the slopes of Gamboa Hill, a meeting point for dockhands. Baeta was watching a group of street toughs gathered in a circle, keeping rhythm with their clapping hands and making up impromptu verses, when he heard a voice from behind:

"Looking for me, boss?"

It was Aniceto. He was blowing cigarette smoke up at the ceiling, his hat cocked to the side, decidedly dressed down— well below what the expert himself had seen him wearing on Ouvidor Street. Baeta was not there to get into silly fights. He shrugged it off, as if his suspicion were absurd.

"That's what I thought, boss. But I'm all yours."

The capoeira's tone was an open challenge. Baeta decided to make light of the situation. The expert was—and knew himself to be—irresistible to the female sex. As if in the habit of boasting about it, he said:

"I have better reasons for being here."

And he motioned suggestively to two unaccompanied women smoking and laughing it up in the corner. Aniceto, who had been getting downright hostile, simmered down. Anyone watching the clash would have concluded that the capoeira was now on his turf, because he answered, with a huge smile:

"Those are my girls!"

Before the expert could stop him, Aniceto, laughing and in high spirits, called the girls by their names, and announced that he wanted to introduce them to a policeman. Baeta, furious at being called out publicly, was invited to the table by the women themselves, with excited gestures, and was stunned when the capoeira politely offered him a seat:

"Make yourself at home, boss!"

Already walking away, Aniceto said to the girls:

"You're doing me a big favor."

This was going too far; it was highly awkward. Baeta, flustered, tried to apologize. And he was surprised that they did not seem even remotely offended. On the contrary, they looked at him with a certain degree of pity.

"We're good girls, sir. But we do whatever he asks."

For a proud man like Baeta, this was hard to take. At a loss for words, he left the girls and went to the bar to lean on the capoeira. By now, however, other people had witnessed the scene, and they started talking, cracking jokes, even laughing.

"I don't need help with women!"

Aniceto shrugged his shoulders and threw his arms open:

"Whatever you say, boss."

While the expert closed out the bill, the capoeira initiated a chant in the middle of the circle of drummers.

> *"Every monkey has his branch,*
> *Every king, his deck."*

About two weeks later, Baeta left police headquarters on Relação Street, walked up Inválidos Street, crossed the Campo de Santana, and rounded the Central Station toward Favela Hill, where his new girlfriend, the flag-bearer of Rancho das Sereias, lived.

He climbed the stairs, greeting old ladies and tousling kids' hair. The fact that he had already shown his face around there did not lessen the hostility with which the men eyed him. He was forced to stare down a group of toughs, just to put them in their place.

The houses on Favela Hill were almost all made of wooden boards and slats left over from the abandoned crates in the harbor, covered with zinc sheets, rarely more than one room in size. Baeta's girlfriend lived in such a house, on a steep hill next to a ditch, with her grandmother. The grandmother broke the news to him:

"She's not in, sir."

Her tone was grating. The expert did not like the old lady, who was always tepid toward him. Maybe because every time he visited the same scene repeated itself: the flag-bearer would send her grandmother off to the neighbor's house, for however long their tryst lasted. Baeta once brought a coffee pot with him, but the old lady never even thanked him.

So, he waited outside, standing in a puddle, angry at the girl. He learned more only from the next-door neighbor:

"She's probably still up there at the Galician's bar, by the shrine."

That was hard for Baeta to swallow. He could not accept a girlfriend of his consorting with lowlifes. So, he headed over there, hot under the collar, ready to square off with her.

The Galician's bar had the architecture of a classic early 20th century dive: a low, rectangular establishment, with more front than back, zinc sheets for a roof, rarely more than one room in size, the entrance in the corner, and, instead of windows, two large wooden planks, occupying about two-thirds of the façade and opening out like two tongues, doubling as counters—all of which, essentially, constituted the bar.

Customers never went in. Most stood outside, leaning on the counters, chatting with the owner, while others congregated on the street itself.

That was the scene when the expert arrived. It took a while

to find her, because she was not actually in front of the establishment but by the entrance of the simple oratory that marked the top of the hill. Half hidden in the shade, hand on her waist, skirt thigh-level, she had her back to a group of men playing *porrinha* in a circle. She was talking to a man.

Baeta approached and had his second surprise:

"Look who's here—the boss!"

The man talking to Baeta's girlfriend was Aniceto. It's hard to describe the look of shock on the girl's face and Baeta's anger. Aniceto, however, was thoroughly enjoying himself, blowing cigarette smoke up at the sky. The expert took her by the arm, staking his claim.

"Get out of here. I want to have a word with this bum."

The two men sized each other up.

"Tell me, boss: Is it a crime now to chat up a single girl?"

Baeta started to reach for his gun. But he noticed Aniceto shift his body slightly, as if to conceal a kick. From that distance, and in that position, the expert understood the futility of the gun—the same foot that would rise in a half-moon, to disarm him, would give the capoeira the necessary momentum to spin on his axis and unleash the fatal "leather hat" kick with the opposite leg. He did not want to give him the pleasure.

"The girl's mine. Lay off her."

Aniceto goaded him:

"It's not my fault if they love my chatter."

Baeta had already turned his back and was walking down the street, demanding an explanation from the flag-bearer. Contrary to what he had expected, he found no repentance or remorse.

"Slavery's been abolished, Sebastião!"

Outraged, holding up a stiff finger, she swore her innocence. She had not noticed the time pass, and besides, the capoeira was not what Baeta thought. The expert cursed, threatened, and even gave her a shake. The old lady stepped in, inserting the flag rod between them.

Baeta was a defeated man by the time the grandmother went off to the neighbor's house, after they had made up. Later, when he arrived home, he thought it best not to wake up his wife.

Anyone walking by that graceful man in his English cashmere vest, bow tie, and bowler hat, looking down at the pavement as he passed the Colombo Café, might not detect the tough-guy swing to his gait, or suspect that he also frequented the piers dressed in a striped shirt, silk scarf, and baggy pants—traditional capoeira garb.

I speak, of course, of Aniceto. The townhouse on whose door he knocked—and entered straightaway, as a person known to the proprietor—belonged to a widow from Macaé, distantly related to the sinister Coqueiro Mota family, whose patriarch was the last free man hanged in Brazil.

The widow had a half-niece, half-cousin, born on a farm in Quissamã, an heiress, married to an illustrious industrialist who made his fortune in the textile business. It was she, the half-cousin, half-niece, who discreetly knocked on the same door half an hour later.

An observer watching these two enter that same house in the same stealthy manner, at the same time of day, would presume that this was a case of adultery. And he would be right.

The incident is of no small importance to this narrative, since it is the first time we see Aniceto having relations with a respectable lady. Therefore, it is interesting to delve deeper into this affair, and learn how it unfolded.

The heiress, the wife of the eminent industrialist, was not unhappy in her marriage. She had been coveted in her youth, for her beauty as well as for her money. And, since she was a rich heiress, she could choose whomever she wanted at the parties and receptions given by her parents.

The industrialist was older. And, as often happens, his

maturity impressed the girl. That was not all: the industrialist was the most successful of all her suitors. He had a fortune of ten thousand *contos de réis*, and his conversation was not the most foolish in the room.

If one lie persists—left over from nineteenth-century novels—it is that pure sentiments cannot involve financial interest. For the heiress, however, as well as for many women like her, a man's wealth was the material expression of his ability to win; it was a mark of virility.

The heiress liked seeing him in expensive cut tails and feeling his face, recently shaved with lavenders imported from France. She was proud of having been chosen, of being considered a worthy match for that mighty man, whose decisions influenced the lives of thousands. And she loved it when he had his way with her without asking permission.

So, then, how to explain Aniceto, and their presence together at the townhouse?

When the capoeira approached her the first time, they were on Ouvidor Street, in front of a women's clothing store. She was coming out, he was on his way in. Aniceto invaded her space with a piercing look.

"Need me to call you a cab, ma'am?"

He was coarse in appearance but not poorly dressed. She passed by him without answering, thinking that the correct thing would have been for him to offer to carry her parcels. Farther down the street, at the glove shop near the Notícia newsroom, the capoeira called out to her again, his eyes fixed on her, this time proposing to drop her off at home. She thanked him, but curtly, making clear that she disapproved of his audacity.

"Come for a stroll tomorrow. I'd like very much to talk to you again, ma'am."

It was the height of insolence. But the heiress returned the following day, because she thought herself to be a free person, and she would not be held hostage by a common womanizer.

And, sure enough, there was Aniceto, walking leisurely along Ouvidor Street. He smiled when he saw her leave the perfumery on the corner of Gonçalves Dias, and he resumed his pursuit.

"Should we go get something to drink, ma'am?"

His vulgar language, his mannerisms were in all aspects completely inappropriate for a woman of her status, or of the status she believed herself to be.

But it was precisely this exhibition—being wooed in this crass manner by such a brash fellow—that led to her capitulation. She began to enjoy being the object of that lothario's attention.

"Who knows, maybe next time?"

And there was a next time, on that same street. Little by little, things evolved. Until one day they met at a discreet café on Central Avenue—she, wisely, accompanied by the widow from Macaé. It did not take long for the widow to open her house to the lovers.

On that day, in a bedroom without windows on the second floor, the heiress was naked, facedown. Aniceto lay next to her, his outstretched hand wandering over the nape of her neck and the swell of her buttocks, sometimes drifting to the shoulders, sometimes the back of legs, in a motion that was rhythmic and gentle, but firm.

He did this while whispering in her ear, foreshadowing the obscenities he would demand of her. There was another element to this game: the capoeira would tell her that these obscenities had to be done in front of people present in that room who were hidden, watching them. She, with her legs slightly open, sighed, and writhed, and raised her hips. And these people, this small audience, did not only include strangers. In her imagination, there was someone very special there, a privileged spectator, watching everything, all of the vileness: her industrialist husband.

Let us go back in time a little, to the moment when Aniceto passed in front of the Colombo, head down, and proceeded to knock on the townhouse door. Dressed in a style that mimicked all of the elegance around him, no one paid him any mind.

The heiress, in turn, arrived in a poplin wire-frame dress, with silk gloves and a lace hat, and was much noticed by passersby as well as the clientele at the café.

The open admiration of beautiful women is a tradition in Rio de Janeiro. And the heiress, who was accustomed to that type of attention and liked to show off in public, did not realize that she was being followed, and that she had been from the moment she left her majestic mansion in Botafogo. It is not difficult to guess that it was by the industrialist himself.

The heiress's husband was very nervous, lifting his collar and looking at his watch every chance he got. He seemed to want to register the exact time when the adultery would be committed. In the café, he drank three glasses of the best pomace brandy. And he began to sweat. Many knew him in that café, and his nervous demeanor was attracting plenty of attention.

So, when he tossed too much money on the table, and did not wait for the change, and knocked on the same townhouse door, many eyes were upon him.

Of course, the industrialist knew the widow. The owner of the house could not help but open the door, and invite him in, though she must have been terrified. But these saucy old ladies are cunning: she imagined that from street level he would not be able to hear anything upstairs, and that she would be able to send him on his way quickly, because a man like him would not have much to discuss with a distant relative of his wife's. She realized her mistake when he drew his revolver:

"Where is she!"

It did not take long for the industrialist to kick open the door and rush into the room, catching the adulteress by surprise in that unmistakable position I have already described, just as she was in the throes of her exciting fantasy. Destiny truly has amazing coincidences.

The industrialist—though he was armed, though he had long suspected everything—trembled when faced with the truth, and was slow to act. Thus, he missed with the first shot he fired at his rival, and when he tried to fire a second one he felt the blow: his wife struck him with a wooden Saint Anthony, adding two or three additional blows to the head once he was on the ground.

Meanwhile, the widow had sounded the alarm, which coincided with the shots. There was a commotion in the street, and the entire café emptied out, hoping to intervene, but the police arrived straightaway. The heiress was arrested then and there, naked, bloodied, and in tears.

Aniceto did not even try to escape, hoping to avoid getting charged. After all, the man had fallen on the chair, spattering the capoeira's jacket all over with blood. Aniceto was also taken to the police station.

The crowd huddled in front of the house included the fine Colombo clientele. They did not know quite what had happened, and they applauded the adulterers and jeered the industrialist, noisily shouting, "Here comes the cuckold!" A few minutes later, though, there were plenty of embarrassed faces as they saw the corpse being carried out, its skull shattered.

The case would have proceeded unexceptionally except for the behavior of the woman, which mortified the police. Still in the bedroom when they went to arrest the capoeira, she threw herself on the officers, scratching and biting them and trying to prevent them from taking Aniceto away. She cried hysterically all the way to the police station, saying he was innocent, demanding that he be freed. She had to be restrained when Aniceto was taken away to jail, and she screamed and let it be known that she would pay for her lover's lawyer.

Forensics made quick work of their investigation, and concluded that the woman acted alone. The police captain, however, tried to lay the groundwork for another version:

"All you have to do is give your statement, and I'll arrange something with forensics. Just say he smashed your husband's head with the saint."

The offer was made in the presence of the killer's lawyer, shortly after the woman's arrival at the precinct. Her reaction was to cause another scandal, saying she would leak the setup, demanding the presence of journalists.

Appalled by the heiress's attitude, and with no good argument to challenge her detention, the defense lawyer began instead to represent Aniceto, as per her orders, with great success. According to Article 279 of the Penal Code, the crime of adultery was a private matter, and there had been no complaint.

The idea, which someone floated, that he could be framed for vagrancy also went nowhere. Article 399 was clear: despite not practicing the profession of typesetter, he had a livelihood, as the law prescribed, for he had converted his inheritance from Fortunata into bonds, which gave him an income, albeit a modest one.

Aniceto, thus, was freed, though not before meeting with Baeta again. The expert wanted to do a "reconstruction" of the crime committed at the townhouse. Nobody criticized him for excessive zeal; nobody saw this as personal. Baeta wanted to intimidate the capoeira.

"I have no idea how a woman like her can get involved with a lowlife like you."

Aniceto thought it very funny.

"Women are very strange, boss."

And it was really very strange—a streetwise thug from the hills, with barely a grade school education, raised amid capoeiras and drummers, snagging himself such a wealthy lover.

And Baeta, who had admired the industrialist's wife and saw her as one of the great beauties of Rio, began to reflect seriously on that mystery and that power.

So much so that, days later, while walking down Favela Hill, after finally being dumped by the flag-bearer, Baeta could not get one name out of his head: Aniceto.

Adultery is not, of course, a Rio institution in the chronological sense. Nor are its origins specific to any one city, or to a specific people. In fact, this notion is what differentiates us as modern humans from *Australopithecus*, *Pithecanthropus*, Java men, *Homo erectus*, and Neanderthals.

In the history of cities, however, though it is never absent, its importance varies. Cities like Beijing, Jerusalem, Timbuktu, or Calcutta are not remembered for their cases of adultery. The same cannot be said about Paris or San Francisco and certainly not of Rio de Janeiro.

At least eight thousand years ago, a group of highly skilled sailors approached the Rio de Janeiro coastline. These original inhabitants (called "Sambaquis," and, later, "Itaipus") were a seafaring people, peaceful and fond of leisure, but completely dominated by the spirit of risk-taking.

At the time, the sea level was much lower, so neither the coastal outline nor the natural landscape was the same. But it was Rio de Janeiro, nonetheless.

These first arrivals—about a dozen men, women, and children—were not pioneers, but rather fugitives. Living in an anarchic society, devoid of the concept of property, the only crimes possible in the world of the Sambaquis were incest, to which they had an overwhelming aversion, and adultery. The founders of Rio de Janeiro were fleeing this last crime: half of the Sambaquis' wives had been stolen.

We know little about them, but what is certain is that they prospered. Archaeologists have been fascinated by their delicate ornaments made from shells and bones. In this book, they will be remembered as inventors of Carioca literature.

It is said that the Itaipus were of the sea, but they also learned to exploit the rivers. Thus, since they always preferred water, they never made great expeditions into the depths of the forest, and considered the mountains to be the limits of the physical world.

However, it was sometimes necessary to pick fruit, find new mangroves or streams, and maybe catch some small animal. This was a dangerous adventure, because the forest was inhabited by evil and mysterious spirits who had a penchant for pursuing women and embarrassing them into practicing shameful acts.

Life involved certain strictures: just as fishermen preferred to go at it alone (except when they went out onto the high seas in search of *xaréu*), groups that entered the woods, mostly women, sought not to spread themselves too thin or travel too far into the thickets.

Occasionally, however, a woman would disappear only to reappear a few hours later. In the evenings around the campfire, gathered around a shell mound or under an overhanging rock, or on a sand dune, they would tell amazing stories, in which virgin girls were impregnated by water snakes, or wives were seduced by salacious lizards.

This tradition did not disappear with the Itaipus. In fact, invaders coming by land or by sea kept repeating the same legends. The invaders belonged to two great nations of fierce warriors. They arrived at about the same time, some three thousand years ago, and they had so many differences that they hardly ever intermarried. Their laws concerning adultery were also in conflict.

The first ones, from the Unas Nation—ancestors of the Puris, or "the crowned ones," and of the Goitacás, to a lesser extent—failed to prevail for very long in the city of Rio. Though much given to games and competitions of strength and dexterity, they took a very serious view of things, and were very attached to their social hierarchy and rigid customs. Not surprisingly, they considered adultery a serious offense, a question of character.

The individual caught in the act was beaten terribly by the betrayed partner, with no right to self-defense.

Often, such punishments were applied with war clubs, which could be lethal.

Thus, the invaders who remained were those of the sea, those of the Tupi nation—ancestors of the enemy tribes that, in historical times, called themselves Tamoios and Temiminós, or "grandparents" and "grandchildren."

Lovers of art, good food, good drink, and plenty of revelry, the Tupi had developed a philosophy of contradiction and absolute celebration of life, whose ultimate expression was the cannibalistic rite wherein the enemy was transformed into the redeemer.

The Tupi were compulsorily happy—so much so that they only cried when receiving good news.

In cases of adultery, though wives were entitled to create an uproar, husbands would play dumb to avoid disagreements. But at the next feast—when they would drink plenty of the famous cassava beer—one or more men would go on a rant and pummel the unfaithful woman. The ancient Tupi in Rio de Janeiro would take revenge on their women only if they were drunk.

In the 16th century, two more savage hordes joined the Tupi: the French, who built a fort on the island of Serigipe in 1555, with the endorsement and assistance of Tamoios, and the Portuguese, who considered themselves owners of the land, and who with the help of the Temiminós managed to gain definitive dominion over the city in 1567.

This period was one of tremendous wars, and culminated in

the defeat of the Franco-Tamoian coalition, which was forced to withdraw into the high mountains of the interior. Thus the Temiminós—hitherto most populous in the bay's eastern rim—moved into Carioca territory, and even mixed with the remaining Tamoios.

The Europeans—both the Portuguese and the French—though deeply attached to their superstitions, assimilated much of Tupi culture. For example, having come from a strictly monogamous society, they adopted indigenous polygamy—which, according to their laws, would have constituted a crime.

This ambiguity is typically Carioca: every relationship between Tupi women and European men was both legal and illegal. Rarely did this happen the other way around; Tupi men found European women very repulsive.

Thus, the first *mamelucos* of Rio de Janeiro appeared, resulting from the Tupi women's acceptance of French and Portuguese men. From their fathers they inherited the notion of the willful lie and a very buoyant sense of honor, born of the asymmetries and antagonisms of the city, which some-times led them to punish adultery by death, as specified by the ordinances of the kingdom and the ancient traditions of the Unas.

This did not, however, diminish the impulse to commit adultery. As a matter of fact, Hector Furtado de Mendonça, Visitator General of the Holy Office in Brazil, declined to come to Rio de Janeiro in 1591 because (according to a letter by the Rio de Janeiro Prelate to the Bishop of Bahia), "under the maximum influence of the tropics, judging by the amount of fornication and concubinage that goes on, it is feared that the venerable priest will order us to burn the whole city down."

Naturally, there was another encounter between the expert Baeta and the seducer Aniceto, which is vital for the continuation of the story. The scene takes us back to the beginning, to the House of Swaps. Perhaps it would be worthwhile to describe it in detail.

The building, of palatial dimensions, was built and decorated by artists of the French Mission. It is almost a two-story quadrilateral, subdivided into halls, rooms, corridors, and chambers that communicate with each other via any number of doors, arcades, and passageways.

I described it as almost a quadrilateral because its architects, in designing the rear facade, rather than tracing a line parallel to the front facade, instead gently inserted, at about the one-tenth mark from each corner, two curved walls projecting outward, which then again resolve into straight lines, but are interrupted anew, this time by a large protruding semicircle. This appendix, spanning both floors, is incorrectly labeled as the "oval halls." It is, in fact, the building's true entrance.

Therein lies the genius of the building, whose form discovers the character of those who inhabited it. The side seen from the street, while classic and elegant, does not have the grace of the rear façade in three planes, which overlooks the garden, and whose intimacy is invisible to passersby because of its position behind a wall of leafy trees.

A visitor entering the lobby would head straight to the imposing staircase, which, after reaching a half landing, divided into two flights, one to the right and one to the left, leading to the second floor. All of this was lit by a huge skylight with a stained-glass dome.

It was below this staircase, across from the oval room on the first floor, that the exit (or entrance) to the secret tunnel was located, excavated to connect the Marquise's House to the Quinta da Boa Vista Palace. It was in this tunnel that Dr. Zmuda created an impromptu wine cellar. And this was the wine cellar where the prostitute Fortunata took the bottle of wine on the day of the secretary's death.

As I already mentioned, all illicit activity took place upstairs, therefore it is there that our story resumes.

On that day, the House of Swaps was receiving couples. To provoke the senses—and ensure confidentiality—light was kept at a minimum, except for the natural light from the skylight, and a few gaps in the curtains allowing in a faint stream from the street. Pairs arrived in cabs or rented carriages. As per the rules, the drivers were instructed to leave immediately. The housemaid, an inconspicuous girl, stood in the garden in front of the iron stairs leading to the second floor with a candle in hand as she greeted the visitors.

When Baeta arrived with his wife, Guiomar, it was still early. They followed the receptionist up the stairs to the oval room. It was there that the guests were prepared before entering into the house proper.

The expert and his wife stripped naked, handing their clothes to the girl with the candle, who placed them behind a folding screen so as not to be recognized by others. He donned a robe, and she a slightly sheer tunic, in the style of a Greek maenad.

Although there were rare exceptions, Madame Brigitte and Dr. Zmuda preferred that couples always kept their identities concealed in public spaces. To that end, they provided guests with special hoods of very soft silk, reminiscent of the executioners of old. They could be adjusted with an elastic band, and exposed only the eyes and mouth, with a discreet opening at the nose. There was also enough space in the hoods for women with large manes to wear their hair loose.

In the front hall, there were already half a dozen couples, besides the hosts and a few nurses (the only ones who always kept their faces uncovered). In general, people drank and talked, getting drunker and drunker and breaking out into groups, and then proceeded into the nearby rooms.

Baeta took an interest in a lady, apparently young, probably blonde, whose skin, even in the dim light, seemed extremely fair. Guiomar, for her part, tried to distract the man so that Baeta and the blonde could make the arrangements alone. That was their game: Guiomar was a fierce and jealous woman, unaware of her husband's adventures, who would never stand for an affair, and who could not even suspect, for example, the existence of a flag-bearer on Favela Hill.

And yet, she loved to see him with other women, especially the white ones, which was when his powers of seduction became most evident. Therefore, she consented. Therefore, she looked forward to their visits to the House of Swaps, where Baeta could show off his virility, which so enraptured her.

However, Guiomar would never allow anyone to touch her. Not only because this was a condition set by her husband, but because she felt better that way, as though she were worth more, knowing that she belonged to just one man, a man who could have any woman.

Things had begun well enough that night; that is, until something seemed to irk the expert—a new couple had just arrived, and Baeta heard a familiar greeting:

"Evening, boss!"

The greeting was addressed to the doctor, the owner of the House, who responded in a familiar tone. There could be no doubt concerning the identity of the newcomer: the timbre of the voice, the subtle body movements, and especially the insolent manner he had of blowing cigarette smoke. Aniceto was the last person Baeta expected to meet at the House of Swaps.

Everyone noticed Baeta's anxiety as he excused himself and pulled the Polish doctor aside.

"This guy may be implicated in the secretary's death!"

Dr. Zmuda was always discreet, but the vehemence with which Baeta addressed him, and the fact that he was police, led him to talk.

"He is the widow Palhares' guest. They've been here several times before. The nurses love him."

Baeta had never noticed the capoeira's presence there before. He insisted that the man was a lowlife who preyed on women, and that he had just led an honest woman to kill her husband. He was also probably involved in some very shady dealings because it was inconceivable that a mere typographer's apprentice could have so many opportunities to meet and conquer rich lovers. The doctor looked surprised:

"From what I understand, he works on Ouvidor Street, at La Parisienne. He is Madame Montfort's right arm."

So that was Aniceto's secret: he had found a job at a store that sold luxury items in order to seduce society ladies. But even if this helped explain the question of opportunity, it still could not elucidate the fascination the capoeira exercised over the female sex—a phenomenon that extended even to prostitutes.

The expert also did not understand why the capoeira had omitted this fact—his "working" at Madame Montfort's establishment—which would have been enough to have the charge of vagrancy against him dismissed in his latest encounter with the police.

Dr. Zmuda interrupted the conversation, pointing to a group that was getting up. Baeta and Guiomar accompanied the other couples to a room that had once been the Marquise's dressing room. There was a bed at the center and benches against the walls for observers.

Onto the bed climbed Aniceto, the young widow Palhares, and another, very tall lady, who was there for the third time but who had only been a spectator until then.

Brazen, and forceful, the capoeira put on a show. The two women, in a sudden surge of desire, were completely tamed by him; he orchestrated every action, every initiative. However varied his movements, at no time—and perhaps this is where his great artistry lay—did their bodies lose contact. There was some shyness, some reticence on their part. The two tried to disguise their excitement and pleasure, as if everything were unfolding by chance.

Baeta noticed a detail that might have escaped the others: Aniceto never ignored the widow, but he also never looked straight into her eyes. The high point of the night was when he, with a gesture of contempt and dismissiveness, held her by the hair and made her explore, with her mouth, the entire body of the tall woman—who suddenly overcame her shyness and offered herself up, swearing all the while.

Lastly, the audience watched yet another impressive feat: putting the tall woman in a supine position and openly turning his back to Palhares, he brought them to simultaneous orgasms, entering the first one with force, while stretching his arms to caress the widow.

That earlier comment by the doctor about Aniceto's success with the nurses, and the great excitement he had just observed in his own wife, definitely shook the expert's pride. Guiomar, however, did not perceive this slight change in his mood, and the couple returned to the salon because she insisted on a drink.

When the rogue walked by arm-in-arm with Palhares, recomposed and smiling, Guiomar's quick swerve in his direction did not escape Baeta.

In almost every crime novel in which the investigator is the protagonist, there is an element of improbability seldom noticed: the investigators seem to have nothing else to do, no other cases to solve other than the one central to the story. This, of course, is a mistake.

In this novel—constructed from real events—the policemen have plenty of work to do, especially because the action takes place in Rio de Janeiro, a city prone to very sophisticated crimes.

And that is why officers of the First District, accompanied

by the first lieutenant, were obliged to put aside work related to this book's plot to perform an investigation at the piers.

In the early morning hours, some boatmen found the body of a teenage female floating in the bay, her hands tied behind her back with strips of thick denim. When they returned to report the discovery, they saw, a few meters away, hitting up against the pier's ladder, the corpse of an adult man with his hands tied in the same way, with the same type of fabric.

Baeta appeared on site and concluded (foreshadowing the coroner's report) that the two had been drowned no more than four days earlier. They were probably immobilized and thrown into the water from the pier itself. And he concluded that the strips of denim came from the same pair of pants. The only problem was there was no apparent connection between the victims, especially because he lived in Niterói, and she in Itaguaí.

The police considered it almost impossible for anyone to have murdered those people at that location without being seen or heard, because the victims most likely cried out for help. It must, therefore, have been a group job. And the immediate suspicion fell on the stevedores or other dockworkers. At least, that was the opinion of Officer Mixila.

"This area, lieutenant, especially at night, is frequented by a bunch of bums."

What the officer said was true. And Mixila went further: such a murder could only have been committed by hired assassins—the type that threaten witnesses.

"We still haven't rid ourselves of the scourge of capoeiras."

At that moment, everyone agreed with Mixila's thesis, especially the first lieutenant. And soon thereafter they decided to pay a visit to the pier, to round up some suspects: street thugs and capoeiras that could be found there every night, participating in the well-known *pernada* sparring circles.

That was the First District's sense of justice. I am not sure we can blame them, because revenge—the basis of the legal systems of the Talion and Hammurabi, for example—is perhaps the most ancient of prehistoric man's sentiments; perhaps it is our most legitimate and inalienable right. And even Yahweh was taken up by this impulse, in the episode that culminated with the peopling of Earth.

Those policemen did not have to be convinced of any of this, though they had arrived at their conclusions by other means. Their conversation was confidential, as, by the way, were all the conversations of the Brotherhood of Mauá Square, when planning any operation that did not strictly follow procedures or comply with the law.

That is why Baeta, someone close to the investigation, who had personally examined the crime scene, did not hear of the plan. If he had, he would not have gone back to the pier at night, as he had intended to do since the previous Thursday, when he recognized the capoeira at the House of Swaps.

For the reader, it is easy to understand the expert's intentions. Although he had no proof (because he did not want to endure the shame of going back to Favela Hill), he was convinced that the flag-bearer had dumped him due to Aniceto's interference. And as if that were not enough, the *malandro* was now a great celebrity at Dr. Zmuda's parties—not to mention that he had aroused the curiosity (and perhaps the interest) of Guiomar.

Vanity leads men like these to extremes. Baeta was counting on catching Aniceto in some criminal act. What's more, he was itching (consciously, even) for some type of resistance, for a skirmish where shots might be exchanged. In such a situation, he would not hesitate to aim a gun at his rival.

The piers in Rio de Janeiro at nighttime are a deserted, gloomy place, and are therefore full of danger. But those who visit them after dark see very little: everything bad or illegal that may occur on the docks is concealed inside the warehouses.

That night was no different. Lit by only two or three candles, a dozen men had been gathered since early morning between stacks of boxes and burlap bags, drinking cachaça and sparring for keeps. Among them, of course, was Aniceto.

A feature of the true *pernada*—which cannot exist in any state but one of illegality—is that there is no singing or clapping. Time is only kept by an abstract, corporal rhythm that manifests itself by the shuffling of feet.

The game is simple: a man stands still, awaiting the blow, which could be in that circle, a sweep, a *banda*, a *tapona*, or a *cocada*. He has to hold his ground or dodge; what he cannot do is fall to the ground. The other *malandro* comes shaking his hips, circling, as though dancing samba in front of his standing adversary, waiting for an opportunity, when the opponent's defenses are down, to apply the blow.

It was precisely at such a moment that the police broke up the circle. They gave no warning; a shotgun blast blew the lock open.

"Everyone on the ground!"

To the frustration of the police, however, no one resisted. As it happened, no one was even carrying a gun, or cash—bets were made with toothpicks, and could only be traded in the next day. The warehouse foreman, who also played, came up with the strategy himself.

"They were tipped off, lieutenant."

It was, in essence, an attempt to console themselves, because the facts did not look good for the police. First, because the crime of *capoeiragem* could only be charged if practiced in a public place; second, because the officers had just endangered the property of several merchants—the warehouse gate had been blasted open.

Still, they arrested just about everyone for questioning. And then, just as they were leaving, the police and the street toughs noticed Baeta approach. He had been prowling the neighborhood, trying to surprise the capoeira, and was attracted by the noise.

Aniceto sneered, as he passed:

"Still jealous, little boss?"

It was too much for Baeta. Beside himself, he flung Aniceto against the wall and pointed his gun at him. Aniceto simply wiped his shirtsleeve clean, and, almost whispering, made the following wager:

"Ten *contos de reis*, if boss man can take one of my women from me!"

Baeta nodded and returned the prisoner to his captors. His anger was such that he did not notice the intense glare of the Brotherhood hanging over him.

The next day, all were released: the drowned girl's mother implicated her husband, a fisherman in Niterói, who had walked in on his daughter practicing manual obscenities with the other victim.

In the First District, however, the case did not die down completely. The new twist was the strange presence of the expert alone at night by the piers.

When the Visitator General Heitor Furtado de Mendonça refused to come to Rio de Janeiro, in 1591, there was no capoeira yet. There is much debate about its origins, both the word and the martial art. The first problem is easy: "capoeira" comes from the Tupi word *cäapuera*, which means sheared grass. Cutting weeds consists of sweeping an ax or scythe, striking low, near the roots, which perfectly describes capoeira's most elemental and characteristic blow.

"Capoeira," was thus the name of this sweeping move, which can also be called *arranca-toco*, *rapa*, *corta-capim*, and, almost universally, *rasteira*. It was only in the early 19th century that the name "capoeira" came to designate the martial art as a whole and, soon afterward, the martial artist himself.

On the other hand, writing the history of the martial art

itself is impossible. One legend links capoeira to a secret brotherhood organized around the cosmogonic thoughts of Queen Jinga Mbandi. Another turns to prehistoric times and tells us that capoeira was a secret society of men who joined forces to fight the Amazons.

In fact, there is something to be said for all of these, because there is the abstract capoeira, which coincides with the very concept of Rio de Janeiro, and the concrete capoeira, the corporal and philosophical expression of this concept, coined by Africans.

According to Father Anchieta, slaves from Guinea had been present in the city since at least 1583. However, until the mid-17th century, what impressed travelers most were the many natives. It was only in the 18th century that the nations of the Congo, Camundongos, Angolas, Ganguelas, Benguelas, Quiçamas, Rebolos, Monjolos, Cambindas, Cabundás, and Caçanjes took over the landscape. Accounts of the martial art of capoeira appear precisely around this time.

The oldest capoeira we have news of was the slave Adão Rebolo, who alone routed a detachment of regular troops in front of the palace, in the Terreiro da Polé, during the reign of Count da Cunha. The feat is remarkable not only because the African handily kicked and head-butted soldiers, knocking them all to the ground without suffering a single bruise himself, but because the attack was not initiated by the guards.

Before moving ahead with the narrative, I want to inform you that the slave was never arrested, either at the scene or after the fact. For the history of capoeira, though, what is important is Adão Rebolo's motives in perpetrating such a bold act.

The capoeira Adão had a wife—a free woman, the daughter of a judge and his slave. The young woman received an annuity from her father and opened a small grocery store on Latoeiros Street. Adão Rebolo would go there to eat soup. The judge's daughter took him as a lover, though she would not consider marriage.

At that time, in Rio de Janeiro, to seduce and bed a free woman was almost unthinkable for an African. Especially because there was a scarcity of women, especially African women. But Adão Rebolo had courage, he was brash—and few male qualities are as valued as brashness.

For almost one full year there was no trouble at the grocery store on Latoeiros Street. All lewd comments directed at the owner were avenged on the streets; customers began offering to pay their debts, and runaway slaves passed through the house only once.

But women are an unpredictable lot. And the African Adão found out, or rather witnessed, the unfaithfulness of the grocery store owner with an army sergeant. If he were Portuguese, he would have slapped her, but Adão Rebolo was a capoeira, and his response confirms the capoeira's ethical foundation in Rio: no woman can be guilty of adultery. Any dispute of this nature is to be dealt with among men.

Adão Rebolo was hurt, but he left the grocery store without breaking a single mug. Then, as soon as he identified the sergeant who commanded the unit at the Terreiro da Polé, he moved against him, and, consequently, against all of his subordinates.

Capoeiragem, therefore, came to introduce in Rio de Janeiro a new way of dealing with adultery, transforming the mores that had prevailed since 1591.

Although these early capoeiras were Africans, the institution is legitimately Carioca, because it was conceived in the city. Why here and not there? The reason is simple: with slavery, there were profound changes in the patterns of relationships between men and women brought from Africa, the result of the numerical discrepancy between the sexes and the dissolution of traditional family relationships.

Thus, the Rio de Janeiro capoeira—the only one that genuinely deserves that name—did not emerge as a game or exhibition of acrobatics, as is the case of similar martial arts in Bahia, Cuba, Martinique, Pernambuco, or Venezuela; Carioca capoeira is a tactic of war—one in which fighters vie for, and win, the favor of the female sex.

We do not know exactly how the art spread, but the process was rapid. By the time of the reign of the Marquis of Lavradio, between 1769 and 1779, there was already a Brown Regiment, made up of capoeiras, foreshadowing, in a way, Emperor Pedro II's famous Black Guard.

Also dating from this time is the legend surrounding the viceroy himself, a product of the imagination—or the self-indulgence—of novelist Joaquim Manuel de Macedo. He wrote of how the Marquis Lavradio used to go out at night, in disguise, and visit homes hoping to win over false maidens and married women while pretending to be Lieutenant Amotinado, an officer of the militia and an extraordinary capoeira, whose reputation prevented fathers and husbands from seeking revenge. What Macedo did not realize is that the marquis trailed a path that had actually been blazed before by the very same Lieutenant Amotinado.

Many powerful individuals and members of the nobility were, or said they were, capoeiras—for example, Major Vidigal, auxiliary of the superintendent of police of the Royal Court and, ironically, charged with rooting out the evil of capoeira; Emperor Pedro I and his adviser Chalaça; the generalissimo Duke of Caxias, whose military strategy owes much to capoeira; Marshal Floriano; and other historical figures like Father Perereca, Paula Brito, André Rebouças, and José do Patrocínio.

But the stories of men like these, although interesting, overshadow the art's true protagonists: African slaves and Creoles, who, in the early decades of the 19th century, gave capoeira its definitive form.

Immediate heirs of the Tupi philosophy, by then already ingrained in the city, according to which an individual only becomes whole if he has an enemy, the capoeiras began splitting up into gangs, with defined territories and specific emblems like colored ribbons, whistles, and guardian spirits. The female population of these territories, naturally, was the property of the local gangs, and wars would break out on account of women seduced in enemy territory, or as revenge for adultery committed.

Great effort was also invested in wresting control of churches and public buildings away from other gangs, but there were never any reports of capoeiras assaulting women or hiding in ambush to attack their victims from behind.

On occasion, however, there were deaths during these clashes, which allowed for the use of white arms and sticks, and even thefts—for, as is commonly known, some women are very fond of gifts. For these reasons, capoeira was ruthlessly persecuted since before the exile of the Portuguese crown in Brazil.

But the power of these gangs, the *maltas*, was so devastating that it was only during the republic, over a century later, that the police action had some success against them, with the offensive led by Sampaio Ferraz.

Even though he managed to arrest and deport hundreds of capoeiras to the island of Fernando de Noronha, he failed to eliminate them; by that time, eliminating capoeira would have meant destroying the city itself.

Names like Prata Preta, Ciriaco, Manduca da Praia, Master Canela, Gabiroba, Bernardo Little Hand, Mano Juca, Cabacinho, and Madame Satan (who also fought for the love of young men) are testament that capoeira survives, and even evolves, into the 20th century.

There is no need to extol its greatness as a martial art here, nor the importance of its legacy to the ethics of *malandragem*.

But it does not hurt to remember, to honor those who nurtured it, that the capoeiras were the western world's first feminists.

The bet—or, perhaps better said, duel—that pitted Baeta against Aniceto did not include, as would have been natural, the necessary witnesses, or even an individual to hold the prize, for that matter. It was, above all, a question of their word.

If he were to lose, the capoeira would give his rival all of Fortunata's assets and an additional sum of cash, which Aniceto would obtain from Madame Montfort. However, should Baeta be defeated, he would be unable to pay, because ten thousand *contos* was a considerable sum, far superior to what he had in his savings at that moment, or could honestly obtain as a public servant.

Thus, the tranquility exhibited by the expert the day after the meeting at the warehouse was strange. If the reader remembers the scene, he can imagine a few reasons: first, at no point did Baeta expressly agree to the bet. In fact, the expert did not say a single word. His gesture was limited to putting his gun back in its holster before the officers took the capoeira to the precinct.

Clearly Aniceto took that motion—the silent placing of the gun in its holster—as a gesture of assent. For Baeta, it could not be otherwise: his pride and vanity prevented him from backing down.

Actually, my point was another one. In the strict construction of the bet, there was no time limit: Aniceto agreed to pay as soon as he, Sebastião Baeta, had conquered one of his women, but without specifying how long he would wait for this to happen. If it happened, say, after five years, he would still be entitled to the ten thousand *contos*.

I spoke of vanity, I spoke of pride. The expert was vain. He might not have thought he was the best of men, but he was sure he was among the most attractive. Even in London, even in Buenos Aires, and especially at the House of Swaps. This for him had an almost existential meaning: having his way with the women of others while seeing his woman spurn the advances of males was a kind of triumph that made life worth living for him. So, for there to be someone like Aniceto on earth, in Rio de Janeiro, simply annihilated in him what was supposed to be one of his greatest merits as a human being.

The flaw in the bet as it was set up, therefore, allowed the expert to plan the attacks calmly. It gave him the opportunity to study his adversary's terrain—i.e., to make a map of the women Aniceto had seduced. Baeta wanted his victory to be complete. Thus, the first address he paid a visit to, of course, was Doctor Zmuda's clinic on ancient Imperador Street.

The doctor was surprised by the expert's visit and somewhat upset with his insistence on rehashing the case of the secretary. For Dr. Zmuda, the crime was political in nature, and the individual who ordered it had to be a very powerful individual because the murderer had vanished without leaving a clue. This view was identical to that of the highest police authority in the city, who, incidentally, had since returned to the House and told Zmuda as much.

Baeta was a bit startled by the doctor's attitude. But he had no honorable way to get to what he wanted without the pretext of an investigation. Thus, he tried the less deceitful path: he told him he needed some information about Aniceto, who had been with Fortunata on the day of the murder (as the earrings proved), so as to illuminate some obscure information obtained in his forensic analysis.

Miroslav Zmuda was a foreigner, but he was not stupid. The expert's reaction at the last couples' party revealed that he had something personal at stake in this. But, since he was confident, he decided to reveal what he knew, which, in the end, was very little: Aniceto had been there three or four times, always for the evening gatherings, as an escort of the widow Palhares—a debauched Rio socialite whose husband probably had committed suicide in shame, although the death certificate stated pulmonary failure.

Palhares had frequented the House for many years, and she had had numerous lovers during that time. But a truly remarkable thing that Dr. Zmuda had realized was the widow's allegiance to her new partner—an unusual and unlikely phenomenon in such a dissolute woman.

Another fact, no less noteworthy (and which surprised everyone), was the scene between Palhares and the tall woman at the last orgy; no one had ever suspected that both women enjoyed pleasures of Lesbos.

As for the nurses, he had heard from them that he was an expert lover. One of them even confessed that Aniceto had been the first man (because she had always preferred girls in this respect) to give her orgasms with his tongue.

For Dr. Zmuda, that a man should please women so was not entirely surprising. What seemed far beyond the norm was his talent for seduction, the speed and vehemence with which he attracted the female sex, especially being such an ill-mannered and lowly type.

"It truly is supernatural."

Words have a certain power: Baeta understood that the Polish doctor had employed the word in the sense of "unusual" or "extraordinary." But he could not help but make some associations. And suddenly, changing his approach somewhat, he asked the question again:

"When exactly did this street thug come here for the first time?"

Miroslav Zmuda recalled the date because it had been a scandal for him and Madame Brigitte: the presence of Palhares, so enamored with Aniceto, a few days after the one-month mass for her dead husband.

"It was the end of July . . . if I'm not mistaken, by my count . . . the 24th."

To Baeta, all of this was starting to make sense.

I interrupt the narrative here to remember another predicate crime, appearing in a Carioca novel called *The Throne of Queen Jinga.*

I will summarize it briefly so as not to waste time, especially for those who have already read it. There was, in Rio de Janeiro around 1626, a series of crimes perpetrated by a secret brotherhood of African slaves and Creoles, but which also included emancipated slaves and even Indians. The most obvious characteristics that these crimes had in common were their cruelty and apparent lack of motive.

This brotherhood promulgated the renowned heresy of Judas (in the ignorant parlance of the free people), according to which the redemptive mission of the Crucified One had failed miserably despite such immense suffering. For the great betrayer Judas Iscariot had also suffered from regret and shame, having hanged himself on a fig tree—which is the Devil's tree, according to many traditions.

In fact, the brotherhood and its heresy were based on the metaphysical thoughts of the Queen of Matamba, Jinga Mbandi, who considered evil to be one of the physical quantities of the universe, being finite, measurable, and constant. Manifestations of evil were, naturally, emotional or physical sensations, such as pain, disgust, fear, sadness, anger, or guilt.

So, the more physical pain felt by a group of individuals, the less pain, consequently, would be felt by others. Therefore, the crimes of the brotherhood were barbarous and bloody. Because they were slaves, subject to the highest possible punishments, they sought to eliminate that possibility, inflicting on the free a very intense preventive suffering.

None of the crimes of the brotherhood, however, concern

us here. I want to mention the incidental episode of one of those heretics, a certain Cristóvão—a slave for hire, a black-smith from Congo or Angola (now I cannot remember which).

Cristóvão was in love, madly in love, with the brotherhood's leader, the slave Ana, also known as Camba Dinene in Kim-bundu, the group's liturgical and official language.

Ana, however, was the lover of an enslaved Indian who Cristóvão despised. This Indian, known in the brotherhood as Lemba dia Muxito (born Boicorá, though he channeled Cobra Coral when possessed during ceremonies), was versed in the sci-ence of the forests and taught Ana the active principle of poisons.

What made Cristóvão indignant, and suffer even more, was that Lemba dia Muxito would have his way with Ana as he would have his way with any other woman: with contempt, as if it made no difference to him if he had her or not. What Cristóvão failed to understand was that this was precisely why, because of this premeditated contempt, Lemba had become so desirable, to Ana and to others.

Caught in the dilemma of impossible love, Cristóvão was unfaithful to Camba Dinene. He tore his own eyes out, so as not to see her; he cut out his own tongue, so as not to kiss her; he inflicted a series of punishments on his own body, so as to become repulsive; and, like Judas, he assumed all of the blame, not just his own.

I presumed, when I read this story, that he wanted to draw to himself all the pain, all the evil in the world, and thus redeem humanity, fulfilling the ideal never attained by Jesus Christ.

However, I now see another intent: Cristóvão was jealous of the *caboclo*. And he made the following association: he con-cluded that love, too, was constant and finite, that it was one of the quantities of the physical universe. So if he, Cristóvão, felt the most love, an absolute love, there would be no more love in the world for anyone else.

This crime, this suicide, of course, was insane. Nonetheless, there has persisted among people the saying that the one who loves less has the most power.

Of course, Dr. Zmuda had not told all. So, after bidding the expert farewell, he took out a black notebook from a locked bookcase and sat at his mahogany desk with ivory details.

On the cover, at the top, there was a label, and written on it in flowery handwriting was the German title *Das Aníketos Problem*, which I have ventured to translate as "The Aniceto Problem."

Seeing our character so absorbed while leafing through this notebook, we begin to unveil a new and even more mysterious universe among the various ones that coexisted in Dr. Zmuda's house.

A curious man, the Polish doctor: he could have been one of the most famous scientists of the late 19th century, had he committed himself to this purpose. At seventeen, he entered the University of Vienna, where he obtained his medical degree in 1879. He was, as you can see, a contemporary of Sigmund Freud, sharing with him an admiration for the same professor, the famous physiologist Ernst von Brücke.

Miroslav the student, as I said, from the beginning of his studies showed interest in the physiology of coitus, guiding his research from the female angle. One of his first articles linked Darwin's theories to the characteristics that he imagined distinguished the various human races, proving woman's sexual role to be the determining factor.

In this paper, now seen as obsolete, Zmuda claimed that steatopygia among African women—associated with the "on all fours" position, typical of inferior cultures and most mammals—evolutionarily produced a higher than average penis size in Africa.

On the other hand, institutions like the geishas of Japan and other forms of female sexual servility existing in East Asia would have generated, due to the absence of orgasm in women, a progressive reduction of the male members in that region.

Along the same lines, the higher performance indices among Arab males, as measured by "rigidity," "erection time," and "recovery time," would be linked to the ancient polygamous traditions of the Semitics, preserved by Muslim civilization, based on a conditioning bordering on insatiability.

The Europeans, on the other hand, stood out for an absolute balance of sexual functions (i.e., pleasure and procreation), which corresponds to the high evolutionary stages attained by the Aryans, manifested in their almost universal preference for the "face to face" position, dictated by the imperative of monogamy (at least after Rome and Christianity), and by the respect for motherhood.

This led him to then study the Myth of the Large Penis, to better understand the female reaction to the relative dimensions of the male member. By measuring length and girth, Miroslav Zmuda identified five penile categories: minuscule, modest, respectable, robust, and colossal. The first and last were pathologies, and their effects were inconvenient because they either produced pain or did not provoke a reaction.

The three intermediate categories, in turn, showed interesting differences: modest sizes were capable of inducing orgasms on occasion, depending on several competing variables of an emotional nature.

Meanwhile, respectable and robust were more consistently successful, but with one difference: several female patients reported that, even if the orgasms produced by these two types were of equal intensity, if they had to choose, they preferred the robust size.

This fact was so important that it helped explain an apparent contradiction in the research: being that minuscule and colossal were organic deformities, one would expect for them to be rejected in the same percentages. However, colossals were more accepted and in some cases even preferred, which never was the case with minuscule.

Miroslav Zmuda thus concluded in favor of the Myth of the Large Penis and wrote the classic passage for which he would forever be criticized: "The human spirit was molded for great things, to idolize immensity; we admire palaces, cathedrals, monuments, mountain ranges, and oceans, and for that same reason women prefer a well-endowed phallus."

It was around this time, while strolling in Vienna, that Dr. Zmuda met the Brazilian woman whom he would marry and with whom he came to Rio de Janeiro in 1883. And it was in Rio, a true melting pot of races and a major destination for immigrants, that his theories were perfected.

I have stated that Dr. Zmuda was a Pole, a Slav. Hence, he held to the superstition of Aryan superiority. Therefore, he added certain elements to the first version of his theory surrounding the Myth of the Large Penis, giving more emphasis to the affective phenomena of sexuality (which his colleague Freud would call psychological). These were the subjective aspects of attraction between couples that would prepare or predispose women more to a man's contact, greatly increasing the likelihood of orgasm.

Thus, penile volume did not merely have a physical or sensory aspect. It was the vision of the member, the optical seduction, that was the key element, which explained the success of the colossal among some women, even when anatomically uncomfortable. And this also explained the preference for robust with respect to respectable, when they were equivalent on the physiological plane.

Nevertheless, a large penis produced this effect because it evoked the perception of power—a perception that could be aroused, even jointly, by other manly traits subject to admiration, such as strength, intelligence, eloquence, sophistication, artistic skills, social projection, wealth, or (and here the Aryanism comes in) the superiority of a race, perhaps the most expressive quality (in the opinion of the doctor), because it was directly associated with natural selection.

Miroslav Zmuda found that sexual attraction reproduces power relationships: a dominant woman will not accept a sub-servient man. On the other hand, men in general crave to dom-inate the highest number of females possible. Therefore, an Aryan, being the member of the superior race, would have an advantage and would not need to be robust or colossal, pro-vided he is not minuscule. He will always be preferable, and will better predispose his partner to orgasm.

So it was with the Brazilian he met in Vienna, and so it was with Brigitte from Espirto Santo. The doctor smiled slyly, remembering that he was not only Aryan, but also belonged to the class of the robust.

What Dr. Zmuda did not want to tell Baeta were all these scientific secrets, which he could no longer publish. Especially because—and it is important that this be made clear—he would have had to commit an unspeakable indiscretion, he would have been forced to reveal another mystery concerning the House of Swaps.

For you see, in the shelves and drawers of Dr. Zmuda's office, under lock and key, were all the data on the intimate sexual secrets of the clients of the House of Swaps, transcribed into black notebooks, identical to the one he was leafing through.

Contained in these notebooks were all the fantasies clients had requested of Madame Brigitte, descriptions of firsthand observations gathered during the communal sessions and on couples' night, and (herein lies the crime) transcripts of the verbal reports regularly required of all nurses concerning everything they had done with their clients.

Sebastião Baeta, his wife Guiomar, and all of the other people who had passed through there had their names very safely stored in these notebooks, in which their sexual behaviors and predilections were described in painstaking detail.

The former house of the Marquise of Santos was not only a gynecological clinic, a maternity ward, a brothel, and a place for clandestine affairs and orgies. It was also, we now know, the most secretive and complete observation laboratory and repository of records of the sex life of a city anywhere in the world.

Thus, Miroslav Zmuda could not reveal to the expert the details of the "The Aniceto Problem"—which had subverted crucial points of his theory.

Since early July, when Baeta first began tracing Aniceto's wanderings, the map that emerged contained vastly different, and even contradictory, areas of the city. Each one with their own chain of lovers, antagonistic and isolated, which made his rival's amazing talents even more apparent.

The first one had Ouvidor Street as its epicenter. It was where, at one of the most elegant and sophisticated addresses in Rio, Aniceto had seduced the French owner of La Parisienne, Madame Montfort. From this conquest, he initiated a network of relationships with store customers, such as the wife of the industrialist residing in Botafogo, and the widow Palhares, a resident of Laranjeiras (where rumors were beginning to emerge about a certain neighbor, happily married, who was cheating on her husband with a shady type).

From Ouvidor Street, Aniceto would bridge into the rich neighborhoods and operate within the highest social circles. Moreover, Palhares helped him open another vector, which led the capoeira to São Cristovão—more specifically, to the House of Swaps.

From there, his potential for seduction grew exponentially.

But so did the possibilities for the expert, who needed to have access to places where the capoeira had conquered his lovers so he could then take them away from him.

However, while the House of Swaps was a territory where Baeta had traditionally had great success, the fear of losing in front of witnesses caused in him a certain inhibition. And it led the expert instead to the second zone in which Aniceto operated.

It was the poor side of town, where washerwomen, maids, street vendors, cooks, candy makers, seamstresses, factory workers, and newsgirls lived. This was not an unknown universe for Baeta. As a matter of fact, he had actually had lovers there himself, as was the case with the flag-bearer. Unconsciously, perhaps, he felt this environment was more conducive, because, in theory, women such as these should prefer a policeman to a street hood.

The capoeira's stomping grounds in this sector, excluding the port itself, were essentially comprised of the neighborhoods of Saúde and Gamboa, the streets of Senador Pompeu and Barão de São Felix, more or less following the western edges of Livramento and Favela up to Pinto Hill—including the actual hills themselves, of course.

Aniceto lived on Harmonia Street, near the square, in a rooming house just a notch above a tenement (therefore the building had escaped the fury of the city's sanitary engineers at the turn of the century). It was a sober building, originally one-story, to which a second story was added, with eight rooms on top and four below, leaving ample space for the kitchen and bathroom. The expert's probes began there in mid-September, on a day when Aniceto was not there.

A policeman in Saúde asking questions scares people. Baeta was not well received. And he had to win over the Portuguese landlady, patiently assuring her that he did not have anything against the tenant, that in truth he was actually there looking for one of his girlfriends. The expert evaluated what kind of regard the landlady seemed to have for Aniceto:

"He doesn't bring them home out of respect for me. But his collection's been growing ever since he came back."

This was an important fact: the landlady had no recollection of Aniceto being such a womanizer before his time in Alagoas. This information was consistent with Dr. Zmuda's statement of July 24th. It was clear, therefore, that the capoeira's talent had been acquired after Rufino had rendered his services. The conversation ended with the landlady giving Baeta two or three addresses.

The expert would not, of course, knock on these girls' doors. But the leads clarified a fundamental feature of the capoeira's ethics: in that region, at least, no one knew of his involvement with any married women. This facilitated things, apparently. First, however, Baeta needed to lay the groundwork, making himself even better known in the area, lessening the resentment that his position as policeman inspired in everyone.

In subsequent days, Baeta made incursions into very many bars and dives in the area—anywhere he might find Aniceto's women, while at the same time avoiding his rival. He even ventured into a drumming circle on Proposito Street.

However, it was at an old warehouse in Santo Cristo—where codfish, sausage, and dried beef were sold off of hooks from the ceiling, infesting the air with a suffocating smell of salt and fat—where he met the capoeira's first avowed enemy.

"Stinking bastard. One day he'll be dead, and no one will have a clue why."

His tone was one of pure hatred. Baeta also detected a foreign accent. The man turned his back to the expert and returned to his conversation with two companions lounging on potato sacks. That's when a fourth man from the same group folded his hand in a round of *sueca,* and motioned to Baeta, indicating that they should go to the rear to talk.

Antonio the Mina, the man with the accent, owned his own home on Hospício Street and was one of the last African *babalaôs* of Rio de Janeiro. The other Ifá priests disliked him intensely because he went around saying that he was the sole legitimate heir to the tradition, the only one who knew the two hundred fifty-six paths of each of the two hundred fifty-six *odus* (or individual destinies), which equaled more than sixty-five thousand memorized poems he could recite.

The man who explained these things was the African's apprentice. Baeta had never heard that the Mina people had a god of knowledge, and a kind of alphabet—represented by complex symbols whose meaning could be deciphered by arithmetic analysis of their strokes—used to write the *odus*. He began to realize that these sorcerers had their own principles and methods. Perhaps for that very reason, because of the rational nature of that activity, all of those men, including the Galician, the owner of the warehouse, venerated Antonio the Mina, the *babalaô*.

And the expert went on listening, paying for more and more rounds of cachaça and chorizo, until finally Antonio joined them to narrate what he knew about Aniceto.

Antonio had consulted for Aniceto forever. The capoeira had been abandoned by his mother as a newborn, and then lost his father, which was when his brothers disowned him. At the time the *babalaô*, out of the kindness of his heart, helped support him. They did not know or even remember a sister named Fortunata—which was natural, considering the age when the two would have been separated.

Incidentally, no relative, except his father, had ever shown any interest in the capoeira. For this reason, the Mina could not forgive Aniceto's betrayal. As he explained it, before the capoeira disappeared for a while up north, he had sought out another sorcerer from a different line, an old *macumbeiro*, a charlatan and a scam artist.

That was the reason for the fight: Antonio had refused to initiate Aniceto as a *babalaô* because the *odu* prohibited it.

"He came up *Odi-Otura*. They say that whoever performs *Ifá* on this individual will attract shame or disgrace."

The expert was impressed with this schism between sorcerers—similar in many ways to what one encounters between scientists advocating divergent theoretical tangents.

"Now he struts around like a big shot. They say he has lots of women and money. People think it's the work of *macumba*. Don't believe it. If he has women, it's because he got rich. And if got rich, it's because he's a thief!"

By then, Baeta had already knocked back a few cachaças. But he could still easily deduce the identity of the old *macumbeiro*: power like that—money, women—really was worth a pair of gold earrings shaped like seahorses.

It was not the first time Baeta had been draw into a world of fantastic realities, of esoteric knowledge, and of magic. His mother, a laundress, had been permeated by the supernatural in her daily life. She liked to recite supernatural incidents, mostly crimes, which she had heard from neighbors at the grocery store and at street fairs.

In Catumbi, Baeta's birthplace, they had lived next to a fortune-teller, Mrs. Zeze, who took in an old man who channeled the spirits of dead African slaves, a *preto velho de quimbanda*. Young Sebastião had been with that old man, Father Cristóvão das Almas, only once, secretly taken there by an aunt when they said he had rabies after a dog bit him.

He never forgot that scene: Mrs. Zeze, possessed by the spirit, wrinkled skin, her body all bent with age, contorted, sitting on her adductor muscles, her legs folded back, a position that in theory should have been unbearable for anyone her age. And Father Cristóvão, with his ancient and pentatonic voice, channeling chilling melodies while wielding a machete and knife, puffing bitter smoke from his pipe, exploding huge *fundanga* wheels, drinking liters of cachaça, and staying clear-headed all the while.

The washerwoman's son was healed and heard even more stories, about people who died on the day and in the manner predicted by the old man; about messages from beyond the grave, with details so precise and so intimate that they could not be mere coincidence; about diagnosed diseases, which were later confirmed by medical doctors; plus many other wonders.

But he never paid much heed to any of these things. His father had been an engineer who, even from a distance, had instilled in him the illusion that everyone who came out of this universe was a failure. The engineer, seeing the boy's extraordinary intelligence, invested heavily in his formal education and inculcated in him a mindset we might call "scientific."

Perhaps this was why Baeta had never given any credence to the more heterodox strands of science. His vehement rejection of Lombroso's criminal anthropology, for example, stemmed not only from numerous counterproofs collected in Baeta's own work, but also because the Italian doctor had studied spiritualism, having attested to the veracity of the mesmeric and magnetic experiments that were all the rage in Europe at the time. The expert found such an interest incompatible with the scientific mentality, and therefore disqualified it as theoretical.

The *babalaô* Antonio the Mina was both a disturbing and conciliatory element for Baeta. First, because Baeta realized that magical thinking surprisingly sought support in numbers theory, and second, because the expert now had no doubt whatsoever that Aniceto's seductive power had been obtained supernaturally. The testimonies of Antonio the Mina, and of the Portuguese landlady, and of Miroslav Zmuda himself confirmed that those feats were recent, and that they coincided with the date of the services rendered by Rufino at the English Cemetery.

We know that great mathematical minds have a great propensity toward mysticism: Baeta was the son of an engineer, and he had grown up on supernatural stories from the laundress. At that moment, these lineages merged; logic and magic began to inhabit the same world, and all of the fantastical inclinations of his intellectual constitution blossomed inside of him with great energy.

The expert felt that if he resorted to witchcraft to win the bet, he would not be betraying his essentially rational nature.

Consulting Mrs. Zeze, however, was impossible—Baeta had gone to her funeral, years earlier, in the company of his mother. Antonio the Mina was even less of an option. Although he had not clearly understood the *babalaô's* objections to Aniceto's plans, Baeta intuited that the capoeira had only sought Rufino because he could not accept the Mina's rejection.

Therefore, the one who possessed that power, the one who could transmit the power he so coveted, was the scam artist, the charlatan, the *macumbeiro* Rufino.

One of the fantastic stories Baeta had heard his mother tell in his childhood was published under the title *Maria do Pote's Unexpected Revenge*, and it was still well known in 1983, when the late Beto da Cuíca transformed it into a samba.

It tells the story of Dito (short for "Benedito"), a trickster, drummer, and resident of Rato Hill who attended the samba circle of the sinister Terreirão, in San Carlos. This place—a sort of step, naturally cut out of the hill's steep slope—had been cursed ever since they cut down a *mata-pau* (or laurel fig) tree there, thus opening the ground as if it were the very gates of Hell.

Whoever walked through the Terreirão, and specifically dragged his foot over the area where the tree had once stood, was stricken by irreparable misfortune, and would be haunted until his dying days.

At the time of the events narrated, however, this phenomenon had not yet been perceived. For that reason, no one who lived nearby ever missed a jam session there, and even people from Andaraí came down to verify the reputation of the hot-shots from Estacio.

Dito was not just a drummer and a *malandro*. He was also, above all, a bandit. The robberies he committed were not of his own initiative, but were killings he would do for hire. The latter fact, of course, did not prevent him from performing some killings whose motivation was, shall we say, of a personal, rather than financial, nature. If he was not getting paid, Dito only killed for revenge.

There were certain rituals associated with each case. For example, when for hire, Dito complied with his client's calendar. Revenge killings, however, he performed only on Saturdays in March or April.

So much art, so much premeditation, went into these crimes that Dito was not concerned that future victims might get wind of their sentences. No one escaped—especially because they had not uncovered the principles underlying the choice of the fateful Saturday.

The consequences of having stepped onto the Terreirão, for Dito, began as soon as he laid eyes on a lively mulatta in the samba circle, who transfixed the *malandro* with a very eccentric, very provocative swing in her hips. As you may have surmised, it was none other than Maria do Pote.

After the samba, Dito, a bandit and a drummer, became intimate with the girl right there on the slope.

Maria do Pote was a local, but she attended a *candomblé de inquices* at Barão of Itaúna, and had been shaved for *sinhá Bamburucema*—similar to a Iansã or a Santa Barbara. They say the women of Santa Barbara are very hot-blooded—and better than those of Oxum.

Her friends warned her that she should reject him, that men like him were no good, that they were only trouble. They had no idea, these women, how good it is to be with a bad man. Dito claimed Maria do Pote as his.

In a story such as this, whose theme is betrayal, which begins with talk of revenge, which involves a man (a villain) and a woman (a seductress), there can be no outcome that does not involve adultery. And that is exactly what will happen.

First, however, it must be said that Maria do Pote was not a loose woman, a whore, as many insist. It is important to remember, first, that she was a young lady, and second, that she had danced on the spot where the root of the *mata-pau* had once been.

They are impressive, these fig trees. Their vast, confused, and irregular thicket of branches appears to reflect the very unpredictability of life. Contradictorily, the branches resemble roots, and they appear to extend deep into the earth. Because of this ambivalence, the trees are a gateway into the underworld and into the tombs where disembodied spirits dwell. The tree itself, the *mata-pau*, the "kill-stick," feeds on death, as the name itself suggests, because it only germinates over the corpses of other trees.

Maria do Pote—like many others, like Dito himself— seemed infused by the spirit of the fig tree. And on one occasion, one single time, after a samba, when her man did not show up, she curled up with another man in that gully. Dito, being streetwise, got wind of everything, but he kept quiet, taking full advantage of the few days Maria had left.

It was April 15th, 1911—Holy Saturday, the day of the Great Revenge—where they would beat up on Judas and then go drink and beat their drums in the Terreirão, that Dito cut Maria do Pote's throat, right there in the middle of the circle.

Her girlfriends mourned, and no one else dared even touch the subject. What people did begin to talk about was the thug's behavior. First, he would go to great lengths not to pass by the São Francisco de Paula Cemetery, instead taking Doutor Agra to get to Itapiru Street, always avoiding Catumbi Square. Then he started fearing all intersections, which he only crossed with his eyes closed. It was then that it was revealed that Dito was seeing apparitions.

No father or holy person had a solution to his problem. The *batuqueiro* was a hopeless case, until a new Holy Saturday came along.

Dito was at the Terreirão, fighting off the blues, when it happened: the *malandro*, the crook, this evil and murderous thug, suddenly jumped into the center of the circle, hands on his twisting hips—dancing in the exotic, seductive, and unmistakable style of the late Maria do Pote. They say even his laughter had the exact same timbre as the girl's.

Let us get back to Rufino now. The house, atop Santa Teresa, seemed to be carved out of the forest right above where Antonio Valentim had once built his imposing castle, in an area that was being settled little by little, and already had a dozen shacks on it.

Rufino's house was the most isolated of them all. But it was not built from scrap lumber and demolition materials like the others: it was of a much older construction, made of wattle and daub, low and without windows. The precarious ventilation was achieved by way of a small gap between the walls and the palm fiber that covered the roof. A meandering coral snake was painted on the front door, which was shut with a wooden latch. There was a second door in the back, with just enough room for a crouched man to enter. This door faced the dense forest.

This was an important difference: while the other residents tried to clear the forest around their homes, to make the environment increasingly urban, Rufino preferred the shade and humidity of the jungle. And that was not all—he threatened anyone who appeared with a scythe, a machete, or an ax, saying that the exuberant nature that surrounded them had not been the work of God, but rather that it was he, Rufino, who had built that forest, just like Antonio Valentim had built his castle. The old man claimed he could identify all of the palm trees, the *jequitibás,* the *jatobás*, the *jacarandas*, the *tapirirás*, the cinnamon trees, the cedars, the *perobas*, *ipês*, begonias, orchids, the *angelins,* and *gameleiras* he had planted there in a labor that had lasted forty years.

It was one more story that circulated about him: that he had been one of the slaves utilized by Major Archer during the reforestation of the mountains of Tijuca, an effort which started in 1861, by order of the emperor, with the intent of recovering the sources of the Comprido, Maracanã, and Carioca rivers to end the city's chronic water shortages.

Rufino actually completed his duties, but only after leading his fellow slaves to escape into the surrounding hills. Thus emerged the mysterious Cambada Quilombo, a community of runaway slaves never destroyed or located, which Rufino headed.

While the major continued with the work (this time with salaried employees), the fugitives did the same thing, replanting the forest at different points on the hillside.

The replanting of Tijuca Forest, for Rufino, served to rescue not only the rivers but also his favorite prey: pacas, peccary, the macuco, and the lizards. The old man also wanted to create a maze, inside of which the Cambada Quilombo could resist forever.

Thus, Rufino's house, which was built in the *quilombo* style, was from an architectural standpoint more important than the castle, because it was one of the last of its type in the city.

When Baeta arrived at the house, Rufino was not in, and it was raining. It had been a long hike up from Guimarães Square, where he had jumped off the streetcar. He would have preferred to wait a little before approaching the house, but there was nowhere to stay dry there, especially since the neighbors, who lived just down the hill, did not seem to like the old man very much, and pointed the way very grudgingly.

Just when the rain began really coming down, when it was turning into a full-blown storm, the expert noticed a movement in the bushes, and he walked around the house, gun in hand, expecting find an animal of some kind. Then he saw that the back door, protected by a fence of bromeliads, was open. He could not resist.

The furniture consisted of a mat, covering a bed of leaves, and a wooden stool covered with tapir leather. There was also the stump of a jackfruit tree, which must have doubled as a chair, and a stove with an iron trivet over it. The rest were various wicker baskets hanging from the roof, a *candongueiro* drum made of *jararaca* skin, and the skulls of animals hanging from the walls. The expert thought he recognized fourteen: a jaguar, a giant anteater, an agouti, an alligator, a peccary, a pygmy owl, a howler monkey, a capybara, a sloth, a spider monkey, an armadillo, a toucan, an ocelot, and a paca. Finally, objects lay scattered on the floor: ropes, candles, bottles, primitive tools, knives, a rapier, and even a large shiv, which could be used in hunting or even warfare.

"Looking to die, young man?"

Baeta turned to face Rufino, who was standing, drenched, barefoot, and shirtless, machete in hand. Some solemn looks can scare you more than a machete. Despite being armed, and despite being police, the expert trembled.

The old man recognized the expert. In his mind he was of the same ilk as the Mauá Square thugs. He stared Baeta down with a steely gaze, awaiting an explanation. The expert, very carefully, began apologizing before getting to the subject at hand:

"I came to talk to you about the man who gave you the earrings."

Rufino, was skeptical. He settled down on the tapir skin bench, his legs open. Suddenly, he hurled the machete, lodging it into the jackfruit tree stump with a thud. It was his way of telling the policeman where to sit.

"What does the man with the earrings have to do with this story?"

Baeta did not understand. He knew nothing about any story. He had come with a very specific objective concerning Aniceto. That is what he intended to talk about.

"Don't think you can fool me, mister. You're all the same."

It was clear to the expert, once again, that being police spoiled everything. But he didn't feel like justifying himself and went straight to the point: he spoke of the *babalaô* Antonio the Mina; of Aniceto's countless women, and of his own suspicion that the service rendered for the capoeira in the English Cemetery, and paid for with the earrings, had something to do with that power.

"I came to get myself the same thing."

Rufino did not answer immediately. He dried his hands with a wad of tow, took a pipe from one of the *samburás*, filled it with a pinch of tobacco, and only after his third puff, declared:

"I don't strike deals with the police. Never again."

That's when Baeta understood: his home had been broken into, his belongings had been ransacked and scattered like trash, he himself had been tortured. He still had bruises from the blows to his back, not to mention the burns on his face, hands, and the soles of his feet. All of this because of a treasure they said was his.

The officers who wanted to extort him (Baeta did not suspect the captain was one of them) were now poking around, prowling his house, following his every footstep and those of his clients.

The expert—who had already accepted the abstraction of

magic—still could not believe in stories of such palpable wealth, in such vast quantities of stones and precious metals. And he told the old man as much, to try to convince him that he had not gone there to rob him. Rufino, however, remained interested only in his pipe, making it very clear that the subject was closed.

"So then, does this treasure really exist?"

It was just a taunt. When the old man opened his mouth it was only to spit on the ground. Baeta stood, angrily. Before slamming the door behind him, though, he played one last card:

"I'll take care of the police. We'll talk soon."

Rufino, who up until then had maintained a fierce expression, laughed for the first time.

The Aniceto Problem—as Doctor Zmuda had termed it— was actually a set of observations that could be looked at from the prism of three distinct topics, related to the areas of female sexuality that had most interested the doctor in recent years.

We saw that in Vienna, Miroslav Zmuda emphasized the physiology of intercourse, the sexual evolution of the races, and the Myth of the Large Penis. His ideas at the time brought with them the implicit assumption that the action of the phallus in the vagina was the primordial element of female pleasure, albeit assisted by other factors.

By overly stressing one aspect, you run the risk of neglecting another one. Thus, the Polish doctor belittled the importance of clitoral functions, both in stimulation as well as during coitus, as he regarded manual induction of orgasms as secondary and dispensable, particularly in women. Who would have thought? Miroslav Zmuda, skilled masturbator, who had won over Brigitte at his former clinic in Gloria in precisely that manner.

It was Aniceto who began to change the doctor's thinking.

It was couples' night. July 24th. The usual guests were there. Guiomar and the expert Baeta were there. Zmuda was shocked to see Palhares, with her new partner, less than two months after her husband's funeral. Few realized it was she, though, so the couple sparked little interest. Baeta, then in the throes of lovemaking, did not even glance at them.

But Aniceto was playing close attention. His gaze was firmly fixed on the women, especially the nurses. He soon attracted one, and, with Palhares, took her into one of the bedrooms that guests were allowed to lock from inside. It was this nurse who narrated the following series of events to Madame Brigitte.

Not only did Aniceto guide the widow to kiss her on the mouth, and to explore her entire body, but he produced in her an orgasm through penetration that she had never before experienced with a man at that intensity. Lying on her back, the prostitute felt Aniceto's full weight focused on his pubis, and, by vigorously pressing against her vulva, he could swivel his hips, introducing the penis at the same time and with the same force that he massaged the clitoris.

"I was so shaken, I could barely move," concluded the girl, at a loss for words to describe the sensation.

Because she was a prostitute with vast experience, Zmuda gave much value to that technique. And a few months later he was able to watch it live, for it was exactly the technique Aniceto used on the tall woman at the party where Baeta took notice of the capoeira for the first time.

That, however, was not what most impressed Dr. Zmuda about Aniceto. It was in the field of sexual attraction that he was truly working wonders.

To seduce a nurse was perhaps not so difficult; but by then, Dr. Zmuda already knew that Aniceto was not exactly Madame Montfort's employee, that he had been the cause of the crime committed by the industrialist's wife, and that he had a certain facility in seducing very fine ladies, like the widow Palhares and her neighbor in Laranjeiras, not to mention the women he met at the House of Swaps.

Although there were exceptions—and Madame Brigitte had already arranged some fantasies to that effect—females in general (so the doctor believed), preferred males of a superior social rank to their own, which in Rio de Janeiro was often confused with the notion of race.

Palhares and many of the other women who had been seduced by the capoeira had already shown a tendency toward brutish, poor, or ignorant men, which for Zmuda belonged to the realm of individual fantasy, so there was no real surprise there. The surprise lay in Aniceto's being accepted by so many superior partners, which gave his achievement the air of a real feat.

This was one reason why Aniceto's presence at the House of Swaps was so essential. Miroslav Zmuda wanted first to understand his method and then to discover the scientific foundations that made it possible.

The second reason was more pressing: the capoeira, besides being an irresistible seducer, had an unimaginable capacity for entering the minds of women and discovering their most intimate sexual desires, which he would then turn around and expose and exploit.

A good example was how he had managed Palhares and the tall woman: Aniceto seemed to know things beforehand—that both liked being with women, too, that the widow enjoyed being treated with a certain contempt, and playing a more submissive role, that the other preferred the more dominant role, and that being passive, in that kind of situation, was her way of humiliating her partner.

Even supposing Palhares had revealed such desires to the capoeira (which Zmuda considered very unlikely), there was no way to explain the tall woman, other than amazing coincidence or deep intuition. The doctor leaned toward the second hypothesis, while revising his notes and confirming that neither of the two had exhibited those tendencies, those symbolizations, before.

This was the third major theme of Dr. Zmuda's research: the constancy of the phenomenon he called "sexual symbolization," the discovery of which he owed to the city, Madame Brigitte, and the House of Swaps.

It was in Rio de Janeiro that Miroslav Zmuda discovered— or, rather, became fully convinced—that female orgasms were extremely affected by the symbolic components of attraction and sex. These symbols could operate merely in the realm of fantasy, for example in individuals who secretly imagined certain scenes during intercourse. Or these scenes could be fully carried out, and then they became real-life experiments and tremendously influenced pleasure levels.

Since then, the Polish doctor had been cataloging and classifying a large number of these symbolizations. Both the specialized literature and public opinion in general tainted these as aberrations, perversions, fetishes, addictions, vices, abominable practices, and deviations. Nobody inhabited these dark areas so familiarly as did Aniceto.

In 1916, when the composer Donga filed for a copyright at the National Library for a score to a song entitled *Pelo Telefone* (the first composition to earn the name "samba," although it was, in fact, a *maxixe*), he may have committed a series of omissions, or even told lies regarding the genre, the authorship, and the dates of its composition.

However, the song was truthful with regard to the content of its lyrics. At least since 1913, the police chief had known of the presence of a roulette wheel at Carioca Square. And that such a roulette wheel was located at the Hans Staden Bar—the popular nickname of a traditional German brewery, which never officially went by that name, and at its height served the best lager in the world at an address that today houses a cutlery store.

Whoever entered Hans's could not help but notice the round marble table where they displayed (for the use of the customers) playing cards, dice, boards, and the pieces of various games of chance. It was not exactly a den of gambling, but the bar had become famous for being one of the main centers of banned games in the city, even boasting of a secret room, where said roulette wheel was located.

For this reason, the patrons of Hans's felt uneasy when Baeta and the captain of the First District crossed the entire length of the bar, and sat at a small table in the back, and ordered draft beer, pickles, and assorted sausages.

The captain's invitation had come as a surprise to the expert. It must not have been work they had come to discuss; otherwise, they could just as well have talked back at the division. The matter, thus, must have been private, giving Baeta a unique opportunity to address his problem, the case of Rufino the sorcerer.

The expert imagined that the captain, a skeptical type, would not give any credence to the treasure story. So, without revealing his true reasons, he would ask that his colleague impose his authority and force his officers to lay off the old man. He would say it was arbitrary, he would use the police chief's name, perhaps even that of the minister of justice. What he did not know was how to do this without disclosing his personal stake in the matter.

So he was taken aback when the captain went straight to the subject, after the first sip:

"I know you were in Santa Teresa, at the sorcerer's house."

So it really was true: Rufino was being kept under round-the-clock surveillance by officers of the First District. The movement in the bushes the expert had noticed, before entering the old man's hut, was a spy. Baeta simply could not have imagined that the captain himself was behind this hunt.

"Something big is going down in my district. I have a right to know what it is."

This was a checkmate of sorts on the expert's plan. Baeta could not allow them to suspect that the secretary had been murdered (and therefore could not say that the case of Fortunata had occurred in São Cristovão and not in Mauá Square, which perhaps would have relieved tensions). He needed to maintain the same posture that he knew nothing, that he had gone to the old man as a forensics expert, in search of evidence for other cases of stolen corpses that he had begun to review. It was rot, and the captain saw right through it.

"You need to know something: the First District is a brotherhood."

Baeta understood the implied threat. In the department, the sense of honor and loyalty of the Mauá Square gang was legend. Not that they were really a gang. They had no kickback scheme or anything of the sort. What existed between them—beyond the vanity of thinking they were the town's finest—was merely a pact of mutual defense and of unconditional support, like the Freemasons or other secret societies. There's no need to mention here the kind of punishment that befell traitors and enemies.

"And what were you looking for at the wharf two weeks ago?"

They must never know in the First District that Fortunata was the capoeira's sister. Baeta said dismissively that his problem with the scoundrel was of a personal nature. As soon as he gave this answer, though, he realized he was not lying, that he, Baeta, really did have a personal issue with Aniceto.

The captain, however, was a good cop. And he was in the habit of saying what was on his mind: that Baeta was conducting an investigation in his, the captain's, jurisdiction; that the capoeira had some link to Rufino; that Rufino had links to the woman named Fortunata; and that the woman was related to Aniceto, which closed the circle. And said circle certainly involved a very big story.

"Speaking of big stories, why were the earrings returned?"

Baeta read into the captain's smile a suspicion. And he responded with an accusation of his own, a frown. The captain, who knew how to read facial expressions, hastened to retort:

"No one steals at the First District."

It took a while for the expert to understand what his colleague was thinking: at Mauá Square they thought Baeta had returned the earrings to serve as bait. Rufino—who everyone knew had a treasure—would not take long before visiting his hideout to add that piece, or any of the others he had received from his many clients.

So that was what they had against Baeta in the First District.

The expert, however, had an essentially mathematical spirit. For him, it was more difficult to believe in concrete wonders (such as Rufino's treasure) than in abstract entities such as points, lines, circles, and other geometric figures nonexistent in nature that make up the fantastic universe created by Euclid.

That, more or less, was what he hinted at to the captain: he was not hunting for any treasures because he could not imagine a more pointless idea.

It is amazing the affect treasures have on people. The captain did not accept the expert's explanation, because those who believe in treasures simply cannot admit that others might not believe.

"And why exactly did you pay the old man a visit?"

It was an answer Baeta would not give. And such insistence, at that moment, infuriated him. Perhaps the captain had not noticed that the expert did not like to be intimidated. Baeta was a man. He had been born a man. Being afraid was not in his makeup; he did not care if he were going against the entire Brotherhood.

He was faster than the captain, and he angrily stabbed the last sausage, leaving the other with his toothpick hanging in the air.

"You invite, you pay," he said, standing to leave.

He had just declared war.

One of the stories recorded by Dr. Zmuda, and brought to life by Madame Brigitte, illustrates how the House of Swaps proceeded in cases of the sort. It began when Brigitte received an anonymous letter in which the female sender (because it was surely a woman) described a fantasy she needed fulfilled, but stated that she would only let her identity be known if the House administrator first consented to make it a reality.

Madame Brigitte wrote yes and set the price and also gave instructions regarding certain arrangements necessary for the implementation of the plan, particularly the delivery of the money—to be made on a certain date and time, to a certain individual who would be dressed in a certain manner, at a pre-determined spot on Machado Square.

A few days later, the following scene unfolded: on a dark street by Flamengo Beach, near Catete, a horse-drawn coupe pulled up beside a woman in a muslin dress with a tight corset and feather hat, walking in well-measured steps, so that the driver, very politely, could ask a question.

The woman's anxiety was visible. Approached in such a cordial manner, though, she seemed to relax, and as she was about to answer, suddenly, from a nearby alley, a man grabbed the lady's arm and shoved her into the carriage.

And the coupe drove on, from Catete downtown—not to a public place like Central Avenue, but to the worst part of Alfândega Street, where the old Quitanda do Marisco used to be, and there it stopped. The woman—who had suffered verbal insults and some physical abuse during the trip—was dragged to an old two-story apartment building and taken upstairs. There she would be handed over to another man, who would then unceremoniously have his way with her.

But we will leave that story for later. Let us now examine the first man, the abductor, actually a young man of twenty-two. He was a kind of an external arm, an advance guard, so to speak, for the House of Swaps, there to perform the risky and somewhat more unusual services.

I do not know if I made clear that, though there were men for hire, unlike the nurses they were not on call at the House. Madame Brigitte would summon them when needed, and depending on the circumstances, they could even render their services at the old Imperador Street (always with great discretion, following strict security procedures). But it was more common to go instead to rented quarters in the old downtown area.

Hermínio, the male prostitute who took the woman from Catete to Alfandêga Street, was not from a wealthy family, but still he could have been a journalist or employed in trade instead, like his father and brothers. He had chosen this line of work because it gave him pleasure, because he enjoyed the risk, and because he did not understand the concept of work.

Though he had participated in his share of melees at America matches (he enjoyed soccer precisely for that reason), what he really loved were the regattas, and he had even rowed for São Cristovão. As for his money, he preferred spending it at Hans Staden's secret back room, or playing the lottery at the Central Station.

It was also not unusual to see him near Mauá Square playing monte, English monte, heads or tails, or *chapinha*—games not frequented exclusively by *malandros*.

It was his ability to move in all of these circles—the secret roulette wheels of Carioca Square and the wooden stools of the Gamboa—that made him an ideal candidate for the major missions of the House of Swaps. Hermínio was well-spoken, dressed finely, and, with his ex-rower's size 18 neck, he cut a good figure. But he also could mix just as easily with the down-and-out crowd, though he was not a capoeira and did not frequent drumming jams.

Thus, while he worked almost exclusively for sophisticated clientele—capitalists, military, high-level civil servants—he also acted behind the scenes, organizing elaborate fantasies, hiring carriages, renting rooms, bribing authorities, taking precautions to guarantee secrecy, and other measures of the sort.

It had been Hermínio, for example, who had managed to convince three unemployed men to accompany him to that same flat on Alfanêga Street, where they found a masked woman, whose identity only remained unknown due to Hermínio's diligence (such was the eagerness with which all three fell on her). It was he, too, who had succeeded in persuading a bankrupt woman to give over her daughter for two *contos*. It was also Hermínio who discovered an immense and evil woman on Cachoeirinha Hill who truly had giant paws for feet, and who became all the rage with the foot fetishists of the House of Swaps.

Accustomed to tasks such as these, it was with regret that Hermínio finished reading a letter from Madame Brigitte, dated October 1st, containing a strange request. In this letter, the house administrator asked that he ascertain as much information as possible about a certain sorcerer named Rufino, who was said to be very well known in the Lapa area. She did not take time to explain the reasons—a courtesy he believed he was entitled to. She only said that it was private, and it that had to do with the security of the House of Swaps.

This was a world Hermínio rarely entered: the *casa de santos* of the *macumbeiros*. He also never knelt in church or sought out priests. He believed that the randomness of life was incompatible with the idea of God. He was disgusted by any reasoning that resorted to superstition, and he never gambled on an animal because of a dream, but rather according to logical principles he thought existed in every game.

But the letter was indeed signed by Madame Brigitte. Still, instead of scouring Lapa for this obscure character, trying not to attract attention, he preferred remaining in his own element. So, on an illegal card game night, in a hole-in-the-wall bar on a Liceu side street where plenty of whiskey was being downed and the main victims were officers of the British Navy, Hermínio thought that one of those players, because of his profession, most likely knew something about this Rufino, and he was imprudent enough to inquire.

"And what exactly is your interest in this man?"

The man who answered Hermínio with another question was a member of the Mauá Square Brotherhood. He was one of the police officers assigned to the First District.

There was a third predicate crime which deserves the title *The Treachery of the Manilha of Clubs*. This crime was at once unfortunate and essential, because if on the one hand it ruined the city, leading to its only military defeat, on the other hand, it allowed for the rescue of perhaps its most valuable document hitherto held in foreign hands: the missing map of Lourenço Cão.

Let us tell the story, then, as it really happened. The earliest decks of playing cards found in Rio de Janeiro date back to the Philippine Dynasty. The decks, in and of themselves, perhaps might not have excited the mood of the citizenry much. However, because gambling establishments were outlawed, the pleasures of chance began to grow.

It was after 1655, when the first wave of Gypsies flooded the city, that the lure of cards became definitive and irresistible.

They were so suited to Rio de Janeiro, and Rio de Janeiro was so suited to them, that here they abandoned millennia of nomadic existence and settled down.

Disdained because they sometimes served as hangmen or slave traders (a disdain which was unfair, because they were not the only ones), Gypsies had a deep impact in several areas: the domestication of horses, the counterfeiting of coins, the dissemination of playing cards and dice, and the expansion of our arts of magic and prophecy.

The greatest contribution of the Gypsies, however, was to have fortified in the city the oriental notion of chance. So much so that chess became unthinkable among us, for it is a game that is won by very tedious calculations. Snooker is also not so welcome, since the talents and techniques needed make it more suitable to the city of São Paulo.

The notion of chance is so inherent in Rio de Janeiro that the two main games native to the city are the *jogo do bicho* and the Carioca version of monte (the *ronda* being a simplified version). They are forbidden, and thus they are popular, as is the case with the *pernada* Carioca, although that is linked to another tradition altogether.

We do not know when, but we do know that the game of *manilha de paus* arose among the Gypsies and then spread throughout the city. Among other things, it was, of course, also a game of cards. However, before long there infiltrated in the Gypsy mentality the archaic concepts of the native peoples of the city—and for the natives, the stakes are life itself.

But let us go over the rules. An equal number of young women and young men participated, all potentially desirable, and of every status except married or enslaved (they say that this exclusion was what spurred the slaves to create capoeira).

The total number of players was necessarily divisible by four, the number of suits in a deck. The duration was one year, beginning and ending on Easter—the day when the cards were dealt. The game had a real life queen, a Gypsy, who drew the cards, using two decks exactly the same: one for the men, another for the women, and whose cards, in ascending order of rank, were the ace, the deuce, the three, the four, the five, the six, the seven, the jack, the queen, and the king.

During Holy Week, starting on Palm Sunday, the Gypsy queen would randomly deal cards from the respective decks, one card for each girl, one for each boy. So, usually by Easter, a card was exhibited atop one of the tents in the camp— located around where the current Campo de Santana is, at the time known as Gypsies' Corral. The card was taken from a third deck, and it was the wild card, which defined the *manilha* and the *trunfo*.

If the card exhibited on the tent were a three of spades, the strongest rank (*the manilha*) would be the three, of any suit, and the strongest suit (*the trunfo*) would be spades. Any spade, in this example, would defeat any other suit; any three, in its particular suit, could defeat any other rank, even the king. But the three of spades, the wild card, would not be, in this case, the strongest card. This privilege was always reserved for the *manilha* of clubs—in this case, it was the three of clubs.

Here it is important to open an aside: for the Gypsies of Rio de Janeiro, the suits of a deck of cards represented, among other things, the four masculine virtues. And the ultimate virtue for them, symbolized by clubs, was luck, to which they linked cleverness and the ability to lie. Hence the greatness of the *manilha* of clubs.

Just below it, in a malleable hierarchy, came the diamonds, representing money, power, honor, the possession of material and abstract assets, and the capacity to influence men; then came spades, encompassing pure strength, dexterity, or other essential physical qualities such as ambition or courage; and finally hearts, reflecting elegance, charm, grace, and a mastery of knowledge and the arts.

The reader may find the following basic rule inconsistent: the young man who was dealt the *manilha* of clubs became the guardian, the grand master of ceremonies, responsible for protecting the young lady who, from the female deck, randomly selected the same playing card—but he did not have the right to touch her. I mentioned that he was a guardian because the ultimate prize was precisely this young lady who drew the *manilha* of clubs.

One day I will write a book (perhaps a wearisome novel) about this intriguing Rio tradition. For now, if the reader is not familiar with the card game and has difficulty understanding the rules, please follow the author's instruction: observe the unfolding of one match which began on Easter of 1710, when the Gypsy queen drew and put on display on her tent the ace of diamonds.

For our purposes, it will suffice to follow the movements of a single player—Fernão da Moura, a young man, a student, the son of a surgeon who rented houses in less wealthy parts of the city where emancipated slaves lived. The father was an elderly widower, but his great sadness in life was having been denied the ability to serve Christ, because he was unable to establish cleanliness of blood and because his ancestors were said to have suffered from a "mechanical defect," (i.e., they were suspected to have engaged in manual labor). Fernão, of course, cared little about such trifles.

Fernão da Moura's problem at that moment was his luck: he had been one of the first men in line to see the Gypsy, and he unfortunately drew the deuce of hearts. Not only did he not draw clubs, not only did he not draw the *trunfo* card—for the wild card was the ace of diamonds—his card, the deuce, also happened to be the lowest rank in the four suits.

Let us understand Fernão's dilemma: like any other player, to win over one of the young girls he first had to be alone with her (a move appropriately called "ravishing" in the Gypsy slang).

If he were successful in performing this feat and presented that card—the deuce of hearts—and the girl had clubs or spades, he could not touch her, because the suits do not coincide and because hearts was not the *trunfo*. If, by misfortune, the young lady were *trunfada* (i.e., if she had diamonds), he would have to pay a penalty and maybe even be suspended temporarily, if she chose to seize his card. And if, by chance, this young lady, who he had managed to be alone with, had hearts, it would have been just as bad luck for Fernão to have deuce—that year, it was worth less than the ace itself—and it would have eliminated his last chances at success.

His only option, therefore, was to take a playing card away from an opponent via a challenge. Fernão da Moura, however, was coolheaded. Instead of proposing challenges left and right, as many did, he preferred to carefully analyze the behavior of others. He, Fernão, believed that each player was his own playing card. The ones who proposed challenges right away, in general, were those who did not have clubs or the *trunfo* suit. The ones fortunate enough to be the *trunfados*—the only ones who could try approaching young ladies of any suit—would throw themselves at all of the girls eagerly. Those who had drawn clubs—the only ones entitled to "ravish" the trump of that suit—would normally adopt a defensive posture, because they were also the ones who received the most challenges, since even those with a *trunfo* card needed clubs in order to obtain the big prize. This was a key aspect of the rule: the young lady who held the *manilha* of clubs could only be "ravished" by someone who also held clubs.

The fascinating part about the game was not just the duels to seize the playing cards; the art resided mainly in the intrigue, the deals, and the deceit (as allowed by the rules). Women, for example, though they were potentially available, had their own desires, their own romantic interests, and they would rather choose, spurning those they saw as unworthy.

Fernão da Moura, patient and cool, also observed them, particularly to discover as quickly as possible who the lady *manilha* of clubs was.

Thus, Fernão's first step in the game was to spy on the grand master of ceremonies. This player—whose only job it was to protect the *manilha* of clubs until the end, when he would conquer her and thus win the game—was the only player who was obliged to declare his status (and there were agreed upon signs to that effect), and he was also the only one to know the playing cards drawn by the others (information given to him by the Gypsy queen).

He also served as referee for challenges, which needed to obey the nature of the suits in a dispute, and he surreptitiously served the other girls too, in exchange for favors in schemes that naturally served their interests.

The grand master of ceremonies also had the duty of announcing to all the preconditions imposed by the lady *manilha* of clubs. Besides the possession of a card of that suit, only the fulfillment of such preconditions empowered players to try to "ravish" her, and anyone who dared do this without fulfilling one or another condition was excluded from the game. It was common for the lady *manilha* of clubs to establish four preliminary tasks, each according to the nature of one of the suits.

That year, in April 1710, the grand master of ceremonies was Estevão Maia, a member of the powerful Maia clan and a foe of Fernão, for his family had testified before the Council of Conscience and Order against the claims of old man Moura. As per the rules, Estevão declared the preconditions of the lady *manilha* of clubs. However, in August, there was a twist in the game and in the city's history: the invasion led by pirate Jean du Clerc.

Four hundred French and seventy Cariocas died in the fighting. Captain du Clerc was arrested, but not before inflicting some of those seventy casualties, including that of Second Lieutenant Gaspar d'Almeida, who had drawn the jack of clubs.

Although cheating was, to a certain extent, permissible, the grand master of ceremonies would hardly, if ever, accept a card taken off of a murdered man, unless there was a valid explanation and an even better witness. However, in the case of Gaspar d'Almeida, who died in battle, things were much simpler: and everyone knew that the killer was one of the pirates, and many claimed that it was du Clerc himself. And French pirates, of course, did not play.

Hence, the mystery: Gaspar's brother—a cadet, who had drawn the seven of diamonds—was the first to be called to rescue the wounded solider. He could not do so immediately, because the French were advancing. When he arrived, his brother was already dead. His first step—to preserve the secrecy of the game—was to search for Gaspar's card, which, as per the rules, players were bound have in their possession.

However, after searching him from head to toe, he found nothing.

Of course, everyone wanted to know what had happened. Either the second lieutenant had simply lost the card, or he had not complied with the rules (thought to be very unlikely), or there had been extenuating circumstances that needed to be brought to the fore. That is when the big news was revealed: Grand Master of Ceremonies Estêvão Maia said the lady *manilha* of clubs had replaced the four preliminary tasks with one single task: to discover the whereabouts, or the holder, of the jack of clubs.

The life of Fernão da Moura—which had gone from Hell to Heaven—was sliding back into Hell, for it was he, Fernão, who held the jack of clubs. To understand how, we need simply to go back to the battleground: at that skirmish, Fernão da Moura, hidden behind the walls of a church that was under construction (the future church of the Rosário), witnessed the death of Gaspar d'Almeida. Because the French kept advancing, pursuing fugitives, Fernão came out of his hiding place, unnoticed, and went to the second lieutenant's body, where he wasted no time in taking possession of the card.

Of course, he was counting on the fact that such theft would be deemed legal. After all, he had not killed anyone, and he had witnesses to that effect. But, being somewhat fearful of Estêvão Maia's reaction, he took his time in reporting the incident, hoping to concoct a version that would not bring dishonor to himself and which omitted mention of his hiding behind a wall.

Once the decision had been enacted by the *manilha* of clubs, which made it clear that they had a suspect, Fernão da Moura found himself in a tight spot, because one could arrive at the conclusion—or Estevão Maia might argue—that he had found the lieutenant still alive, and had killed him in order to take possession of the powerful card.

While awaiting an opportunity to display the jack with a compelling story, Fernão da Moura was challenged twice: once in spades (which he won, to his surprise, in a game of ring toss at a horse show), and again in hearts (defeating his opponent in a test of Latin grammar).

The match extended into 1711. By then, about twenty girls had been "ravished" and were out of the game (because they had delivered their cards to the boys, for the final calculation of points). Thus, by process of elimination, many should have already deduced the identity of the *manilha* of clubs. Fernão da Moura, however, did not have sufficient information to work out such computations. The actions of the grand master of ceremonies, however, revealed once and for all (and not only to Fernão) the identity of the *manilha* of clubs.

Estevão Maia, who had been in the habit of attending Mass at the army's Santa Cruz Chapel (because he was a cadet and his family had quarrels with the Jesuits), amazingly began instead to attend services at the old church at the college at Castelo Hill.

It so happened that, at around the same time, a beautiful young girl broke with old habits and also began attending the same church: Brígida, Little Brígida, daughter of Lieutenant Castro e Torres, political ally of the Maias.

Fernão da Moura, like others, had no doubt that Little Brígida was the *manilha* of clubs. Gypsies say that the greatest virtue in a man is luck; and Fernão's luck began to turn when the pirate Jean du Clerc—hitherto detained at the Jesuits' college—was transferred, by his own urgent insistence, to the house of Lieutenant Castro e Torres.

This, as far as Fernão was concerned, seemed to be a plan concocted by Estevão Maia, because the lieutenant's house, Brígida's house, actually a three-story palace, was now patrolled by soldiers. Plus, there was something untoward between the girl and the pirate, which the grand master of ceremonies, contrary to the rules, was concealing, perhaps because he was only interested in the card.

However, the presence in the palace of Jean du Clerc, the killer of Second Lieutenant Gaspar d'Almeida, gave Fernão da Moura an occasion. Now he only needed to contrive a way to enter the mansion.

The surgeon's son reasoned like a Gypsy: in that game, he had already proved his mettle in hearts, and he had also shown his skill in spades. The episodes involving the second lieutenant's murder and the transfer of du Clerc showed his valor in clubs. What was necessary now was to demonstrate his talent in diamonds.

Do not think, however, that Fernão da Moura needed to resort to bribing guards. His father, old man Moura, had rented houses in the less wealthy parts of the city, and his blood stain and the other defects attributed to him were perhaps explained by the fact that, in his capacity as a surgeon, he provided medical services to many of his tenants, free of charge, especially the emancipated slaves, members of the fellowships Our Lady of the Rosary and Saint Benedict of Black Men.

Thus, Fernão da Moura, alleging matters of the heart, asked a very small favor of one of Lieutenant Castro e Torres' slaves: that a tiny attic window be accidentally left open, where he could enter from the neighboring rooftop.

The scene that ensued is classic and, to some extent, even clichéd: Fernão da Moura, late at night, armed with a dagger, after jumping from roof to roof, surprised the pirate, naked, in the arms of Little Brígida.

Jean du Clerc was a murderer, an enemy of the city; Little Brígida was a traitor, false and insidious—not just because she lay with a pirate, but because it was forbidden, strictly so, for female players to give themselves to men who were not in the game.

So, Fernão da Moura stabbed du Clerc. And he could have ravished Little Brígida, because it was his right, because the mere possession of the Jack represented the fulfillment of two conditions: that of the suit of clubs and that of the completed challenge, for he would allege that he had found Gaspar d'Almeida's card in the pirate's bedroom, and that he had killed him to avenge the second lieutenant. Little Brígida would not be so crazy as to tell the truth, and Estevão Maia would not confess his complicity either.

So, Little Brígida, who had wrapped a sheet around herself during the fight, let the sheet drop, surrendering to the winner. But she did not expect the humiliation that followed:

"I just want the *manilha* of clubs."

Needless to say, Fernão da Moura was merciful, he was a gentleman. He carried the pirate's body back to his quarters and helped dress him.

The story of the masked intruders, which to this day everyone believes, was a touch suggested by Little Brígida. And, for it all to be believable, she needed to disappear with the Frenchman's papers. Among those documents was Lourenço Cão's map.

There was another occasion when the destinies of Baeta and Aniceto intersected randomly, and of which they had no knowledge. The location, of course, was the House of Swaps. The date, August 21st, was a Thursday, when one of Miroslav Zmuda and Madame Brigitte's communal sessions took place.

The police narrative, strictly speaking, could just as well omit this passage, but it is deeply relevant to another aspect of the book: the difficulties that the "the Aniceto Problem" posed to the Polish doctor's sexual theories.

The reader should keep in mind the layout of the upper floor of the House of Swaps: beside the Oval Parlor (which functioned as reception and coatroom), there was the front room, where the guests could drink and speak before selecting their partners. The two side wings had rooms—some which could be locked from the inside, some which could not. To the right was the showroom (where we saw Aniceto's performance with Palhares and the tall woman), and to the left, in the room today known as the music room, there was a large area that could accommodate several couples for parallel explicit relations, where the emphasis was not so much on the show but on greatly increasing the opportunities for swaps.

I mentioned that it was preferable for guests to introduce themselves while wearing hoods (excepting the proprietors and nurses). This had the effect of hiding (as much as was possible, or desirable) the identity of the participants. However, each disguise, or hood, was unique, and had its own distinct design embroidered on it with a golden thread, representing an animal or a plant, or sometimes an abstract figure. There was the tower, the anteater, the water lily, the hummingbird, the crown, the sword, the spiral, etc.

Madame Brigitte obviously arranged for hoods to be randomly distributed to encourage a certain level of intentional confusion. She would tell participants a story that all accepted, that their logo was only for the purposes of that particular event, hence the rotation.

The real reason, however, was different altogether: the nurse who handed out the hoods would write down the individual's name so that Dr. Zmuda could then record in his notebooks the exact behavior of each patron.

On that day, Baeta and Guiomar (he wore the palm tree; she, the jaguar) found themselves in this previously mentioned room. They were in the throes of a deep kiss, and next to them was another couple, the wife of which was wearing the dove hood. The goal, as we know, was to attract women for Baeta, with Guiomar acting as bait. And things were headed in that direction when another group began gradually getting closer.

This other group was also made up of two couples, but how they were approaching was somewhat unusual. One of the men—there for the third time, and who that day had on the diamond mask—seemed to be intimidating, even trapping the other couple, particularly the woman, who had the water lily design and seemed terrified, as if she were actually fleeing.

Her husband or partner was retreating with her, without even hinting at putting up any resistance. Suddenly, the diamond, demonstrating a certain impatience, spun the water lily around and threw her hands against the wall. Abruptly raising her tunic, he had his way with her, as if riding her, even simulating whipping her hips and pulling on the reins.

These moves distracted Baeta, Guiomar, and their respective targets. Guiomar stared at this man who was imposing his will so sovereignly. At that exact moment, he, the diamond, returned her glance, and for a brief instant he stared deeply into the eyes of the jaguar.

Baeta had not noticed because he was still busy trying to

conquer the dove. But he heard Guiomar, who had assumed a position similar to the water lily's, against the wall, ask him to take her in that manner.

Baeta did not refuse, but he found little excitement in such a change, because he had been born a protagonist, and he felt a certain embarrassment at copying others. Just then they heard louder spanking, as the evil, predatory diamond abandoned the natural avenue for the path that had made Sodom infamous. By now, Guiomar could not contain herself, and begged her husband:

"Hit me!"

Baeta, however, did not respond well to such a request. Perhaps he did not want to see the jaguar debased in public. What excited his interest in her was not the image of female submission; on the contrary, it was the haughty air with which she refused other men that excited him. It was the most attractive aspect of his wife's sexuality.

The Polish doctor, of course, was watching everything closely. Since he knew his clients in intimate detail, and since he had a greater interest in all of this, Guiomar's reaction did not escape his notice, and, in a certain sense, her reaction contradicted the hitherto dominant trends of her eroticism.

He did not, however, immediately associate her behavior with the man wearing the diamond: none other than Aniceto. He considered only the stimuli of the scene itself, not giving due importance to the actors in question.

Minutes later, however, Aniceto would give Dr. Zmuda cause for reflection: he achieved the rare feat of producing an orgasm in the water lily by the method of penetration he had chosen—a climax so intense and so sincere that it infected bystanders, inducing a series of subsequent orgasms, including in Guiomar herself.

The symbolizations, or sexual fantasies, that Miroslav

Zmuda considered promoters of female orgasms, although they were unique and specific to each individual, could be divided into four categories, plus a fifth, as yet misunderstood, provisionally called "residual."

The first—perhaps the most important—was comprised of the symbolizations of violence. Here I must digress in order for the reader to grasp the doctor's thinking.

The Polish doctor began from the assumption, or prejudice, that human beings in their natural state, in their primitive and tribal life, had a very simple, very elementary sexuality because, paradoxically, it was very free.

It was civilization and its moral coercion that, after elevating the family to the position of the basic cell of society, had sophisticated sex.

Zmuda, therefore, believed that prohibition, censorship, was the foundation of pleasure. And that it was this constriction of desire that had led to the development of certain techniques of sexual stimulation in human history—for example, the kiss, where the emphasis is on lingual friction. And the Polish doctor chafed at the notion that this component could have ever figured, for example, in the sexual practices of savages such as the Botocudo people, and he produced arguments as to why it did not.

Studying primitive collections of erotic art as opposed to that of the ancient civilizations of the Mediterranean and the Far East, Zmuda concluded that masturbation, fellatio, sodomy, and cunnilingus had arisen among advanced peoples, and were probably contemporaneous to the invention of writing.

Miroslav Zmuda, a Slav and an Aryan, was an enthusiastic champion of civilization. He even went so far as advocating (in one of those articles that were always so abhorred) that virgin girls, in the interest of family, should practice in their youth all of the highly civilized modalities (because they were, in fact, civilized), such as manual, oral and anal sex, thus avoiding unintended pregnancy and the embarrassment of wedding night surprises.

The great legacy of civilization, therefore, as far as human sexuality was concerned, and particularly female sexuality, was providing the conditions for the expansion of fantasies. And the symbolizations of violence, Zmuda's first category, illustrated this well.

For the Polish doctor, mere penetration already represented an act of aggression. And not a small number of women enjoyed vigorous, forceful movements that subjugated them, approaching rape.

Well, it was in the primitive world that such scenes should have been considered trivial. Savages and barbarians routinely treated their women exactly this way, with the brutality that, according to Zmuda, was peculiar to them.

Therefore, when a civilized woman wishes to be taken forcefully, she is at heart yearning to be free from restraints, from the fetters imposed by civilization. It was, therefore, a pleasure whose origins were atavistic. Madame Brigitte and Rio de Janeiro revealed to Dr. Zmuda that most women felt nostalgia for barbarism.

Sexual fantasies involving staged violence—as described by the nurses or as orchestrated by Madame Brigitte—covered a vast symbolic spectrum, from those who wanted to copulate with their wrists bound to those who essentially liked to be beaten—a desire that Guiomar expressed, surprisingly, at the party of August 21st.

There were those that liked go down on all fours like beasts (almost always slapped by the man), or those who preferred verbal humiliation. Even fellatio or sodomy could involve a sense, or an atmosphere, of abuse and female submission, particularly with regard to anal intercourse, which presupposed, at least in theory, some degree of pain.

In some cases, this real physical pain was considered necessary, and accessories such as whips, neckstraps, or ropes could also be brought into the mix.

Among the most frequent fantasies (still in this same sphere) was being seduced or even forcibly taken by strangers, generally men of inferior status—the stronger, cruder, and more brutish the better, such as longshoremen, sailors, or gangsters. Madame Brigitte had made several fantasies of this type come true, with Hermínio or other individuals hired specifically for that purpose.

Women loved to feel prostituted—this could be achieved by the use of intimate, characteristically obscene apparel, or by more direct gestures, such as the offering of money. Fortunata was an extreme example of this: she wanted to be a real prostitute (this was the only way that Dr. Zmuda could make sense of her coming to the House a virgin).

The prostitution fantasy was, for the doctor, very symptomatic, because this was not a primitive institution, a custom of savages; on the contrary, for Dr. Zmuda it represented one of the seminal achievements of high cultures. To understand this apparent impropriety, it was necessary to analyze the symbol.

Indeed, symbolically, prostitutes are people to be used, and are available to anyone who wants them or can pay. In the barbaric world, women were also available, in that case for use by the strongest, which in today's societies are those who can pay.

It was clear that, for Zmuda, the symbolizations of violence included what might be called psychological violence or humiliation; in other words, any situation wherein women are put on a level below men.

On the other hand, another type of fantasy that reaffirmed this idea was that of women who preferred to be in charge or to harm their partners. For Dr. Zmuda, they represented dangerous, vindictive personalities: they were women who sought revenge for barbaric sexuality by reversing roles.

And the best proof of this was the fact that they almost never allowed penetration, for the one who penetrates, dominates. Women who exhibited their feet to their worshipers were engaged in such behavior, and the same is also true of those who beat or humiliated males.

Zmuda concluded that the secretary probably had not penetrated Fortunata on the fateful evening of the crime.

The first dead woman appeared on Pinto Hill, the place still known as Nheco's Ramp, on Saturday, September 13th—officially dawn of the 14th, since days begin at sunrise according to the Carioca calendar.

Police were notified on Sunday, on account of the scandal raised by the mother of the victim, a girl of fifteen, who—having snuck out of her home on Senador Eusébio Street to go to a samba party with some unsavory types on the 13th—had still not returned by the next morning. Some dockworkers recognized the body and then called her mother.

The first complications were as follows: the body had been removed at dawn, around 4 AM, from the scene of the crime to the entrance of Santa Teresa Church, one of the city's landmarks, built atop a hill around 1760. It was there, in front of that church, that three or four mourners kept vigil and stayed with the body until authorities arrived.

Two quite contradictory facts should be mentioned. First, all of the people deposed by police along that route, between the seat of the First District in Mauá Square and the summit of Pinto Hill, where the church stood, spoke only of murder, without any direct testimony or evidence to that effect.

However, according to the forensic report, the cause of death was "total cessation of life"—an expression that, although pleonastic, meant that the death had not been an accident or suicide, much less a murder—in other words, it was a natural death.

The death, however, still bewildered examiners. Besides the presence of semen in her vagina (confirming recent copulation), the contractions in the facial muscles, the sphincter, the quadriceps, and the glutes indicated that she appeared to have been frozen, even mummified, at the moment of ecstasy. For this was exactly the impression one had: her face had immortalized the rictus of orgasm, and none of the mourners, perhaps out of embarrassment, dared cover this up, even going so far as leaving the deceased's eyelids open.

But there were no injuries, toxicology exams were negative, nor could the hypothesis of homicide by suffocation (with the classic use of a pillow, for example) be raised because that would not account for the expression of ecstasy.

It is important to make this clear: the lewd expression on the girl's face was incompatible with the expression of someone who had sensed, as necessarily would have been the case in a murder, the coming end.

What's more, it defied all known thanatological laws because, even more than twenty-four hours after the cessation of life, the muscles mentioned remained rigid. One of the examiners said something very striking, heartbreaking even, to the mother: that her daughter had died with pleasure.

When Baeta received the inital information concerning the case, even before the report had been filed, he declined to examine the scene, not only because it had been tampered with when they moved the body, but principally because the death happened at the famous Jereba's *muquiço*.

It is worth interrupting the narrative here to explain precisely what a *muquiço* is. Even the best dictionaries erroneously spell the word with an "o" and say it is a synonym for a hovel. Indeed, the meaning has very little to do with the appearance of the dwelling that makes up the *muquiço*. Rather, it is what the house is used for that defines it as such.

The *muquiço* is a denial of the very idea of a house: it is a house with open doors, a home where everyone can enter. If houses, or residences, are defined as intimate spaces, the *muquiço* achieves the supreme contradiction of public intimacy. It is also important not to confuse it with a tenement or a rooming house. In the *muquiço*, no space is private, however minimal.

Incidentally, for historical reasons, *muquiços* were, and still are, poor. Although they must have first appeared on flat paved streets, it was in the hillsides of Rio de Janeiro that the institution really developed. And no case is more emblematic than Jereba's *muquiço*.

Jereba had initially rented the house on the Nheco slope hoping to make it his home and simultaneously the seat of the carnival association of his dreams, for which he had even found a name: Rancho das Morenas. It was a spacious, though rustic, house. However, as fate would have it, Jereba struggled to pay the rent.

It was neighbors, friends, and drinking companions who helped him not to lose the house. There was no implicit intention behind this help. However, the generosity was so spontaneous that, little by little, Jereba began opening the doors to his home until finally it became a *muquiço*, with its doors permanently open.

At night—whether or not Jereba was at home—the *muquiço* was frequented by couples who went there to engage in illicit affairs. There was no swapping, there were no orgies. In this, and in many other ways, it differed from Madame Brigitte and Dr. Zmuda's commercial establishment.

The couples at the *muquiço* merely took advantage of its impenetrable darkness (Jereba had no artificial light) in order to give cover to their activities. On more than one occasion, husband and wife were present at the same time, with their respective lovers, without knowing it, committing the same crime and sharing the same space.

Baeta—who had been familiar with the *muquiço* since he was thirteen—knew that once the body had been moved from its original position it was useless to collect fingerprints or other evidence. First, because it would turn hundreds of people into suspects, and second, because not even the occasional witnesses, even those who dared confess to having been at the *muquiço*, could identify the dead girl's companion. The coroner's report put an end to the whole story, certifying death due to natural causes.

In the First District, this outcome was met with animosity. Ever since Rufino's release by order of the chief of police, there was strong resistance to the Relação Street people—and it is worth remembering that the events narrated now occurred before Baeta and the captain's conversation at Hans Staden, which transformed antipathy into outright war. Therefore, Mauá Square made a point of challenging all expert opinions issued by headquarters.

For this reason, their officers continuously pitted the mother against Relação Street, and they made the rounds, asking questions, wanting to know who had seen the girl and whom she had been with before entering the *muquiço*.

On the point of the dead girl's partner, nobody said a thing, though they may have actually known his identity. The less shy, those daring enough to confess they had been at the *muquiço*, insisted on one thing: that the deceased had groaned abnormally throughout the whole act, ending with a scream so piercing, never before heard in that tone and at that intensity, that everybody shut up and stopped to admire it.

What followed was total, absolute silence. And after that, a man's voice, who seemed to be whispering something, as if trying to awaken someone—a man who then (noises indicated) stood and walked away. It was Jereba who found the girl, after everyone had left.

It was the cry, that cry, which led everyone to claim—even

though the body did not show any signs of aggression—that it had been murder.

The reader surely will remember that on September 11th, at the House of Swaps, Baeta recognized that the widow Palhares' new lover was Aniceto, and that Baeta was quite upset not only with the capoeira's success with the audience, but particularly with the look Guiomar gave him, eyeing his rival as he left, arm in arm with the widow.

The crisis actually began two weeks earlier, when for the first time, Guiomar expressed that desire, that inclination, to be hit that her husband grudgingly complied with.

A fascinating woman, Guiomar. Not just because she was pretty, and had those shapely ankles, but because she was highly sexual, very excitable, a level of lust verging on debauchery. At the same time—and perhaps precisely for that reason—she was faithful, even in her innermost thoughts, and I have described how the Baetas' fantasy operated at the House of Swaps.

Guiomar did not work outside the house, but she had girl-friends and neighbors who visited her often, and helped ease the boredom and unpredictability of the life of a policeman's wife.

Women talk a lot about sex when they are alone among themselves, and Guiomar and her girlfriends were no different. Such conversations, of course, can get quite lively, and when certain taboos are confessed they can really go all out—as if it the mere act of narrating were a compensation for the unfulfilled desire.

One of the neighbors, for example, on one of those afternoons they spent together after August 21st, told how she yearned to give herself to a famous, rich, tall, blond man who could speak French, a language that she did not speak. As far as he was concerned, she would be just another stranger, but she would wear the sexiest lace lingerie, like the cabaret dancers.

And he would speak his incomprehensible French, dressed in the most luxurious tailcoat of the day, and he would have his way with her, without undressing her, exposing only the necessary organ. And she would stroke the tailcoat, relish the majestic texture of the expensive cloth, and feel the varnish from his shoes on the bare soles of her feet. And they would come to ecstasy without sweating a single drop, without dissipating the aroma of imported essences.

And a second neighbor would weave even more absurd plots: she wanted to be surprised by her husband as she masturbated, or while she slept, uttering the names of others. And her husband would get furious and be rough with her the next day, never commenting on the incident.

Guiomar was always the quietest. She only said things that could not be considered extravagant, even though she was the only one who ever really ever did anything sordid. That day she went a little farther:

"What I really like are strong men."

And Baeta was strong. Her confession (which revealed little, as always) did not raise eyebrows. No one found it unusual that Guiomar yearned for a little rough play. Besides, it was with her husband, the neighbors thought, since he was the only man in the few fantasies she shared with them. What was new about her statement, though, was the subtle use of the plural, which went unnoticed.

A few days later, on account of these same conversations, a girlfriend—who crackled with passion—asked for Guiomar's company to pay a forbidden visit to an old palm reader on Marrecas Street. Not even I, the author, can explain exactly why Guiomar, after her friend had finished, decided to have her own palm read.

They say soothsayers in general—palm readers, fortune-tellers, necromancers, augurers, astrologers, kabbalists, *babal-aôs*, seers, prophets, *caraíbas*, pythonesses, presagers—have a talent for predicting the future. No one today disputes the validity of the concept of destiny, or that a lifeline really does exist, dating from time immemorial, for each individual.

However, in Rio de Janeiro (and this remains one of the city's mysteries), soothsayers do not predict the future. Fortune-tellers never predict, never anticipate coming events. They do something even greater: they change destinies. They alter the course of the lives of the people who consult them. It is closer to gambling than prophecy. You need to be willing to take risks to play; to be willing to change the course of your existence, without knowing what that change will be.

With her palm open, Guiomar listened to the woman who stared at it with almost blind eyes, but who nonetheless could identify very distinctive traits in one of the grooves:

"Over the lifeline, there's a cross; next to it, five lines: two up, three down. You're about to cheat on your husband."

This was an outrage. Guiomar left the cubicle regretting even having come, having succumbed to her curiosity. In disbelief, she dropped ten *mil-reis* in the wicker basket awaiting her on the sideboard as she exited.

September 11th would come, and Guiomar—who had since forgotten the omen—stared for a few seconds too long at Aniceto (without knowing who he was as he walked by haughtily, arm in arm with another woman). It was perhaps the third symptom, or effect, of the words of the Marrecas Street palm reader.

Everything became clear the following Saturday, when they were at home in Catete. Guiomar had just bathed, and lay facedown, almost naked, ready for the taking. Baeta approached, more or less as he always did, with that air of a man ready to take what is his. And then she evaded him slightly and, pointing to her own body, as if selling a piece of merchandise, asked:

"How much would you pay for all this?"

Baeta was not playing along. She insisted:

"How much would you pay, if I were a whore?"

Baeta—a good lover, an experienced man—would have played along if it had been any other woman. But it was inescapably Guiomar. At that moment, he felt as if he had just lost something. And he had a feeling (do not ask me to give his reasons) that this unprecedented behavior had to do with September 11th.

He was high-handed with his wife, and he did not satisfy her, which for a man is a serious offense. Nonetheless, when she got ready to go to the next party at the House of Swaps (the following Thursday, the 18th), her tears had already dried, and she was actually thrilled at the prospect. The expert, though, was even more ill-mannered by then, saying flatly that they would stay home. In the early morning hours, it was Guiomar who tried to reconcile:

"Hit me! Go ahead!"

Hitting a woman is an art. This time Baeta actually tried. It was not the strength, though, that was missing—it was the attitude.

The next day after work, Baeta—who truly loved Guiomar—searched through items stored in a reinforced locker marked "Confidential," to which only he had the key. Not all of the objects collected at the House of Swaps were significant and indispensable to identifying the murderer. So, in a brash move, in order to appease his wife's lust, he took the silver-handled whip back with him to his home in Catete.

Another fantastic story that influenced Baeta's reunion with his primitive world happened in the Formiga neighborhood. The case became infamous in the northern part of town, and if this were a separate short story, it would be called *The Timbau Hill Crossroads*.

There is no Timbau Hill anymore in Formiga. At the time, that hill was an eerie place. It ended in the outer confines of the neighborhood, at a dead-end crossroads, deserted, dark, abandoned, haunted by the memory of sad people who went there to die. Since it was a crossroads, it was also a place where offerings were left.

The story involves two main characters: Tião Saci—a troublemaker, *quizumbeiro*, a matchmaker, and an inhabitant of Quersoene—and Lacraia—a *jongueiro*, drummer, *macumbeiro*, born and raised in the hills of Madureira, who moved to Formiga for a woman, Deodata, who offered him lodging in her home.

Calling him Tião Saci, deep down, was mean-spirited: the mythical trickster Saci Pere had only one leg; Tião had both legs, though he was lame and dragged his left foot. He was not loved, and he was not a person held in high esteem. But he was not a bad person. It was during his wanderings in the hills that he came upon Deodata's house.

It would be a blatant lie to say that Tião Saci went to Deodata's expressly seeking her. No, he had heard stories about the *jongueiro* Lacraia, and he went there looking for him.

Those who know *jongo* know it is a spell, a song, and an initiation dance. A verse of *jongo* never says what it seems to say: it is always an encrypted message that even a good *jongueiro* cannot understand. In a *jongo* circle when someone ties a stitch, that stitch (which is a verse) only ceases to be sung if someone else unties it—in other words, if he interprets it. That is why it is called a "stitch" in the sense that it is synonymous with a "knot."

Lacraia, who had been born limber of body and mind, would untie one stitch after another on Madureira Hill. He knew the entrails of words, he saw what lay behind them. It was a talent he had possessed since birth, an inheritance from the ancient spirits.

Laypeople are greatly impressed by esoteric things: fetishes, rituals, and mystical symbols, demonic images, sacrificed animals. They ignore that the real magic lies in speech, in human language.

So, being the *jongueiro* that he was, having mastered the secret of words, Lacraia also became a *porteira*, a gatekeeper. I took such a tortuous route to say one simple thing: in Deodata's backyard they built a shack where Lacraia channeled a shadowy entity.

Before the famous pronouncement by the *caboclo* Seven Crossroads, the founder of Umbanda, which took place in the hinterlands of São Gonçalo in 1908, and which codified some of the laws of *jira*, the spirits of that religion were all anonymous. We do not know, thus, exactly who possessed Lacraia's body.

If, for Seven Crossroads, there were never any closed paths, the *jongueiro's* entity had the opposite line: fewer openings and more locking of paths.

Tião Saci often went to Deotada's to consult the spirit that possessed Lacraia. Although he continued to be lame, dragging his left foot wherever he went, Tião Saci was still able to resolve many personal issues during these sessions. However, everything has its price.

One night, all three were in the shack in the backyard. The details are as follows: Tião Saci, Deodata, and the disembodied spirit were present—technically speaking, Lacraia's soul was suspended, and he was totally unconscious. Deotada was the *cambona*, the assistant, and she tended to the spirit in whatever way she could. Suddenly, Tião Saci, who was splayed out on the floor listening, heard:

"Beware of my horse."

The sepulchral tone of the warning, coming from so terrifying an entity, terrified the two.

"My horse has already seen you."

So, it was true what they had been grumbling about around

Formiga: Tião Saci had fallen for Deodata, head over heels—and it was reciprocal. What amazed and disgusted people was not just the fact that Tião was lame (while Lacraia had such a sensual swing to his body); it was that the cheating had occurred in the house, in the backyard, of his benefactor.

Tião Saci, however, had a clear conscience—he owed nothing to Lacraia, only to the disembodied spirit. And it was the spirit itself that had warned him:

"He will set a trap for you. Up the hill, near the crossroads at Timbau."

He even stated the date and the time; there was no need to state the motive. But the mention of the hill left Deodata in a panic. It was a ghastly place, and she had a foreboding sense of doom. She would look at the disembodied voice, but only saw Lacraia's face, flushed, unrecognizable. She had been a *cambona,* a priest's assistant, for a long time, but she had never heard of anything like this. And, in a sense, the way the disembodied spirit treated its own horse, or its medium—warning an enemy that the medium had a legitimate right to kill—absolved her of guilt. Deodata had preferred Saci's mutilated gait, to the sprightly step of the *jongueiro.*

Knowledge is always an advantage: Deodata knew Lacraia did not know that she already knew. And she noticed how he had become increasingly impatient and sly with Saci Tião. A short while later, Deodata heard a snippet of a conversation between the two men, and she probed her lover the next day.

"He asked me to go with him up the hill, to Timbau."

The request made sense: Lacraia would offer a goat at the crossroads, and needed someone to hold down the animal. Tião Saci was lame, but he had strong arms. The problem was the date and time, which coincided with the withdrawal of the disembodied voice. As a matter of fact, the spirit had spoken of a blade: the same one used to bleed the goat would be used on him, Tião Saci.

Deodata said to Tião Saci that he should try to back out, saying he had another commitment. But the man had mettle, and he planned a second betrayal.

On the appointed day, Tião Saci, with a borrowed revolver (not easy to get back then), stood in front of Deodata's door and clapped loudly. Lacraia appeared, but he said Deodata was sick, and that he would be late. It was his cue: Tião Saci, realizing that she was pretending in order to facilitate the ambush, volunteered to go ahead, carrying the bowl, the machete, the candles, and the cachaça. He would just have trouble dragging the goat all the way up the hill due to his miserable defect.

Lacraia agreed, and Tião Saci proceeded up the hill. The Timbau Hill crossroads was a terrible place because, as I have mentioned, it led into blind alleys, and at that time of night the silence was so great, the darkness so absolute, that Tião Saci was scared he might miss his target.

Thus, taking every precaution, he decided to throw his machete into the bushes to avoid any unexpected move on Lacraia's part. So he went into one of the alleys, lurching all the way, and tossed the blade meant to execute the goat, and then probably himself, as far as he could over the quarry.

When he returned, he had arrived at the appointed time and place.

"Put the money on the ground, and come down, but don't turn your face."

Tião Saci could not make out the face, but he was able to deduce where the voice was coming from—and it was certainly not Lacraia's. Not knowing who he was dealing with, not knowing what it was about, he made a subtle motion with his right hand toward his waist, where the gun was.

The stranger, however, fired first.

Later, Deodata—even though she had managed to keep her husband at home much of the night—spread the rumor that it had been a crime, plotted by the perfidious spirit of the cunning Lacraia.

In Formiga, however, the saying goes that God is the Devil from behind. So they did not believe her. These were people already accustomed to dealing with spirits. They knew that strange things happened, especially in those bad places, at a crossroads, on a hillside such as Timbau.

We are now only a few days from the end. This, of course, is the point at which the narrative speeds up and events become jumbled together, and the best technique is to lay out the facts in chronological order (with a few exceptions, here or there), in order not to ruin or frustrate the effect of the last great revelation.

Between October 7th and 9th three important incidents occurred, all figuring prominently in the city's police annals. My difficulty as an author is to choose which of the three I should begin with.

Let us then report the case of the second woman who died under mysterious circumstances. This time it was not a poor young girl, but rather a lady, who was set up with her own business on Ouvidor Street. Her body was found naked on the second floor, in between the small office and a storage room. She had that same orgasmic expression and the same intriguing features: the sphincter, the buttocks, the thigh and face muscles exhibited signs of rigor mortis—even more than twenty-four hours after death.

There were no signs of bodily injuries, and there were no signs of burglary—nothing had been stolen from the shop. It was also impossible to find witnesses: nobody saw or heard anything in the nearby buildings.

They knew that since she was French she had a lover right under her husband's nose. The lover was one of those bums, one of those capoeiras, who had appeared three or four months before at the store, offering his services as security, mainly to provide protection against thieves. He won the "job," and, shortly thereafter, won over his employer. Of course, we are speaking of Aniceto, Madame Montfort, and La Parisienne.

However, forensic tests were never performed because, technically, there had been no murder, and because finding fingerprints or other evidence of the presence of individuals who could enter the facility without needing to break in (for example, Aniceto or the victim's husband) would not mean much.

The forensic examiners thought that the two women—the poor girl and the rich woman—must have ingested some kind of drug capable of causing those surprising symptoms, but since they were dealing with an unknown substance, drug tests were inconclusive.

Unfortunately, physicians in Rio de Janeiro were still under the spell of scientific superstitions, and although ancient African and native beliefs still survived in the city, and many healers still sold potions and other preparations, all of this ancient knowledge of the manipulation of herbs, leaves, and roots was no longer incorporated into the officially accepted medical canon, which hindered the experts' actions.

However, attention was soon turned in another direction because, at that same time, a dire scandal was exploding in police circles, one that it was no longer possible to suppress: one lieutenant and two officers stationed at the First District had gone missing. The captain was called in to give a statement as to why he had not referred the case to his superiors, and he provided an explanation only very grudgingly: he had preferred to act behind the scenes, and the mere announcement of the fact would lead—as was indeed happening—to a big commotion, which would only serve to endanger the success of the investigation.

At police headquarters, the matter was treated with the

utmost seriousness, especially after Baeta, on the 9th, had personally gone to the office of the chief of police to report the strange attitude of Mauá Square and that his home, a street-level house in Catete with green doors and windows, had been robbed.

Baeta himself had surprised the officer known as Mixila near Baeta's home, apparently on a surveillance detail, on a Sunday. Baeta crossed the street and went to question Mixila, who responded by being evasive and outraged and walking away.

Baeta took no immediate action because he was having difficulty even conceiving of such brazenness. This, of course, was a serious accusation. His suspicions were confirmed by the fact that there were no fingerprints—he himself had done the forensics—other than his and his wife's on the broken window and the dresser drawers, which had been overturned, and from which some savings and a small jewelry box belonging to Guiomar had been removed.

In Rio de Janeiro in 1913, hardly anyone had any knowledge about the science of fingerprinting, or the revolution that this technique represented for forensic investigations. Only the police, probably using gloves, would have been able to commit a crime like this without leaving a trace.

These facts were sufficient to trigger an institutional crisis within the police. The expert only failed to mention that among the objects stolen from his home was the silver-handled whip—one of the pieces of evidence in the crime committed at the House of Swaps.

The second category proposed by Dr. Zmuda had to do with symbolizations of infidelity. It is important to distinguish here, as the Polish doctor had done, between adultery resulting from dissatisfaction—when the original partner is unsuitable or sexually inadequate—and the adulterous fantasy itself—which is a necessary, constitutive element of the primordial relationship. Fantasies of infidelity, as you can see, presuppose this primordial relationship, without which they would be meaningless.

Zmuda divided women who fantasized about infidelity into two almost distinct categories. The first were those with the desire to enjoy this pleasure secretly, because having a secret, carrying this crime in their inner depths, of course gave them a sense of power. These are the women who cheat for pleasure, because it is what excites them.

Although Dr. Zmuda did not focus so much on male symbolizations, he did have data and could compare the two. According to the doctor, unfaithful men often claimed to seek other women just to escape routines—in other words, for variety. This was not the case for the adulteress, however. Female fantasies of these types were actually quite elaborate.

In general, they involved very specific places, partners, or circumstances: women who spoke of being alone at home in the company of strangers or dangerous persons; of wanting to seduce beardless young men, or men in uniforms; who would easily allow themselves to be seduced by any great dancer (the type of artist to whom Madame Brigitte attributed the greatest power of seduction); who dreamed of a deserted beach or the dark trails of a secluded forest; who imagined meeting someone during a voyage in a city they would never return to.

Although one could say that the notion of jealousy has existed forever—and the primitives at times went to war over women—it was only with civilization that rigorous and definitive moral sanctions became associated with adultery. So, fantasies of infidelity in women, or rather this first subset of women, were also the result of a nostalgia for barbarism.

But there was a second group of cheaters. This was made up of those who cheated openly, in front of their partners or husbands. The couples' parties at the House of Swaps were places where this modality was given free rein—and it had many variations. There was a simple swap, where the pleasure was to cheat and to be cheated on—a practice of considerate people with a great sense of justice.

There were those who preferred to be the center of attention, making a point of being seen by their spouses—a group Baeta took advantage of. These women were of two types: those who wanted to humiliate their husbands by enjoying another man in front of them, and those who did the same thing, but who were sending another message alltogether. This second type wanted to prove that they were the most seductive, the most interesting, the most coveted, the wildest, and the most sexual. They wanted to demonstrate that their husbands really should be proud of them after all because they would try all men, lightly, fleetingly, but always ended up preferring their husbands, because their husbands were the best. It is curious how the same subject can be understood in such antagonistic ways.

And there were plenty of women who wanted to be with two men at once, or more than two: these were the so-called sluts, the powerful ones, the nymphomaniacs, the cannibals, the man-eaters, who embodied the primitive myth of the *vagina dentata*.

In one variant of this symbolization, there were those women who wanted to be in the middle of one or more couples. This would extend all the way to what the Polish doctor called a full-on orgy: a free-for-all, with the uninterrupted exchange of partners.

What Miroslav Zmuda found interesting concerning group fantasies (besides the fact that they intermingled various categories—for example, one woman and two men, violence and infidelity) was that they did not represent a nostalgia for barbarism.

Even though primitive men behaved in ways that are hard

for us to comprehend nowadays—for example, lending, kid-napping, or raping women—human sexuality was usually private in those societies. There was always a sense of shame, and orgies, when they occured, were linked to very specific and special rituals.

Dr. Zmuda could find only one parallel to such orgiastic fantasies: the behavior of animals—indeed, they are totally devoid of the concept of shame. And this was the third of the categories recognized by the physician: the symbolizations of indiscretion, or publicity.

Orgies, swapping, threesomes—these were composite fantasies, symbolizing at the very least indiscretion and infidelity, but sometimes even violence. But there was the pure form of this category: women who liked to be observed during sexual contact.

One scenario was classic: a woman in the bedroom, with her husband, who notices or sees a maid passing by, or a male cousin, who, in turn, watches through a door left ajar. Or something more daring: a young girl, for example, who lets herself be seen while she undresses, pretending to ignore the observer. The fantasy of indiscretion also includes an active component: as, for example, the maid.

The first three categories of symbolizations established by Miroslav Zmuda said much about the nature of female sexuality. These fantasies constituted downward movements, they were movements of "falling." They consisted, in fact, of de-evolutionary impulses, contrary to civilization. They were either a return to savagery or a reaffirmation of the animal kingdom.

Castelo Hill, in Rio de Janeiro—where the first seat of government, the first school, the first jail, and the first storage house were built—was also the place to which the city's founding landmark was transferred in 1567.

As you know, Rio de Janeiro was founded in 1565, with the

stature of city from the start, practically in the middle of a swamp between the Cara de Cão Hill and Sugar Loaf Mountain.

After the war, when the Temiminós defeated the Tamoios and Estácio, the city's founder, was mortally wounded, Mem de Sá ordered the citizens to migrate to Castelo Hill.

This move, because of the symbolic nature of the landmark being moved, meant much more than a mere change of location: it meant a new beginning, the founding of a new city—homonymous and homotopic.

And Castelo Hill met with an unusual fate. Partly demolished in 1905, during the construction of Central Avenue, it was finally razed in 1921 during the administration of Mayor Carlos Sampaio, and part of the rubble was used as landfill to cover the wetlands of the primitive city between Sugar Loaf Mountain and Cara de Cão.

Thus, Rio de Janeiro is perhaps the only city in the world founded twice, whose founder's tomb was twice desecrated, and that with one sweeping gesture twice destroyed the original landscape of its two foundation sites.

Many people, therefore, accuse Carlos Sampaio of being a traitor to his country, because, under the pretext of building a large esplanade for the Independence Centennial, what he really wanted to do was open the city up to the sea breezes and remove the poor, who, at the time, were the majority of the inhabitants of Castelo Hill.

For me, however, Carlos Sampaio was a mystic. First of all, by destroying the city's foundational landmarks he affirmed Rio de Janeiro's timelessness, its condition as a city that has always existed, not only since 1565. Second of all, by razing Castelo Hill he proved that he believed in and was searching for the more than legendary treasure of the Jesuits.

It is curious how the legend of one treasure always overshadows that of its predecessors. Although there was a fever surrounding this search (Lima Barreto wrote a lot about this), Rufino's treasure, and the growing fascination with it, helped the old Jesuit legend die.

Maybe that is the mystery, the strategy of the guardian spirits of treasures: the imminence of finding a treasure helps the story of a new treasure reverberate. And Rufino's had precisely this function.

For that reason, officers, lieutenants, and the First District police chief himself were obsessed with the sorcerer, and ever since that meeting at the old corner tavern (at what was once known as Cachorros Alley), they decided to mount a full-out treasure hunt.

Since they suspected that the treasure was hidden in the English Cemetery, the first victim was, of course, the head gravedigger. The man was roughed up and threatened, and, for almost the entire month of July, he desecrated graves and turned over almost every inch of soil in that cemetery.

It was strenuous work, because every opened tomb, every hole dug in the middle of the night, had to be restored, to cover up any signs of tampering, by morning. The gravedigger would die the moment the slightest suspicion arose.

Meanwhile, the old man seemed to have guessed that soon their attentions would turn to him. So, he stopped going to the English Cemetery; in fact, he stopped going to all the city cemeteries, as had been his custom. He merely kept to his usual routines, only going to the known points: Misericórdia Hill, Lapa Square, Rosario Church, Pedra do Sal. There he would sell his prayers and his medicinal brews, or perform minor services. And that was it.

The Brotherhood kept a tight surveillance. And some officers—who were as anxious as they were fascinated—committed the folly of assaulting the sorcerer at his home and torturing him, as Rufino himself would later inform Baeta.

It was not, however, the physical abuse—which only

seemed to get worse—that most bothered the old man, but rather the constant and permanent surveillance that seemed to follow him wherever he turned.

But that was the police's strategy: sooner or later (they believed), Rufino would take them to the hiding place. And the plan might have worked, if only Baeta had not shown up in Santa Teresa and, two days later, the rower Hermínio had not inquired about the sorcerer.

These two incidents—which occurred nearly back-to-back—rekindled the Brotherhood's fury. It may seem like an inexplicable reaction, but those who hunt treasures think of nothing else; those who hunt treasures cannot imagine that others might actually think of anything else.

That is when the lieutenant and two of his officers decided to hurry things along: knowing that Rufino was making fewer and fewer trips down into the city, and that he had begun to make more frequent trips into the wilderness, they had the urge to follow him in, believing that what they were after was in the dense rainforest.

Less informed readers might not truly have a notion of what a rainforest is. Especially at night, they are real labyrinths—much more confusing, much more treacherous than any of the mazes of antiquity, such as the Minotaur's, built by Daedalus, or the circles of Hell, discovered by Dante.

The same can be said of deserts, oceans, and glaciers. It has even been said of these that they constitute the perfect labyrinth, for they symbolize nothing. The rainforest inverts this: it is the sign of the absolute—both chaotic and finite.

If in a desert the traveler, or the prisoner, eternally sees the same scenery, and thus experiences a void, in the rainforest he never sees the same landscape twice. The rainforest—particularly a planted one like Tijuca—is a quantum maze: whoever loses his way inside of it interferes with its paths, assuring that its exit is farther and farther away.

We can say that Rufino planned that chase, that he had drawn his enemies into the depths of the rainforest: it was a territory where he ruled, where he knew where to find each *peroba* (for knife wounds), each *maçaranduba* (for diseases of the eye), each *pau-brasil* (dental pain, lumps, and thick urine), each ironwood (for strokes, fatigue, and shortness of breath), each *jequitibá* (for burns, also used to make pipes, and a source of resin and honey), each *ipê* (scabies, ulcers, and gonorrhea), each *embaúba* (to make *fundanga* and protect you from bullet wounds), and each *congonha* (for insomnia).

He also knew where the spirits of birds were in the habit of landing, controlled by the sorceresses of the night—the primordial mistresses of the universe that were never fully appeased and therefore might still interfere in the course of destiny, unable to tell good from evil.

Thus, in the rainforest, in the thick of the night, the police lost track of Rufino. Then they lost track of each other. Finally, they lost themselves, succumbing forever. The old man never expected any other outcome. And he stayed there, too, in the wilderness, in a kind of exile, hoping that another legend of another treasure might spread.

However, an incident that occurred on October 14th— soon to be narrated in more detail—changed the sorcerer's plans: a man who had made certain vow at the foot of a certain fig tree, a man who was fleeing the police, sought refuge in the rainforest, at the very place where he had made the vow, and he unwittingly dragged with him the officer known as Mixila. And Mixila disappeared, too.

The next day, the arrogance, the megalomania, of the First District Brotherhood was no longer tenable. The captain had to acknowledge his impotence before the rainforest, and had to yield. He confessed to the chief that his men had gone into, that they might have gone into, that he had heard rumors they had gone into, the dense Tijuca jungle. And a great expedition was organized during the day, with over one hundred police officers, to cover every corner of the rainforest.

Rufino was captured near Laranjeiras. In one of the hills leading to Corcovado, they found the lieutenant's body lying in a ditch and pierced by caltrops. The last body they came upon (because no bodies were found subsequently) was that of Officer Mixila: he had stumbled aimlessly and lost his life near the top of Sumaré. He was all swollen and purple, held up by a *sumaúma* tree, the bite marks of the *jararacuçu* snake still visible.

Naturally, there was a third dead woman. The narrative once again goes back in time, this time to October 10th, and the focus shifts to the distant lands where Captain Richard would later tear up the streets of bucolic Grajaú. So, it was there, in that great wilderness, at the foot of Elefante Hill, in one of the beautiful farms that bordered the old Cabuçu trail, that the woman died.

To say *woman* is an exaggeration, because she was only a girl of fourteen. She had the same obscene expression on her face, the same lascivious grin, which gave rise to venomous comments. She had not been choked, she had not been poisoned, there was not a single bruise on her body, and no sign of injuries that could have led to her death.

The mother wept and said she would only allow a closed-casket funeral, due to the shame that exposing her face would bring. The father raged, demanding punishment for the murderer. Of course, the coroner replied that there had been no murder. However, as this was the third episode of its kind, they gave the case special treatment.

Baeta went out to the old Cabuçu trail. I spoke of the mother's shame; I spoke of the father's rage. But I have not mentioned the sister of the deceased. It was a sad scene. She was the youngest and only thirteen. However, rumors were starting to spread around the neighborhood that she had seen everything, and that she was next to her sister when it all happened. That night, a loud shriek was heard, which suddenly ceased. Dogs began to bark and the lights in the mansion came on. The youngest came running in all the way from the rear of the garden, and then she locked herself in her bedroom.

Only when her sister was found dead, with her dress up, with signs of having lost her virginity, did she begin convulsively and desperately weeping until she fainted. Neither the father nor the mother, afraid of the truth, wanted to hear what she had to say.

Pressed, however, by the kitchen help, and by Baeta's persistent questioning, she finally gave in, with the promise that nothing would be said to her parents. She gave the following terrifying statement: that the two of them were with a man in the backyard, under a tamarind tree; that they had met him in the city after a day of sightseeing and shopping; that they had strayed a bit from their mother to try some candy a street vendor had to offer; that this was when he approached them; that they laughed and talked; that he seemed to guess their thoughts; that he knew both of them had a secret game they played, that one pretended to be the other's boyfriend, that they pretended how it would be like when they had a real boyfriend; that he said he would be their boyfriend; that they were delighted by him and gave him their address on the farm, and they settled on the day when he would visit them; that on that day they locked the dogs up; that they were scared but did not have the courage to back down; that he arrived, when everyone was asleep; that they led him to the tamarind tree; that he then placed her sister on her side, recumbent, and lay behind her, lifted her dress and showed them how it was done, asking that she, the youngest, kiss her sister on the mouth, close her eyes, and that she hold in her hand what was moving down below; that her sister felt no pain, but suddenly she gave out a cry and appeared to have fainted; that the man became very nervous and told her to run home; that she obeyed without understanding what was happening; and that only later did she learn that her sister had died.

Baeta insisted that the girl give more details; he actually wanted to understand how it was possible, how these two children allowed themselves to be seduced so quickly. Incredibly, not even she could make any sense of what had happened. By the way, there is no need to mention that the expert was able to deduce the man's identity. He did not, obviously, give voice to his suspicions. Admittedly, for him, the case of Aniceto had become personal.

At the very least, a crime had been committed in this case— perhaps not murder, but certainly statutory rape. Baeta let the officers of the Twentieth District try to discover the man's identity. By the tamarind tree he collected a button that had fallen off of a jacket, and based on that single piece of evidence he created his plan.

The expert waited until nightfall of the following day, Saturday, October 11th. He knew that Aniceto would be making his rounds at the pier, attending one of those *pernada* circles, and that, on such occasions, he did not dress elegantly, preferring instead the ragged clothes of the *malandros*. This would be his chance.

At around 8 P.M., Baeta crossed Harmonia Square and knocked on the door to the rooming house belonging to the Portuguese landlady. She was visibly terrified at the sight of the gun. Baeta pulled the woman outside by her dress sleeve, closing the door behind her to make sure they would not be seen.

"I'm going into Aniceto's room. Go and open the window. If he or anyone else knows I've been here, you die."

They say you can know someone by where they live. And that very little room said a lot about its occupant. First, with regard to cleanliness. The expert, who hoped to find soil on the shoes, saw that they were shiny and clean. Second, the contrast of the three elegant suits and the frock coat compared to the overall environment.

It did not take long for Baeta to realize that one of the jackets, still exhibiting a dirt stain on the elbow, was missing a button, precisely the one Baeta had brought with him, which was an identical match. The side of one of the pants was dirty, too.

That was the proof. Right then and there, he should have seized the evidence and filed for an arrest warrant. Instead, however, the expert continued scrutinizing the intimate details of his rival's life.

Aniceto was superstitious: he had pinned an image of St. Expedito to the wall, dressed as a Roman centurion, wielding a sword and a cross. The only piece of furniture other than the bed (the clothes were hung on a wire) was a trunk. On top of it stood a miniature plaster statuette of Saint Sebastian, along with two bottles containing herbs and twigs soaked in an alcoholic liquid—probably prepared by a healer, maybe old Rufino. In the corners, there were candles tied with ribbons, and all sorts of trinkets.

Baeta was not satisfied; he removed the figurine and bottles and opened the trunk. Inside, he saw a bundle of money, perhaps more than five hundred *mil-reis* mixed in with the bedsheets. To his amazement, next to the money were three badly printed volumes: *The Black Book of the Souls of Évora*, the extremely rare *The Invocation of Lucifer*, and *St. Cyprian's Black Hood*.

The expert picked up one of those copies. And what he saw next completely unhinged him. Because, underneath the book, buried even deeper among the white sheets, he recognized the whip with the silver handle, stolen from his home in Catete.

Miroslav Zmuda had relegated to the classification of *residual* a series of symbolizations which, according to him, represented very dark desires. Even though these were also falling movements, it was not merely a movement toward barbarism or the animal kingdom: it was a search for anti-nature. Among them, surprisingly, the Polish doctor included incest. That was when the first major disagreement arose between him and his former classmate in Vienna, the renowned Sigmund Freud.

Something must be said here to bolster the reputation of our doctor. Zmuda, on this particular topic, did not have a lot of data at his disposal. The Austrian's data, on the other hand, although more abundant, were not the result of direct observations, not to mention that they took as their point of departure the false assumption that the Greeks had concentrated in their texts all universal mythological knowledge.

Freud was one of many thinkers to believe the fable of the Greek miracle: that they in fact had been the smartest people in history, the creators of Western civilization. It was for this reason alone that he elevated the myth of Oedipus to the level of fact, considering the crime of incest to be one of the effective pillars of the human condition.

Our luminary Polish doctor, on the other hand, after observing dogs for long periods, did not admit that incest was natural even among animals (because, for them, it only occurs as an accident, and never as the result of intention).

It is up to the reader to judge: Freud spent his life in Vienna and conceived his theory by studying hysterical women. In all likelihood, he did not even take a hundred women to bed. Miroslav had a very different experience in Rio de Janeiro.

Incest, for Zmuda, was an attempt to break with nature. And such fantasies among women were very rare. This entire fifth category—the residual category—consisted of very rare phenomena involving female sexuality. One example would be pedophilia—not to be confused with a desire for beardless youths, it refers rather to sexual relations with prepubescent children—examples of which the Polish doctor could not register a single case.

He was also not able to document in women any tendencies toward necrophilia, nor even among men at the House of Swaps. Only once was this morbid desire ever carried out, when Hermínio managed to steal a corpse from the police morgue, in one of the largest financial transactions they had ever undertaken.

There was only one incident of bestiality or zoophilia: a woman applied gravy to her own genitals and trained her immense São Miguel Cattle Dog to practice cunnilingus on her, and one day this dog attacked her, jealous that her husband was outrageously nuzzling the woman's private parts.

Along those same lines, the popular folktale "The Woman and the Horse," although widely retold around the city, has never been documented, and thus remains only a literary example of the Myth of the Large Penis.

Zmuda was able to isolate a fourth category also comprised of symbolizations contrary to civilization and human nature, but these were not descending or falling movements—rather, they were ascending, or rising: these were homosexual fantasies.

In the House of Swaps (and Zmuda suspected that it was a widespread phenomenon), it was the symbolization that generated the most fascination: many couples actually engaged in swaps only as a pretext for female homosexuality, where the men became mere spectators.

Whenever there was any contact between women in the open environments in the House, almost everyone present, of both sexes, moved in to observe. The show put on by Aniceto, Palhares, and the tall woman had been one example.

Among the nurses, and among prostitutes in general, this was the most frequent fantasy; it was almost universal. Maybe because, subjected to constant degradation, forced most of the time to go against their own nature, they sought a pure eroticism among themselves, without the taint of virility.

The Polish doctor had cataloged a case that he considered

extremely important from a theoretical standpoint, which proved his thesis and therefore could be inserted into this fourth category: that of a woman who had asked Madame Brigitte for an encounter with a homosexual boy.

This would not have been a job for Hermínio, who was very manly; the client wanted a delicate man, with effeminate mannerisms. She had no intention of humiliating him, and she had no intention of playing the role of the male with him. On the contrary, the woman's anxiety was to find—from her perspective—a perfect being: a man who was not masculine.

It must be remembered that Zmuda was Aryan, Slavic, Polish, and, therefore, Catholic. Even great scientists have trouble freeing themselves from the metaphorical pressures suffered in childhood. And nothing exerts so great a pressure on the intellect as the literary and poetic foundational legacies of individual mythologies. In the Polish doctor's case, of course, it was the biblical mythology. It was thus through biblical myths that (even if subconsciously) Dr. Zmuda delineated his thinking.

Although there are very masculine, very patriarchal attitudes in the Bible, particularly in the Old Testament, the biblical God is still necessarily an asexual spirit. Or, more correctly, a hermaphrodite God, which created man in its own image and likeness and then subdivided into two.

These two creatures—man and woman—although sexually complementary, did not have sexual contact until their expulsion from paradise. And the expulsion is especially significant: it was in exile, on Earth, that man and woman propagated. She with labor pains, and he with pain, too, because he had to sweat to extract sustenance from the land for his family.

So, in the biblical myth, the multiplication of the species (only possible with heterosexuality) is associated with pain, punishment, the fall, and the vengeance of God.

There is a bold exegesis that I believe is in the subconscious

of all Christians: that this divine wrath against the primal couple was actually the inaugural manifestation of jealousy. This
God, asexual and hermaphroditic, had a necessary homosexual love for both man and woman.

Therefore, due to such symbols, Zmuda considered homosexual fantasies the most perfect symbolization: transgressive
of civilization and the human condition in being most similar
to the memory of paradise.

There may be those who object to the following: being a
hermaphrodite, God's love for human beings would also be
heterosexual, logically speaking, of course. It is just not true
symbolically. Because the attraction between different sexes—
so banal that is hardly, in and of itself, a fantasy—is not born
of divine work, but of the treachery woven by the snake.

This animal—a phallic symbol, related to the Earth in every
way, especially because it slithers over her—combines the
metaphors of evil and virility. Let us not forget that it is the male
who penetrates, who fertilizes by ravaging, be it the ground or
the woman.

And, thus, the cycle closes: with the fall of paradise, the
divine creatures lose the gift of eternal youth. Virility is one
more of death's metaphors.

If he had only known the specific details concerning the
cases of the dead women, Miroslav Zmuda would have noticed
another complicated slant to his "Aniceto Problem."

I have no idea what associations readers possibly made
when the discovery of the silver-handled whip amid Aniceto's
belongings was revealed. But I do know what Baeta thought: if
the capoeira touched the whip, his fingerprints were still on it.
Soon, the expert's revenge could be colossal; it would go far
beyond using a jacket and a button to frame him for 267,
which carried a maximum sentence of only four years.

Professing to have reviewed the evidence anew, he could

declare that Aniceto had been at the secretary's crime scene. The capoeira could thus easily be charged under 294 and get his thirty years in jail; or, more likely, because of the strict secrecy surrounding the case, he would be summarily executed, by order of the chief, without a trial.

But it was Saturday. The expert would have to wait until Monday to return to Relação Street to lend the story an essential element of verisimilitude. So there was plenty of time: Baeta messed up the room, broke the lock on the window, and pocketed a wad of cash to give the entry the appearance of a burglary. The Portuguese landlady, of course, would say nothing; and Aniceto would suspect a common break-in.

Then, grabbing hold of the leather strap—and not the silver handle—and hiding the object under his coat, he slipped away and headed to Harmonia Square, where he got into a carriage that would take him home.

I might not resist the temptation, were this a psychological or existential novel, to consider at length the constitution of human minds whose first impulse is evil.

If this were a weekday, Baeta would have gone directly to his laboratory to consummate his dark scheme. However, as I said, it was a Saturday. And during the trip, after the first evil impulse had cooled, the expert had a second thought.

If the men of the First District were patrolling his house to intimidate him—and he saw no other motive for the robbery—the fact that the whip ended up in the hands of the capoeira pointed to a hitherto inconceivable link between his rival and officers from Mauá Square. Worst of all, Baeta could not accuse them of this, because to do so he would need to confess that he had brought the whip back home.

Baeta, in fact, had no idea what to make of this. Were these independent actions? Could Aniceto have broken into his home on his own? But if he had, why would he avoid leaving fingerprints?

This last question led the expert to a third, terrifying hypothesis. Aniceto certainly would have never heard of the science of dactyloscopy. In Rio de Janeiro, in 1913, only police officers (and a few government or court employees) were familiar with this crime-fighting novelty. There was, however, at least one layperson, unknown within police circles, who, through special circumstances, knew exactly what this art represented: this person was none other than the wife of the fingerprint identification expert, the faithful and coveted Guiomar.

Individuals imbued with a true scientific spirit are usually well equipped to resist great personal upheavals. Baeta went home, hid the whip, and woke up early on Monday. Just the thought that Aniceto had used this on his wife (even though he had not detected any marks on her body) produced spasms of hatred in him, the desire to randomly shoot people, which his intelligence soon brought under control. But he had arrived at a conclusion: he could not inhabit the same city as such a man, a man capable of seducing children, capable of seducing—and this perhaps he would have the chance to prove in a few hours—Guiomar herself.

The quality of the prints on the silver handle—as the expert was able to ascertain by a superficial exam by the naked eye—was excellent. One of them—a right thumb mark—was especially sharp, and this was where Baeta began, gently sprinkling the black contrastive powder he had helped develop with his fellow forensic experts in Los Angeles.

It was an extremely rare arch formation present in only about ten percent of the population. And the comparison, after photographing the dusted fingerprint, was easier than he had imagined: it was identical to those contained on Aniceto's fingerprint cards, prepared by Baeta himself.

For the purposes of revenge, this would suffice. But the expert still had a question to settle: he needed to know, he needed to be certain, whether Guiomar had delivered the whip to the capoeira of her own free will. Therefore, it was necessary to analyze the other surviving prints on the silver handle—not so well preserved, true, but quite acceptable.

To the expert's relief, a summary examination ruled out Guiomar: his wife had whorls in the corresponding fingers, while those on the handle were shaped like loops. These did not match Aniceto's prints either.

Perhaps they belonged to an officer of the First District, in league with the capoeira in the break-in of his house, a case he could make only if he admitted to having taken the whip to Catete.

Baeta could have stopped there. The scientific spirit, despite offering great comfort in times of inner turmoil, can also sometimes leads us to discover more than is strictly necessary. Baeta conjectured that those could still be the old prints he had examined at the time of the crime at the House of Swaps.

And the expert, who was thinking about writing an article on the controversial issue of the durability of fingerprints on smooth surfaces when exposed to air, decided to investigate further. He pulled the secretary's prints (taken from the corpse) and photographs containing Fortunata's prints (or those he assumed were hers because they were the only ones different from the victim's on the bottle of wine, the wine glasses, and the whip's silver handle).

And, on staring at the prints attributed to the prostitute, in a meticulous comparative analysis, his mental acuity could not help but take over, and soon he noticed an interesting detail: Fortunata's right thumb also had an arch formation, like her brother's. And that was not all. He noticed (it was not for nothing that his visual memory was so renowned) two minutiae, two very characteristic traits, near the center, or nucleus, of the fingerprint, which made those prints more similar than normal: a line interrupted by the so-called "lake" formation, immediately above another line, with an intervening "spur" shape.

Baeta had the strange feeling that he had already noticed those details before, that he had already seen that design. He placed Fortunata and Aniceto's fingerprints side by side.

At first glance, they were the same. The expert, with some anxiety, undertook a thorough, careful analysis to exclude any possibility of error. After comparing twenty-one minutiae of the two thumbprints—a number that would be considered excessive by any other expert (who would have been satisfied with twelve or sixteen)—Baeta concluded that they were the same prints, that, absurdly, they were identical.

I repeat: Baeta concluded that the siblings Fortunata and Aniceto Conceição were the first known case of individuals who had exactly the same fingerprints.

Although dactyloscopy had already convinced most scientists as to its powers of unequivocal identification, and was officially accepted in countries like Argentina (which had the pioneering case solved by fingerprint analysis in 1892) and the United States (with several celebrated cases, such as the Crispi trial, solved in spectacular fashion by Joseph Faurot in 1911), it was still a developing science in 1913. And the main postulate of dactyloscopy—that no two people have the same fingerprints, even if they are twins—was not yet a consensus.

The main opponents to the technique had, I must admit, a good argument: no one had proved, in strictly theoretical terms, the aforementioned axiom; there was merely a lack of any evidence to the contrary. There were no reported cases of two individuals who had rolled the same fingerprint, but that did not necessarily prove the impossibility of such a coincidence in the world, even if it were only one sole example. The discovery of such prints was, perhaps, just a matter of time.

For Baeta, however, the question had to be treated as a statistical problem. He himself, in 1910, had arrived at very similar results to the Frenchman Balthazard in calculating the probability of two individuals exhibiting fifteen minutiae, or fifteen identical digital features, in the same position. This number was so small, so infinitesimal, that between the decimal point and the first significant digit, there would have been forty-four zeros.

Practical evidence of this was revealed at the Crispi trial, when twin brothers exhibited distinct fingerprints before a jury.

Therefore, Baeta—one of the luminaries in the field, who had placed Rio de Janeiro among the pioneering cities in the recognition and employment of this technique—was incapable of believing such a coincidence was possible.

The first thing that came to his mind, a fact that he noticed during the initial investigation, was that the strangulation of the secretary by force applied to the neck would have been more consistent with the actions of a man. The second thing was that legend, still in vogue, that the House of Swaps, which had been home to the Marquise of Santos, had a secret passageway that connected to it to the Quinta da Boa Vista.

Baeta now had a much stronger case, with much more conclusive evidence. Putting Aniceto at the crime scene—with fingerprints on various objects—was no longer simply fraud motivated by revenge: it was laying bare the true facts.

Perhaps, with the complicity of Madame Brigitte and Dr. Zmuda (or perhaps even one of the nurses), the capoeira had entered the House through the legendary passageway, directly under the stairs, where the Polish doctor had improvised his wine cellar.

After all, witnesses agreed that Fortunata had retrieved a bottle of red wine from there. The fingerprints, however, were those of Aniceto. Aniceto and Fortunata were very similar in appearance—they were siblings, they were twins. It had prob-ably been Aniceto who had returned to the room with the bot-tle, disguised in Fortunata's clothing.

When they announced Baeta's presence at the House of Swaps, Madame Brigitte's reaction was one of utter fear. And the doctor's reaction was not very different—he immediately stored his famous black notebooks, which he never ceased to peruse, under lock and key. Baeta was the last person they both wanted to see, or should have. And the reason, which the reader will know in due time, was unspeakable.

Zmuda and Brigitte were already somewhat apprehensive in those days because of problems Aniceto had introduced at the House. First, collective Thursdays were seeing fewer and fewer participants. The husbands and male partners (Baeta included) were discouraged because the women were all focus-ing their attention on the capoeira. Only those who were con-tent to watch the infidelity of their wives—and they were not in the majority—were still attending the parties.

More worrisome still was the hypothesis, suggested by one of the nurses, and which soon had everyone convinced, that Aniceto must be related to Fortunata, that perhaps they were siblings, because their resemblance was so striking.

Madame Brigitte decided, at the time, to confess to Miroslav Zmuda the full story of the letter, whose secret she had concealed so as not to upset him: Fortunata had not, in fact, been a friend of Cassia's. She had been placed at the House by Cassia, but at the request of a certain old *mandingueiro*, a character who was said to be well known in the city, a man by the name of Rufino.

Madame Brigitte, who had asked Hermínio to investigate this man and what interests he might have in all of this this, did not have good news to report: Hermínio had failed to meet with the old man, and he discovered that he had gone into hid-ing in the forest, a fugitive from the police.

This really upset Zmuda. It was very unpleasant that, so soon after the crime had been committed, a likely brother of the killer had begun attending the House. And it was very unfortunate that it had to be Aniceto, his "problem" Aniceto, Aniceto the phenomenon, who was giving Miroslav Zmuda unthinkable opportunities to refine his theories.

The Polish doctor and Brigitte received Baeta expecting the worst.

"I'll be blunt: did you know that Aniceto, who is Fortunata's brother, was in this house on the day of the secretary's murder, inside the victim's room?"

That was not the subject that Brigitte and Zmuda feared most. Still, they were none the more comfortable for it. They admitted that the suspicion had come up—i.e., that the two were siblings, given their resemblance. But never that they had acted together. Nevertheless, they thought it impossible for him to have entered the House on the day of the crime.

The expert recalled the legend of the secret passageway. Zmuda opened his arms:

"Really, Baeta!"

Baeta was not convinced, and they had to take him down to the cellar, under the stairs. The passageway, of course, was not found. But the expert did not give up on his theory, and he went back upstairs to question the nurses. He wanted to ascertain whether they had really seen Fortunata pick up the bottle of red wine, whether it could have been a man disguised as a woman.

People's memories, in general, especially after a certain amount of time has elapsed, and under some form of emotional suggestion, can easily be confused. And some of the nurses, faced with an attractive man who always treated them well, and an important person, the head of a police forensics department, who stated so categorically that the initial version of their story was impossible, began to reconsider and admit that the person who had passed by them with the bottle in hand might not, in fact, have been, certainly had not been, Fortunata.

Baeta seemed satisfied. And turned his attention to the owners of the house once again.

"I have no interest in doing you any harm. Later we'll figure out how he got in. The important thing is that we arrange for the girls to provide new statements."

Madame Brigitte and Dr. Zmuda could no longer cancel certain previously scheduled programming, certain services the House had committed to provide. Thus, they maintained the usual discretion concerning the matter. However, seeing that Baeta's intentions were actually friendly, they decided to return the favor. And they revealed something else, which they figured might be relevant: the contents of Cássia's letter.

The expert, however, did not seem to give the slightest importance to this information.

This novel will end shortly and so far I have reflected little on my favorite character—the beautiful, the true, the coveted Guiomar. Few women have been able to integrate a city so well, so perfectly into their being. Thus, being so much in agreement with the character of the city she epitomizes, it is only natural that Guiomar, too, was founded twice.

The first Guiomar we know well: Baeta's Guiomar, the accommodating wife, who even at the House of Swaps, paradoxically, derived pleasure from *not* swapping. The second Guiomar began on a specific date—August 21st, 1913—at that same House of Swaps, when she felt the irresistible urge to be slapped by her husband, stimulated by the virility of a stranger, who, only a few steps away, was slapping another woman.

This Guiomar, the second one, the definitive Guiomar, is the one that is going to precipitate the final action—an action that was predicted, or even provoked, by the palm reader on Marrecas Street.

"Over the life line, there's a cross; next to it, five lines: Two up, three down. You're about to cheat on your husband."

Guiomar's indignation said it all. Something had entered her psyche; something new was operating within her. And she realized—even though she did not want it to happen, even though she could not admit it to herself—that Baeta would not be at her side at her moment of great transition.

This did not mean that the expert had not been important in the process. It had been his idea to take home the silver-handled whip—even if he had not used it in the best way, in the precise way she yearned for it to be used.

Baeta, however, had always been a great lover. In the House of Swaps, she watched, enraptured, as her husband slapped and spit on a woman. The problem was not Baeta; the problem was not Guiomar. The problem was being Baeta and Guiomar, in those respective roles.

And so, on that fateful September 11th, Guiomar, unknowingly, for all intents and purposes, met the character, and for the briefest of moments she fixed her gaze on him. The man, the chosen character, stared back at her. If not for Aniceto, perhaps the affair would have had a different ending together.

When Guiomar found out, on Thursday, October 2nd, that they would not be going to the House of Swaps—the only place she could hope to meet the stranger again—she lost it. There is no better example of the devastating power of the Aniceto "phenomenon."

I return here to the story that was interrupted a few pages back. I am referring to the woman who, on a dark street leading to Flamengo Beach, by Catete, was pushed into a horse-drawn coupe and was driven to Alfandega Street (in the stretch formerly known as the Quitanda do Marisco), where she was delivered to a man who was waiting in a townhouse to have his way with her.

Before, I told you that Hermínio was our kidnapper. Now, I tell you that Guiomar was the woman. It is not difficult to deduce who the man was.

If some readers marvel at her audacity, perhaps it is because they do not know what she had been capable of a few days before: Guiomar had written to Madame Brigitte, describing a certain man who had done such and such things with two women at the last party she had attended on September 11th. She asked to meet with this man. And she suggested a whip. And Madame Brigitte, as we saw, outdid herself in directing this particular scene.

It was to pay the price demanded by Madame Brigitte, and also to explain the disappearance of the whip, that Guiomar simulated the theft of her own home. The neighbors, of course, would not find it strange to see her force open her own window (which could have just been stuck). Inside, it was easy to turn over the drawers and give verisimilitude to the lie.

One thing is funny: while Guiomar knew the basic postulates of dactyloscopy, it never occurred to her to take any measures to plant the fingerprints that would typically be found in a crime scene of this type.

This error, thus, directed all of the expert's suspicions against the officers of the First District, who loomed over their house in Catete, without her noticing. Unfortunately for Guiomar, they were drawn into the story as well.

I said the neighbors would not think it odd to see Guiomar force open her own window, but Mixila was not a neighbor; he was police. He perceived her agitation, her strange behavior, and he followed the expert's wife when she went off to Machado Square to deliver the whip and pay the fee. The intermediary waiting for her was none other than Hermínio.

The Brotherhood of the First District did not hold women in high regard. The police chief himself was in the habit of saying that a faithful woman in Rio de Janeiro was the one who died before having had the chance to cheat. But adultery never occurred to them in this case. It was perfectly clear to them that this had something to do with Rufino's treasure—so much so that the rower Hermínio had been asking around about the old man, and Guiomar was the wife of a man who, it was well known, was mixed up in this business.

Mauá Square, however, especially after the disappearance of three of its members in Tijuca Forest, could not assign its entire force to monitor around the clock the gang made up of Rufino, Baeta, Guiomar, Hermínio, and perhaps others.

If they had surprised Hermínio the moment when he delivered the whip to Aniceto, the story might have had a different outcome. Instead, the one they followed, the one Mixila followed, was Madame Brigitte's go-between when he rented the mansion on Alfandega Street on Friday the 10th.

The certainty that there was something big there increased when, by Monday evening, neither Hermínio nor anyone else had entered the townhouse. The expectation, however, ended on the 14th, when first the capoeira entered (without the whip), and half an hour later the expert's wife was being pushed and shoved as if it she were a slut by the former São Cristovão rower.

Uncomfortable with three revolvers pointing at him, Hermínio was forced to do an about-face as soon as he exited the building. The three walked back upstairs, Hermínio in front, followed by Mixila and two other policemen, who did not have a clue what was happening. They would have seen much more if they had only arrived a little later.

Instead, they kicked open the door with the immense urgency that only treasures justify, and took in the scene: Guiomar, with her dress lowered, her breasts exposed, her hair pulled back by Aniceto as he wandered with his tongue over her exposed nape.

The three barged in at once. Their mistake was pushing Hermínio onto the bed. It was a mistake because the capoeira needed only one stingray kick to carom one officer off the other and flee down the stairs. Hermínio, the former rower, reached for a fallen gun, which only facilitated Aniceto's escape as the two officers were needed to take him down.

We know how this story ends: Mixila chased the capoeira, discovered he was headed toward Santa Teresa, and went there in pursuit. There he entered the forest never to come out again.

Although it is one of the most studied cities in the world, much of Rio de Janeiro's history still remains obscure. This ignorance is severe for the 18th and 17th centuries. It is extremely severe for the second half of the 16th century. And it is alarming with relation to the entire period previous to that, which includes the city's pre- and proto-histories.

The resulting damage is immense for the native mythology. For example, there is today, in Niterói, an imposing statue of Arariboia—resolutely looking out at Rio de Janeiro as if he were a foreign conqueror.

Although this hero, the first native to wear the vestment of Christ, had received land grants on the eastern rim of Guanabara Bay, he was in fact a Carioca Tuxauu, in the most legitimate sense of the word, because he was born and lived in Paranapuã, the former Cat Island (i.e, "*maracajás*"), currently Governor's Island.

It is possible that, at the time, the Temiminós, or the Maracajás, already inhabited the city's northern coast and the neighboring islands, such as Cobras, Melões, and Moças. So much so that the "Village of Martinho"—as it appears in an old Portuguese map made before 1580—is nothing less than the village ruled by Arariboia (who had been baptized Martim Afonso), erected under the invocation of Saint Lawrence, beyond São Bento Hill, between Prainha and Saco de Alferes. The famous morality play *Auto de Anchieta*, of 1587, was performed in this location, and not on the other side of the bay.

And what about other great forgotten characters, such as Cunhambebe, Guaixará, and Aimbirê? The latter—the mastermind behind the Franco-Tamoia coalition—if for no other reason, deserves to be remembered for the classic scene which so fully embodies the spirit of the city, when, mortally wounded, he chose the fairest among his twenty wives, the stunning Iguaçu, and plunged into the bay with her before dying, fought the tides and swam out to the high sea, and deposited her, safe from his enemies, on Ipanema Beach.

Another attack on the mythical city's memory is making the Carioca River, after many detours and channels, run underground almost its entire length, reappearing as a tiny snippet in Cosme Velho, near the Largo do Botícario. The river's waters were so clear, so pure, that (so the Indians said) it made men strong and women beautiful. This confirms that, at least in legend, there existed a fountain of youth here, the object of Lourenço Cão's lost map.

It is also an unforgiveable crime that not one miserable plaque signals the approximate site of the famous Casa de Pedra—we do not know how, when, or by whom it was erected—a house that is so historically important that from it the citizens of Rio derive their own ethnonym.

By the way, no one knows exactly how Rio de Janeiro's toponym originated, and there is much controversy surrounding it. Varnhagen's thesis—which involves extremely complicated nautical calculations—is that a reconnaissance expedition to the coast, commanded by an anonymous captain, discovered what they thought was the estuary of a great river on January 1st, 1502.

However, as this is merely a logical deduction without supporting documents, conservative historians prefer the year 1504, when the fleet of Gonçalo Coelho would have dropped anchor in Guanabara. However, this is also subject to heated debate.

A strong historiographical strand argues that the name Rio

de Janeiro does not appear on maps before 1520. They present as evidence the fact that Ferdinand Magellan, who passed through here on his famous voyage around the world, gave the location the name of Santa Luzia since he was unfamiliar with any other names.

On the other hand, there are those who invoke the 1513 map of Turkish navigator Piri Reis wherein the outline of Guanabara Bay appears very clearly, surrounding a mysterious Arabic name containing the word "Saneyro." And there are those who remember the voyage of a ship named *Bertoa*, or the expedition of João Dias de Soliz.

This whole controversy attests to the following: that there was intense movement of Europeans—perhaps even Turks—in the regions neighboring Guanabara in the first half of the 16th century, that it is likely that they entered the bay, and that we know almost nothing about the details.

One of the few concrete mentions of this presence is the curious story of the traitor Lopes Carvalho, a Portuguese pilot who served the kings of Spain.

According to at least two sources (Pigafetta's diary and the testimony of the cabin boy Martim de Ayamonte), the traitor Carvalho—who was a pilot in the fleet of Ferdinand Magellan—came to Rio de Janeiro to reunite with the child he had fathered with an enslaved Indian with whom he lived between 1512 and 1517.

Of all of these mysteries, however, the most intriguing, the most impressive, the one most in need of unraveling is the existence, in Rio de Janeiro, of a tribe of Amazons.

Recent archaeological research, done in the area of the Pedra Branca (Jacarepaguá, Bangu, Realengo, Campo Grande, Guaratiba), identified a number of sites belonging to the Tupi tradition, all having in common characteristic ceramics coated with polychromatic decoration of a linear design and a texture of sand and crushed shells.

The oldest sites date as far back as three thousand years and have the following peculiarity: all one hundred and sixty-nine skeletons discovered were of females.

Another remarkable fact is that adult women were systematically buried in their *igaçabas* (or burial vases) with a bone flute and a rare artifact: a heavy, polished stone ring with circular edges. This is an awful and familiar weapon of war, the *itaiça*, with a convenient handle used to smash heads (a fact historically documented among the Guarani of Rio Grande do Sul).

There was another important relic, not necessarily associated with burials: long sharpened bone fragments whose stems revealed they were meant to be attached not to arrows but rather to very thick spears.

Male skeletons begin to appear at sites only a maximum of two thousand years old. And then things get more complicated: although the pottery remains identical, both the *itaiças* and the spearheads disappear, and the bone flutes—without exception—now are buried with men.

It is also during this period that the first axes fit for agriculture appear.

The ceramic records leave no doubt: all of these sites were occupied by the Tupis. What the experts have been afraid to say is that in the first millennium there was a Tupi society made up only of women warriors—the Itatingas, as they were known. They made pottery (always an exclusively female activity), hunted, certainly collected honey and fruit, but refused the tedious work of slash-and-burn farming.

They also had their status symbol: the bone flute, with which they were buried. The men who arrived seem to have usurped such a prerogative for themselves.

One of the mythic themes recurring throughout South America concerns the origins of male dominance. The peoples of Tierra del Fuego, the Pantanal, and the Amazon have very similar stories to explain how men gained dominion over women. And the Tupi versions (as well as those of the Mundurucus and Camaiurás) say that, in the beginning, women discovered the secret of the spirits that inhabit flutes, and this is why they ruled over men. When men finally conquered those sacred instruments, the situation was definitively reversed.

History thus repeats myth, but in the opposite direction. Friar Carvajal's Amazons and Cristóbal de Acuña's Icamiabas—and forgive me if I forget any others because at this stage I do not have the time to consult any more books— were the women who dared to undertake the same course of action of the Itatingas of Rio de Janeiro: they isolated themselves from men, and they armed themselves heavily, they regained control over the spirits of the flutes in order to be free.

And, of course, they took on lovers; after all, a millennium of chastity is simply unsustainable. The vexing question, therefore, is this: why did they submit a second time?

The archaeological remains are clear: the men who arrived in their midst were not necessarily stronger, they did not possess better weapons; on the contrary: they could barely handle the deadly *itaiça*, and they did not use spears in combat.

The Itatingas, for their part, lived alone for at least a thousand years. Of course, they did not reproduce, and they must have abducted girls from neighboring tribes, tribes that they almost certainly oppressed, given their military superiority, and from whom they extorted maize and cassava, which they refused to grow themselves.

And please do not come at me with that old canard that men are naturally stronger and more aggressive. The Itatingas spent an entire millennium hunting and braving the fauna and the wilderness without requiring the help of men.

The riddle may never be solved in strictly archeological

terms. However, there are those who suggest that the Itatin-gas—living a thousand years ago in a superior model of civi-lization—were driven by a simple fantasy, an atavistic longing to try barbarism once again.

While the drama with Guiomar unfolded at the apartment on Alfandêga Street, Baeta had finally managed, at approxi-mately 6 P.M., to see the chief of police at Relação Street. The expert's anxiety was justified: he had just solved, on a strictly logical level, using purely scientific procedures, the crime of the House of Swaps.

Baeta told the following version of events, omitting only a few facts that did not affect the final conclusion: while review-ing the forensic evidence, comparing the fingerprints found on the bottle of wine and the whip handle with those of Aniceto, he concluded that they were identical. Thus, not only had Aniceto been at the scene of the crime, but he had murdered the secretary, because the hands that picked up the bottle by the bulge were of the same dimensions as those that had stran-gled the secretary.

This eliminated the problem with the first theory, in which Baeta himself had pointed out that the force used in the stran-gulation was excessive for a woman.

"But weren't there fingerprints on the wine glasses too?"

It was true. The expert had forgotten this one detail. The police chief's objection was simple: if Aniceto had entered the room with the bottle and the wine glasses, dressed in women's clothing to resemble Fortunata (as Baeta alleged), and then, taking advantage of the fact that the secretary had already been bound, blindfolded, and gagged by his sister (also according to Baeta), had committed the crime, how could one then explain the victim's fingerprints on the wine glass and on the bottle?

"Honestly, I doubt that the secretary proposed a toast to the killer before dying."

Baeta almost laughed at such naïveté. These traditional cops, good men of an older generation, were all in the habit of thinking of crimes as literary works, and sought psychological coherence when the objective evidence, scientifically controlled, pointed them in another direction.

To strengthen his argument, the expert noted that some nurses had already admitted mistaking Aniceto for Fortunata, that the same person who had taken the wine upstairs could have been a man.

The police chief, who seemed visibly uncomfortable as they talked, wanted first to understand how Aniceto had entered the House, and why, since if the secretary were bound, the prostitute herself could have strangled him. He wanted to understand why it had been Aniceto, and not Fortunata, who had brought back the wine, thus increasing the risk of being discovered.

The answers, according to the expert, were pure speculation. There was one material fact, though: Aniceto's fingerprints were those on the bottle, and the hands on the bottle had been on the neck. Therefore, Aniceto had strangled the secretary.

Baeta did not rule out the hypothesis that the whole scenario—the ropes, the gag, the blindfold, a man dressed as a woman, and the wine bottle—had to do with the sexual proclivities of the victim. And he concluded his reasoning with a phrase that could have come straight out of the mouth of Madame Brigitte or Miroslav Zmuda:

"Anything is possible in that house."

The police chief was very circumspect. Deep down, he had a deep admiration for Baeta; he considered him one of his best men, one of the prides of the Rio de Janeiro police force. He could see Baeta's tremendous internal anguish as he struggled with these questions, and his sincere belief in this version, this absurd fable that this was the work of the twins Aniceto and

Fortunata, a view he held only because he was ignorant of one essential fact.

"I need to tell you a story."

The expert sensed something serious afoot.

"Remember that, while you were closing in on the capoeira, we were investigating the political side of the case?"

Baeta nodded. He had suggested as much in his first report.

"The secretary really did have enemies. He'd exerted his influence against important interests and he'd swayed the marshal against certain individuals. One of those enemies was on Fortunata's list of clients, which you yourself obtained from Dr. Zmuda. We also have information that there was a mistress, a prostitute he visited regularly, and whose description resembled that of the suspect's. We tried to identify her, but then it occurred to us that in São Cristovão she would go by a fake name, as all of these ladies do. And that perhaps this was what was hindering our efforts. Then I remembered your report, in which you claimed Fortunata was Aniceto Conceição's twin sister. All we would have to do was check the birth records. We checked the entries for Aniceto: the son of an unknown father and of a certain Maria Conceição dos Anjos. If he in fact had a twin sister, if the mother had gone to the trouble of registering her son, it was only a simple matter of confirming the identity of the daughter born to the same mother on the same day."

There was a short pause.

"The problem, Baeta, is that record doesn't exist: Aniceto Conceição never had a sister."

It is hard to describe Baeta's amazement, and his humiliation. After all, in this case he had failed to apply the principle he always advocated: a continuous and exhaustive investigation. If he had insisted on checking all of these facts, he would have arrived at the same conclusion.

And the police chief went further and said that all Offices

of Vital Records were subpoenaed to provide records of any daughter Maria Conceição dos Anjos might have had, born five years before and five years after Aniceto's date of birth. He really did not have a sister. There really was no Fortunata Conceição.

Stunned, the expert actually considered the hypothesis that Aniceto was Fortunata disguised as a man—perhaps because the mother had made a mistake when identifying the sex of the child, in the birth records. And he was about to utter a response when an officer knocked on the door with an urgent message:

"Mr. Baeta, the captain of the First District just telephoned. He's asking that you go immediately to this address on Alfândega Street. It seems that there's been serious incident there with Mrs. Baeta."

Do not think for one minute that the expert found a woman sobbing and humiliated at the Alfândega Street apartment, in the old stretch where the Quitanda do Marisco used to be. Guiomar had made the crossing—albeit not completely, but she was now free.

Having composed herself by then, though she was still being detained at gunpoint, she denied everything, claiming that she was the victim and the police were the aggressors. Hermínio, who was no less clever, confirmed the lie. The officers were stunned: they really believed that Guiomar was being raped because of the way the rower had roughed her up when he brought her into the apartment and the scene with Aniceto, which did not leave much room for interpretation. They waited anxiously for Mixila to return, bringing the capoeira back, to confirm the truth.

The case was complicated due to the history. On October 9th, Baeta had filed a complaint with the chief against the men of Mauá Square, mentioning Mixila explicitly. Now there was this situation. Baeta did not allow Hermínio or Guiomar to respond to the captain's question about what had brought them there, and he interjected his own question:

"Why were you following my wife?"

Implicit in his question was an accusation. Alfândega Street was outside the First District's jurisdiction. Any action there would be justified only if investigating a crime committed in the Mauá Square area. The actions of the officers, therefore, were illegal and showed that the expert was the real target of this persecution, ever since his meeting at Hans Staden's with the police chief.

Seldom have I seen a man act in this manner. Baeta sensed the truth. In fact, he had known the truth since before, since he had returned home from the Portuguese landlady's rooming house and had had those furtive thoughts about Aniceto, his wife, and the silver-handled whip.

The news of the presence of the capoeira in that apartment was evidence of Guiomar's gross betrayal. Later, he would review those facts in his mind and deduce that she herself had faked the burglary at their home.

The expert's vanity, however, was immense. He could not acknowledge to his enemies any misconduct on the part of his wife—even if it meant they would ridicule him behind his back. He would take care of Aniceto and avenge the outrage committed (even though Baeta had already admitted defeat with regard to the bet). Guiomar represented another prob-lem, one the two could only resolve at their first-floor corner home in Catete. He had so much passion and so much hatred inside of him, he felt an overwhelming urge to pummel her.

Baeta's surprising attitude had the effect of intimidating the officers of the First District. Maybe it was because they now recognized, on an intuitive level, that he was a true capoeira, at least in his moral makeup. At last, Baeta was reconciled with his origins.

So much so that, four days later, when Rufino was arrested

and they found the bodies of Mixila and one of the lieutenants in different points of the dense Tijuca forest, the name of the expert was the first to be mentioned in Mauá Square.

The police chief himself personally organized the search operations. However, with the sorcerer's arrest, and since the presumptive victims were First District officers, it fell on their captain to carry out the investigation.

Baeta was called in and asked to give his opinion as to whether Mixila and the lieutenant had been murdered, as was suspected. Regarding the officer, who exhibited clear signs of poisoning (later confirmed to be *jararacuçu* venom, from perhaps more than one snake), nothing conclusive could be determined.

With regards to the lieutenant, however, who had fallen into a pit and been pierced by caltrops, the intent was clear.

Rufino confessed that he had dug, covered, and camouflaged the trench with dry twigs. However, he said he had not intended to kill the lieutenant; the caltrops had been put there over forty years earlier to protect against bounty hunters, when he, Rufino, was the head of the runaway slave society known as Cambada.

The captain wanted to know if forensics could go down into the hole and determine the age of the trap. Baeta was prepared to go. That's when someone said to the captain:

"Waste of time, boss. The old man doesn't lie."

That was when Baeta let out something he had been holding in for some time. He rushed at the old man, his finger pointed at his face, as if he were about to strike him.

"The old man does lie! And I have proof!"

Nothing could have been more demeaning to Rufino. Outraged, he challenged Baeta to prove it.

"He lied when he said Fortunata was Aniceto's twin sister. Aniceto never had a sister."

The old man let out such a cavernous laugh that he unsettled everyone: "I never said they were brother and sister, much less twins! I said they shared the same belly."

This time, it was the officers who burst into laughter.

"And is it not the same thing?"

With a touch of sarcasm, revealing an ancient contempt for all of that false wisdom, the sorcerer answered softly:

"No, no, sir. They shared the same belly because they're the same person."

The last antecedent crime—whose history is entitled *The Sedition of the Amazons*—can now be presented to the reader for interpretation.

It is 1531, the year that Martim Afonso de Souza, the recipient of the Captaincy of São Vicente, came with his ships and four hundred men into the bay of Rio de Janeiro to replenish their water supplies, dropping anchor near the mouth of the Carioca River, at what is now Flamengo Beach. It was Martim Afonso who ordered the erection, on the banks of this river, of the famous Casa de Pedra.

However, that is neither here nor there at this point in the narrative. The fact is that Martim Afonso was kept busy at the bay for about three months with several tasks. The real intent of the grantee was disclosed by his own brother, Pero Lopes de Souza, a minor captain in the fleet, in a logbook that recorded every step of the journey. In a famous passage, he reported that the Captain General ordered four men into the hinterland, and that these men walked one hundred and fifteen leagues and returned two months later, with quartz crystals and news that the Paraguay River was full of silver and gold.

Martim Afonso, of course, soon departed, heading south. We do not know if he discovered anything in the Rio del Plata. What is certain is that, by his orders, part of his fleet returned to Portugal. Pero Lopes led that voyage, in a mission that we can deduce was a secret one, dropping anchor along the way, once again, in Rio de Janeiro.

What they did in Guanabara, between May 24th and July 2nd, the diary does not tell us. But this is where I come in, to repair this terrible lapse, because I know exactly what happened.

Just as in the first visit, some men were sent into the hinterlands, accompanied, as always, by a native escort. This time, three adventurers were sent—three convicts who had been stationed in forgotten trading posts along the coast, who had lived for years in the land and knew the language very well.

This expedition would not cover nearly the same distance as the first, and they would not need to spend two months in the wilderness. In fact, it was meant to last no more than a fortnight and was confined to city's natural boundaries: the Guanabara Bay to the east, and the Sepetiba Bay to the west.

But they were not be trusted, these convicts. Pero Lopes was actually counting only on the natives' loyalty; however, since he had not mastered the language of the natives, he did not notice a certain tension, a certain estrangement among the natives in the group.

The expedition followed an old aboriginal trail, approximately parallel to the coast, that extended as far as Angra dos Reis. It is likely that the adventurers had coordinates, or even a copy of part of Lourenço Cão's map—hence, they supposedly asked about the Piraquê River. However, when they reached the vicinity of said place in Marambaia, the Indian escorts simply stopped.

There was no discussion: they simply claimed that if they continued along that route, they would end up at an undesirable location, where they would certainly not be welcome. The convicts insisted on knowing what was going on, and one of the guides answered that, if they were to continue in that direction, they would go very near a native village ruled by women, which it was best to avoid.

Unfortunately, I still have not obtained a copy of Lourenço Cão's map, so I really do not know how important it was to keep on the path recommended by Pero Lopes. But I suspect that the mention of women—sovereign women—must have excited the imagination of the adventurers, who by nature were predisposed to risk.

The agreement reached was as follows: the natives stayed back, waiting, while the convicts went ahead to see what fate had in store for them.

The village did, in fact, exist. It was on an elevated stretch of ground, surrounded and protected by mangroves. The hut—because it was not, strictly speaking, a house—combined native and European traits: it was tall and spacious, twelve fathoms wide and six long, covered with foliage and able to accommodate a hundred people in its wall-less interior. The entrance was through a single door, low and in the middle. But the structure was composed of straight lines and it had windows along the edge of the roof, for ventilation and light. I do not know whether it was made clear that this one house was, in essence, the entire village.

The convicts, however, seemed unimpressed by any of this. The savages had spoken of a village made up solely of women, yet there were men there. What's more: with the exception of about one third of the female population, who were very native-looking, the rest of the inhabitants were mestizos, *mamelucos* all of them. Although some women walked around naked, clothing for both sexes consisted of a kind of thick cotton fabric with a hole in the middle to pass their head through, covering their front and back like a clergy's surplice, and tied at the waist with a simple string.

They remembered one or another Portuguese word, but they were unable to understand a full sentence in that language. They claimed to be descendants of the Perós, who came from across the sea in huge *igaraçus*. The three men were taken to the beach, to a sacred spot of sorts, where the ruins of what they recognized as a caravel lay.

In one corner of the hut, the convicts could still see the spoils of that shipwreck, which the *mamelucos* saw no value in at all, and kept as mere relics. There were nautical instruments, such as a quadrant and an armillary sphere; garments, including a tall pair of boots with heels, a doublet of threadbare baize, and two half-corroded belts; weapons, such as a Turkish saber and an inoperative Dutch musket; and all sorts of junk, like shards of mirrors, hooks, clamps, pulleys, mugs, candlesticks, and very ancient coins, to the astonishment of all, many of copper and silver.

The adventurers were amazed with their discovery. But one thing puzzled them: the natives had mentioned a government of women, but so far they had only seen women weaving, preparing food, and even working the land, from where they returned in the evening with beans.

Then came the big surprise: before they could react, the *mamelucos*, with imperious expressions and energetic gestures, disarmed the foreigners and shoved them into the hut, where they had their hands and feet bound and were left abandoned in that state under a tangle of hammocks and storage platforms that constituted all of the interior furnishings of the structure.

At night, the apparent tranquility of the village gave way to great agitation and aggression, harsh discussions and what seemed like fighting, involving men and women alike.

It was the new moon and the darkness only made things worse. No one knew why, but the *mamelucos* decided not to light any bonfires that night; and, in that agitated and harsh environment, the convicts were afraid. Just when they imagined that something very serious was about to happen, it did.

The whole village, filled with a palpable sense of expectation and anxiety, had already retired to their hammocks in complete silence. The voice they heard, which shook a hundred hearts, came from outside:

"Ajaguajucá jeibé! Äé reriguara ixé!"

It is hard to describe the horror of the convicts—who understood the words, but could make no sense of the meaning.

The physical despair that they perceived among the *mamelucos*, however, told them that they were not the only ones in danger. They barely noticed, though, the reaction of the womenfolk, who let out muffled cries:

"Possupara ojur! Possupara ossyk!"

And the voice from outside—guttural, wild, threatening, fascinating—then echoed inside the hut, making the terror reach a fevered pitch.

Naturally, they could not make out the identity of the voice, but he was a man. He wore the rags of what perhaps had once been the noble outfit of a navigator, but he also had huge indigenous plumes strapped to his back, a kind of *enduape*. And this man, this beast, came sniffing and snorting throughout the hut, until he stood right above the convicts. Suddenly, he threw himself into one of the hammocks.

The three adventurers could not believe what their senses were telling them: while other women seemed to chirp like *macucos* on a perch, the noise coming out of the hammock was unmistakably that of copulation—violent, savage, animalistic—and they had no doubt that the woman chosen by the visitor was not, in fact, a victim.

And they were right: that village of *mamelucos*, descendants of shipwrecked Perós, was ravished, every month, every new moon, by this visitor: the *possupara*—who women, it was later discovered, competed for.

Who he was and where he came from, no one could say. And that is what most outraged the convicts, who did not understand such laxity, such unmanliness among those fathers and husbands, who outnumbered him thirty to one.

You would be sadly mistaken to think that the reason the adventurers remained in the village for one more moon cycle was to try to find ways to steal the coins. The native escorts did not wait any longer, and at the Carioca, they reported that all three convicts had fled. Because it had been a secret mission, Pero Lopes omitted these facts from his diary.

Back at the Marambaia, the convicts found out who was really in charge. The invitation came from the womenfolk: if they were to stay, they would receive, as wives, the next three virgins who menstruated.

Certain male instincts, however, are predictable. The adventurers accepted the proposal, but they did not agree, in their hearts, with the implied clause imposed by the night visitor.

So, one week before the new moon—without much fanfare—the convicts began a hushed campaign with every male in the village, delineating the simple plan to kill the visitor. The men seemed to want this death, but all listened with downcast eyes, not daring to act. For the convicts, however, simple consent was enough.

If they were to sharpen the Turkish saber, they would raise suspicions. Therefore, they obtained from the *mamelucos* strong ropes of *embira* fibers with which to restrain and strangle the enemy. There was only one problem: at the chosen moment, there had to be a minimum amount of light.

So, in the new moon, the whole scene, the whole anxiety-ridden experience was repeated. The visitor announced his arrival—*today I killed a jaguar, but I'm an oyster eater*—and entered the hut, sniffing, snorting, until he selected his hammock.

Suddenly, someone waved a glowing piece of wood. The convicts jumped the invader in unison. Nobody knows who died first: three arrows, shot by three females, knocked all three of them down at once.

The *mameluco* who gave the signal was killed, too, plus a few others who had conspired in braiding the rope. But that was the next day, after the visitor had left, after he had peacefully made his selection.

Rufino was able to prove he was not lying. Escorted into the forest by an entourage of policemen, which included Baeta and the captain, he took the trail that led to the majestic *gameleira* tree, the sacred meeting point, or the dwelling place of terrible unnamed witches, night ladies, possessors of bird spirits, and guardians of mysteries of the left side of the world, unable to discern good from evil. And—now I can add—man from woman.

It was there, at that *gameleira*, a place where one fulfills religious obligations, that the old man assumed that Aniceto had sought refuge, since it was the only place in the forest he might be able to reach without getting lost.

"He must be dead now."

This, too, was true. But it was not the labyrinth of the rainforest that had killed Aniceto: he had fallen off a *pirambeira*. His head revealed a bullet hole from a shot fired by Officer Mixila, who also never returned.

The capoeira's corpse was carried to Relação Street, and it is not necessary to inform you that the problem of the caltrops became secondary.

"He's like a seahorse. Cut him open, you'll understand."

No one knows why, but they did not allow Rufino to attend the autopsy that he himself had suggested. This, of course, did not change the crucial, inexplicable fact: Aniceto was not a hermaphrodite. But he did have a uterus. And he was pregnant.

This phenomenon caused great speculation among the coroners. But the fate of the case was the fate of all the great truths, the truths that are unbearable: they turn into legend.

How, I am not certain, but Baeta's old ideas about the presence of the alleged siblings, Fortunata and Aniceto, at the House of Swaps began circulating, and the story of the secret passageway came back with a vengeance, and Rufino's treasure was miraculously forgotten, replaced by the Marquise's treasure.

It was not an unreal treasure, though—those of the city of Rio de Janeiro never are. Nobody imagined, however, that the treasure was merely comprised of black notebooks, filled with scribbling in German and stored, after Dr. Zmuda's death, in a secret compartment under the stairs, behind a stone wall, in a tunnel that once connected the Marquise's house to the palace at the Quinta da Boa Vista.

After Aniceto's autopsy, Baeta experienced a feeling of tremendous anguish. He remembered the things he had done in bed with Fortunata, without knowing she was a man. He had kissed the whore on the mouth, had put his mouth in places—and he was no longer sure if they were exactly those places or not. The expert, in fact, lacked the complete explanation to the mystery: how could that ambiguous body have existed, if it did exist?

It was in order to try to understand these things that Baeta interceded and obtained permission from the police chief to release Rufino into his custody so he could interview him. The old man, who had been a member of a runaway slave community, who had been the head of the Cambada Quilombo, consented to the expert's request.

Aniceto, the old man explained, started in the Ijexá lineage, at the house of the *babalaô* Antonio the Mina. Since the Mina was not widely accepted by the colony of Bahia (who lived closer to Cidade Nova), he sought out adherents among the people of Saúde.

It was Antonio the Mina who first told the capoeira stories of men who were also women. And Aniceto, schooled in the ethics of capoeira, speculated on the sexual powers of a man who had physically known what it was like to be a woman.

The Ijexás, although they had always been ruled by queens, could also be inconceivably narrow: Antonio the Mina would never allow Aniceto to advance very far. And he even refused to initiate him as *babalaô* for fear of things that he might come to know.

That was when the capoeira sought the *macumba* line. And he, Rufino, prepared the ritual, which first began as a pact, signed under a certain *gameleira* tree in Tijuca Forest, with the night ladies, possessors of the spirits of birds.

On a Friday the 13th, the old man took Aniceto to the English Cemetery. Baeta, who by now no longer doubted anything, was impressed by this narrative. After incinerating his clothes and administering certain potions, the sorcerer, with the very bag he used to carry his implements, smothered the capoeira to death.

The old man must have extraordinary strength, for Aniceto struggled mightily, even though he had not forgotten the sacrifice he had agreed to undergo. Aniceto's body was lowered into the pit, where there must have been at least one other recently buried body.

Fourteen midnights, fourteen big hours, went by, and Rufino reopened the tomb, exhuming Fortunata. That was three years before.

It was not necessary to explain to the expert who Fortunata was. On Friday, June 13th, of that year, 1913, what the old man did was simply begin to reverse the process: Fortunata was killed and buried in the same manner to then be reborn as Aniceto after the big hour of the 26th.

The problem was the opening of the mass grave on the 23rd.

Very quickly, the body began decaying inside the grave (helped along by the concoctions ingested). And, just as quickly, it resumed its previous form, reversing only the gender. They were essentially the same person. Hence, the identical (as per the expert's conclusions) fingerprints and handwriting, not to mention the physical resemblance.

Baeta acknowledged that Aniceto had exploited that similarity extremely well. The same was true of the forged note, which mentioned the secretary by name, and the story that it should not be delivered to Madame Brigitte so as not to incriminate his "sister," plus all the lies based on the real facts of his life. The end result was that Baeta had accepted his version without suspecting a thing.

Then there was the issue of the opening of the trench. A metamorphosis, according to Rufino, needed total darkness, a deep immersion into the underworld of death.

The corpse unearthed on the 23rd—although already a man, as forensics had substantiated—had suffered a brief interruption in the transformative cycle, and the resulting defect manifested itself later. Aniceto suffered pain, constantly needing to take potions, because he retained a uterus and a dead fetus, mummified inside of his male body.

Baeta thought back to every sentence the old man had uttered, and indeed, none of them were ever lies: a man had given him the earrings, and he never did dig up a corpse in the English Cemetery.

By now, Baeta could already guess what Aniceto's, or Fortunata's, intentions were when he chose that life, in the House of Swaps.

Rufino simply confirmed the suspicion: the man who plunges deeply into the critical experience of death, and survives, and then, as a woman, completely penetrates the left side of the world, gets to know the secrets of women, acquires the gift of sorcery—but at a level so deep that this man has the power to enchant, to bewitch, to seduce, to intuit, and to know exactly what happens inside of the mysterious and intimate world of women.

The sorcerers who had taught this magic to Rufino warned of the dangers; a man with such powers would be able to have all the women in the world. And what's more, he could even kill them if they were ever to reach an orgasm of maximum intensity—the sensation would be simply unbearable.

"If you divide pleasure into a thousand parts, of that number, surely, nine hundred and ninety-nine belong to women."

The expert still could not understand why Fortunata, or Aniceto, had strangled the secretary precisely on the day when the ritual of return would be performed.

"When the time comes, they are very violent. It's as if the male inside were revolting."

Baeta remembered how witnesses had spoken of the nervous and aggressive behavior of the prostitute in the days leading up to the crime. The one thing he found strange, though, in Rufino's sentence was the use of the plural.

"I've done this with many people already, sir."

And the old man, sensing exactly what the expert was about to ask, went on:

"Aniceto was vain. He wanted to be the best of men. He was the first, though, ever to want to come back. None of them ever wanted to before. Not one."

Rufino never mentioned the old African traditions linking man to light, to odd numbers, to forests, and to the right side. Women are therefore the night, even numbers, deep water, and the left side. They are, as we can see, two completely incommunicable worlds.

In primordial times, however, there was one exception: a hunter, a kind of oxóssi, *a cruel and powerful sorcerer, who made a pact with the Night Women and acquired the ability to transform himself into a woman, hence adopting the emblem of the seahorse.*

This deity inhabits the forest but also the rivers, particu-

larly the flooded banks, the areas where the waters mix with the forest.

And Rio de Janeiro—a city built on swamps and mangroves, from the early shell mounds of the Itaipus to the crude palisades of Estacio de Sá—was fated to belong to this sorcerer, this hunter. So the same adventure is endlessly played out: the ageless struggle of humanity to control one another by controlling the orgasm—which, we now know, is the greatest power of all.

There is a scene from the novel that I have not narrated: when Rufino finished recounting his story, knowing that Baeta sought the same gift that Aniceto once possessed, he offered him that possibility. He asked whether he would like to go through the same experience. However, before Baeta responds, this book will have ended.

And the reason is, since I myself am Baeta, I will not allow the character to venture beyond these our cramped circumstances.

Therefore, all that is left to do is to thank the city and its god, which have allowed me to live, and especially to imagine, which is the most dangerous form of experiencing life.

And if I am granted one last wish, it is that my body remains and dissolves in this fabulous soil, which is that of all of the oxóssis, *the* caboclos *of the forest, and of Saint Sebastian.*

Rio de Janeiro,
March 1, 2010, to January 20, 2011.

ACKNOWLEDGMENTS

Thanks—

to Joãozinho, the first to hear and discuss with me the story in this book, before I even started writing it;

to Elaine, for her constant and engaging inspiration;

to Nilton da Silva Nascimento, a model public servant, who was my guide through the House of the Marquise de Santos, today The Museum of the First Reign;

to José Minervino, who led me through the fascinating gravestones and tombs of the English Cemetery, where I intend to be buried one day;

to Edu Goldenberg and Paulo Klein, for all of the information and resources they shared with me concerning the administrative history of the civil police of Rio de Janeiro (they should not, of course, be held accountable for my small fictional liberties);

to André Luiz Lacé Lopes, for his bibliographical suggestions and for having revived in me memories of capoeira from my adolescence;

to Fred Mussa, an *angoleiro* master and a dear brother, for sharing with me his intellect and his wealth of resources concerning the history of capoeira;

to Luiz Carlos Fraga and Ronald Cavaliere, whose deep literary knowledge and whose immense enthusiasm for crime fiction I have found very inspiring;

to Miguel Sanches Neto, for his striking critical abilities and his profound literary knowledge;

to Stéphane Chao, for his indispensible erudition on all things mythological;

to all the people who directly, indirectly, and emotionally contributed, and will continue to contribute, to this adventure: Adriana Fidalgo, Ana Lima, Ana Paula Costa, Andréia Amaral, Beatrice Araújo, Bruno Zolotar, Camila Dias, Carolina Zappa, Cecilia Brandi, Cécilia Maggessi, Elisa Rosa, Fátima Barbosa, Gabriela Máximo, Guilherme Filippone, Ivanildo Teixeira, Juliana Braga, Leonardo Figueiredo, Leonardo Iaccarino, Livia Vianna, Magda Tebet, Márcia Duarte, Maria da Glória Carvalho, Regina Ferraz, Sérgio França, Tatiana Alves, Vivian Soares;

and to Luciana Villas-Boas, as always, for everything.

GLOSSARY

agremiação: literally, "guild." In Rio, a precursor to today's samba schools

batuque: a musical rhythm of African origins

caboclo: an ancient indigenous spirit, also a Brazilian of mixed white and native or native and black ancestry

Caboclo das Sete Encruzilhadas: the name of a Brazilian native spirit

cachaça: a distilled alcoholic beverage made from sugarcane

Candomblé: a religion of African origins

Candomblé de Inquices: a tradition of Candomblé typical of Angola

capoeira: a Brazilian martial art of African and native roots; one who practices that art

carioca: a person or thing from Rio de Janeiro

Casa da Pedra: the first stone building erected in Rio de Janeiro

Chica da Silva: Francisca da Silva de Oliveira (1732-1796). A real historical figure, she began life as a slave but became a renowned society lady.

Colégio do Castelo: a Jesuit school on Castelo Hill, Rio de Janeiro

corpo fechado: literally, "closed body"; a body that is immune to harm as a result of magic

Iansã: a female deity in the Candomblé religion

jogo do bicho: literally, "the animal game"; an illegal lottery popular in Rio de Janeiro

Macumba: a spell; a religion of Angolan and Congolese origins

mãe-de-santo: literally, "mother of the saint"; a female religious leader who oversees **Candomblé** ceremonies (see **pai-de-santo**)

malandro: a streetwise Rio de Janeiro archetype who lives by his wits and avoids work

mameluco: a person of mixed native and white ancestry

mandinga: a spell; or behavior typical of a **malandro**

Mina: a reference to the Mina Coast in Africa, a region that was the birthplace of many of the enslaved Africans brought to Brazil

pai-de-santo: literally, "father of the saint"; a male religious leader who oversees Candomblé ceremonies

pernada: a primitive type of **capoeira**

porta bandeira: literally, "flag-bearer"; the dancer who carries the flag representing an **agremiação**

preto velho de quimbanda: ancestral spirit of an African slave

puíta: the original name for a *cuíca*, a friction drum

quilombo: a village made up of runaway slaves

Rancho das Sereias: literally, "Ranch of Mermaids"; the name of a carnival **agremiação**

roda: literally, "wheel"; a gathering of **malandros**

rodas de fundanga: circles made of gunpowder, used in sorcery

Saci Pererê: a mythical one-legged trickster and an important figure in Brazilian folklore

São Sebastião: Saint Sebastian, the patron saint and protector of Rio de Janeiro

xaréu: a type of saltwater fish

ABOUT THE AUTHOR

Alberto Mussa was born in Rio de Janeiro, Brazil, in 1961. His father's family originated from Lebanon and Palestine, and he explores Arab-Brazilian identity in his works. In addition to translating poetry and short stories, Mussa has written several novels about the history of Rio de Janeiro. He has won numerous awards, including the Premio Biblioteca Nacional for *Queen Jinga's Throne* (1999) and the Casa de las Américas and APCA prizes for *The Riddle of Qaf* (2004).

EUROPA EDITIONS BACKLIST
(alphabetical by author)

Fiction

Carmine Abate
Between Two Seas • 978-1-933372-40-2 • Territories: World
The Homecoming Party • 978-1-933372-83-9 • Territories: World

Milena Agus
From the Land of the Moon • 978-1-60945-001-4 • Ebook • Territories:
World (excl. ANZ)

Salwa Al Neimi
The Proof of the Honey • 978-1-933372-68-6 • Ebook • Territories: World
(excl UK)

Simonetta Agnello Hornby
The Nun • 978-1-60945-062-5 • Territories: World

Daniel Arsand
Lovers • 978-1-60945-071-7 • Ebook • Territories: World

Jenn Ashworth
A Kind of Intimacy • 978-1-933372-86-0 • Territories: US & Can

Beryl Bainbridge
The Girl in the Polka Dot Dress • 978-1-60945-056-4 • Ebook •
Territories: US

Muriel Barbery
The Elegance of the Hedgehog • 978-1-933372-60-0 • Ebook • Territories:
World (excl. UK & EU)
Gourmet Rhapsody • 978-1-933372-95-2 • Ebook • Territories: World
(excl. UK & EU)

Stefano Benni
Margherita Dolce Vita • 978-1-933372-20-4 • Territories: World
Timeskipper • 978-1-933372-44-0 • Territories: World

Romano Bilenchi
The Chill • 978-1-933372-90-7 • Territories: World

Kazimierz Brandys
Rondo • 978-1-60945-004-5 • Territories: World

Alina Bronsky
Broken Glass Park • 978-1-933372-96-9 • Ebook • Territories: World
The Hottest Dishes of the Tartar Cuisine • 978-1-60945-006-9 • Ebook •
Territories: World

Jesse Browner
Everything Happens Today • 978-1-60945-051-9 • Ebook • Territories:
World (excl. UK & EU)

Francisco Coloane
Tierra del Fuego • 978-1-933372-63-1 • Ebook • Territories: World

Rebecca Connell
The Art of Losing • 978-1-933372-78-5 • Territories: US

Laurence Cossé
A Novel Bookstore • 978-1-933372-82-2 • Ebook • Territories: World
An Accident in August • 978-1-60945-049-6 • Territories: World (excl. UK)

Diego De Silva
I Hadn't Understood • 978-1-60945-065-6 • Territories: World

Shashi Deshpande
The Dark Holds No Terrors • 978-1-933372-67-9 • Territories: US

Steve Erickson
Zeroville • 978-1-933372-39-6 • Territories: US & Can
These Dreams of You • 978-1-60945-063-2 • Territories: US & Can

Elena Ferrante
The Days of Abandonment • 978-1-933372-00-6 • Ebook • Territories: World
Troubling Love • 978-1-933372-16-7 • Territories: World
The Lost Daughter • 978-1-933372-42-6 • Territories: World

Linda Ferri
Cecilia • 978-1-933372-87-7 • Territories: World

Damon Galgut
In a Strange Room • 978-1-60945-011-3 • Ebook • Territories: USA

Santiago Gamboa
Necropolis • 978-1-60945-073-1 • Ebook • Territories: World

Jane Gardam
Old Filth • 978-1-933372-13-6 • Ebook • Territories: US
The Queen of the Tambourine • 978-1-933372-36-5 • Ebook • Territories: US
The People on Privilege Hill • 978-1-933372-56-3 • Ebook • Territories: US
The Man in the Wooden Hat • 978-1-933372-89-1 • Ebook • Territories: US
God on the Rocks • 978-1-933372-76-1 • Ebook • Territories: US
Crusoe's Daughter • 978-1-60945-069-4 • Ebook • Territories: US

Anna Gavalda
French Leave • 978-1-60945-005-2 • Ebook • Territories: US & Can

Seth Greenland
The Angry Buddhist • 978-1-60945-068-7 • Ebook • Territories: World

Katharina Hacker
The Have-Nots • 978-1-933372-41-9 • Territories: World (excl. India)

www.europaeditions.com

Patrick Hamilton
Hangover Square • 978-1-933372-06-8 • Territories: US & Can

James Hamilton-Paterson
Cooking with Fernet Branca • 978-1-933372-01-3 • Territories: US
Amazing Disgrace • 978-1-933372-19-8 • Territories: US
Rancid Pansies • 978-1-933372-62-4 • Territories: USA

Alfred Hayes
The Girl on the Via Flaminia • 978-1-933372-24-2 • Ebook •
Territories: World

Jean-Claude Izzo
The Lost Sailors • 978-1-933372-35-8 • Territories: World
A Sun for the Dying • 978-1-933372-59-4 • Territories: World

Gail Jones
Sorry • 978-1-933372-55-6 • Territories: US & Can

Ioanna Karystiani
The Jasmine Isle • 978-1-933372-10-5 • Territories: World
Swell • 978-1-933372-98-3 • Territories: World

Peter Kocan
Fresh Fields • 978-1-933372-29-7 • Territories: US, EU & Can
The Treatment and the Cure • 978-1-933372-45-7 • Territories: US, EU & Can

Helmut Krausser
Eros • 978-1-933372-58-7 • Territories: World

Amara Lakhous
Clash of Civilizations Over an Elevator in Piazza Vittorio •
978-1-933372-61-7 • Ebook • Territories: World
Divorce Islamic Style • 978-1-60945-066-3 • Ebook • Territories: World

Lia Levi
The Jewish Husband • 978-1-933372-93-8 • Territories: World

Valerio Massimo Manfredi
The Ides of March • 978-1-933372-99-0 • Territories: US

Leïla Marouane
The Sexual Life of an Islamist in Paris • 978-1-933372-85-3 •
Territories: World

Lorenzo Mediano
The Frost on His Shoulders • 978-1-60945-072-4 • Ebook •
Territories: World

Sélim Nassib
I Loved You for Your Voice • 978-1-933372-07-5 • Territories: World
The Palestinian Lover • 978-1-933372-23-5 • Territories: World

Amélie Nothomb
Tokyo Fiancée • 978-1-933372-64-8 • Territories: US & Can
Hygiene and the Assassin • 978-1-933372-77-8 • Ebook • Territories: US & Can

Valeria Parrella
For Grace Received • 978-1-933372-94-5 • Territories: World

Alessandro Piperno
The Worst Intentions • 978-1-933372-33-4 • Territories: World
Persecution • 978-1-60945-074-8 • Ebook • Territories: World

Lorcan Roche
The Companion • 978-1-933372-84-6 • Territories: World

Boualem Sansal
The German Mujahid • 978-1-933372-92-1 • Ebook • Territories: US & Can

www.europaeditions.com

Eric-Emmanuel Schmitt
The Most Beautiful Book in the World • 978-1-933372-74-7 • Ebook •
Territories: World
The Woman with the Bouquet • 978-1-933372-81-5 • Ebook • Territories:
US & Can

Angelika Schrobsdorff
You Are Not Like Other Mothers • 978-1-60945-075-5 • Ebook •
Territories: World

Audrey Schulman
Three Weeks in December • 978-1-60945-064-9 • Ebook • Territories: US
& Can

James Scudamore
Heliopolis • 978-1-933372-73-0 • Ebook • Territories: US

Luis Sepúlveda
The Shadow of What We Were • 978-1-60945-002-1 • Ebook • Territories:
World

Paolo Sorrentino
Everybody's Right • 978-1-60945-052-6 • Ebook • Territories: US & Can

Domenico Starnone
First Execution • 978-1-933372-66-2 • Territories: World

Henry Sutton
Get Me out of Here • 978-1-60945-007-6 • Ebook • Territories: US & Can

Chad Taylor
Departure Lounge • 978-1-933372-09-9 • Territories: US, EU & Can

Roma Tearne
Mosquito • 978-1-933372-57-0 • Territories: US & Can
Bone China • 978-1-933372-75-4 • Territories: US

André Carl van der Merwe
Moffie • 978-1-60945-050-2 • Ebook • Territories: World
(excl. S. Africa)

Fay Weldon
Chalcot Crescent • 978-1-933372-79-2 • Territories: US

Anne Wiazemsky
My Berlin Child • 978-1-60945-003-8 • Territories: US & Can

Jonathan Yardley
Second Reading • 978-1-60945-008-3 • Ebook • Territories: US & Can

Edwin M. Yoder Jr.
Lions at Lamb House • 978-1-933372-34-1 • Territories: World

Michele Zackheim
Broken Colors • 978-1-933372-37-2 • Territories: World

Alice Zeniter
Take This Man • 978-1-60945-053-3 • Territories: World

Tonga Books

Ian Holding
Of Beasts and Beings • 978-1-60945-054-0 • Ebook • Territories: US & Can

Sara Levine
Treasure Island!!! • 978-0-14043-768-3 • Ebook • Territories: World

Alexander Maksik
You Deserve Nothing • 978-1-60945-048-9 • Ebook • Territories: US, Can & EU (excl. UK)

Thad Ziolkowski
Wichita • 978-1-60945-070-0 • Ebook • Territories: World

Crime/Noir

Massimo Carlotto
The Goodbye Kiss • 978-1-933372-05-1 • Ebook • Territories: World
Death's Dark Abyss • 978-1-933372-18-1 • Ebook • Territories: World
The Fugitive • 978-1-933372-25-9 • Ebook • Territories: World
Bandit Love • 978-1-933372-80-8 • Ebook • Territories: World
Poisonville • 978-1-933372-91-4 • Ebook • Territories: World

Giancarlo De Cataldo
The Father and the Foreigner • 978-1-933372-72-3 • Territories: World

Caryl Férey
Zulu • 978-1-933372-88-4 • Ebook • Territories: World (excl. UK & EU)
Utu • 978-1-60945-055-7 • Ebook • Territories: World (excl. UK & EU)

Alicia Giménez-Bartlett
Dog Day • 978-1-933372-14-3 • Territories: US & Can
Prime Time Suspect • 978-1-933372-31-0 • Territories: US & Can
Death Rites • 978-1-933372-54-9 • Territories: US & Can

Jean-Claude Izzo
Total Chaos • 978-1-933372-04-4 • Territories: US & Can
Chourmo • 978-1-933372-17-4 • Territories: US & Can
Solea • 978-1-933372-30-3 • Territories: US & Can

www.europaeditions.com

Matthew F. Jones
Boot Tracks • 978-1-933372-11-2 • Territories: US & Can

Gene Kerrigan
The Midnight Choir • 978-1-933372-26-6 • Territories: US & Can
Little Criminals • 978-1-933372-43-3 • Territories: US & Can

Carlo Lucarelli
Carte Blanche • 978-1-933372-15-0 • Territories: World
The Damned Season • 978-1-933372-27-3 • Territories: World
Via delle Oche • 978-1-933372-53-2 • Territories: World

Edna Mazya
Love Burns • 978-1-933372-08-2 • Territories: World (excl. ANZ)

Yishai Sarid
Limassol • 978-1-60945-000-7 • Ebook • Territories: World (excl. UK, AUS & India)

Joel Stone
The Jerusalem File • 978-1-933372-65-5 • Ebook • Territories: World

Benjamin Tammuz
Minotaur • 978-1-933372-02-0 • Ebook • Territories: World

Non-fiction

Alberto Angela
A Day in the Life of Ancient Rome • 978-1-933372-71-6 • Territories: World • History

Helmut Dubiel
Deep In the Brain: Living with Parkinson's Disease • 978-1-933372-70-9 •
Ebook • Territories: World • Medicine/Memoir

James Hamilton-Paterson
Seven-Tenths: The Sea and Its Thresholds • 978-1-933372-69-3 • Territories:
USA • Nature/Essays

Daniele Mastrogiacomo
Days of Fear • 978-1-933372-97-6 • Ebook • Territories: World • Current
affairs/Memoir/Afghanistan/Journalism

Valery Panyushkin
Twelve Who Don't Agree • 978-1-60945-010-6 • Ebook • Territories:
World • Current affairs/Memoir/Russia/Journalism

Christa Wolf
One Day a Year: 1960-2000 • 978-1-933372-22-8 • Territories: World •
Memoir/History/20th Century

Children's Illustrated Fiction

Altan
Here Comes Timpa • 978-1-933372-28-0 • Territories: World (excl. Italy)
Timpa Goes to the Sea • 978-1-933372-32-7 • Territories: World (excl. Italy)
Fairy Tale Timpa • 978-1-933372-38-9 • Territories: World (excl. Italy)

Wolf Erlbruch
The Big Question • 978-1-933372-03-7 • Territories: US & Can
The Miracle of the Bears • 978-1-933372-21-1 • Territories: US & Can
(with **Gioconda Belli**) *The Butterfly Workshop* • 978-1-933372-12-9 •
Territories: US & Can